Bitter

Uzuri M. Wilkerson

Bitter
by Uzuri M. Wilkerson

Cover by ReBelle Design Studio

www.uzurimwilkerson.com
www.amazon.com/author/uzuriwilkerson

Other works by
Uzuri M. Wilkerson

Bitten:
Sweet
Sour

Bitter

One

Celia smiled for three days straight. Even when she slept—Victor found that particularly amusing. He had announced they were going to Las Vegas for their anniversary. They had never made the plans to go to Seattle, so Victor had surprised her over dinner with the plane tickets. He had even cleared her time off with Bobby, Celia's boss at Cage's Bar and Lounge. *And* she'd found out that Trixie had helped buy her vacation wardrobe, which was a huge step, seeing as how Victor . . . well, he scared her. But she had sucked it up for her best friend.

Celia's face hurt from the constant beaming. Even her coworker Carson couldn't sully her happiness. They had been avoiding each other ever since he'd witnessed Ashleigh's attack.

Ashleigh was a vamp from New York. She'd been kidnapped and drained while visiting Boston, presumably by a nefarious group called the

Night Hawks. The newbie vampire had fallen for Victor and become desperate and upset when he'd turned down her advances. So she'd gone after Celia in retaliation.

Fortunately, a trio of werewolves had come to Celia's aid.

Unfortunately, Carson had witnessed the entire scene.

Celia just didn't know what to say to him. He'd seen huge dogs rip a woman apart, seen Victor and her disappear into thin air. How would you even *start* that discussion?

She and Carson had always enjoyed a sort of combative relationship, but it had been almost two weeks since that night and they both had fallen into a "no speaking" groove. Celia knew she'd have to take care of this sooner rather than later; at the moment, she'd rather be a coward.

Celia took her break at midnight. She found Trixie in the kitchen. Her friend had piled her black hair on top of her head and fanned the back of her neck to cool down. Her skin was flushed a pale pink.

Like she'd done every time she'd seen her, Celia bounced over to Trixie and threw her arms around her, sweatiness and all. Trixie chuckled. "I take it you're ready to leave tomorrow."

"I can't wait!" Celia cried. Trixie seemed glad to see her in such a good mood.

Victor met Celia at the end of the night. Trixie gave her a kiss on the cheek. "Have fun, you two," she said, even smiling to Victor. Though, she averted her eyes when Victor grinned back.

"Thanks, Trix," Celia said. "I'll call you as soon as we get in."

"Yeah, sure," Trixie said, with a playful roll of the eyes. "Like you're not going to immediately hit the slots."

They hugged goodnight. Trixie strolled to the waiting Acura—her boyfriend Lee's car. Celia took Victor's hand as they made their way to the parking lot next door.

"You're all packed, right?" Victor asked.

"Yup."

"And did you get it down to one suitcase?"

She laughed out loud. "Yeah, right."

Victor shook his head in amusement. He got in behind the wheel and zipped down the empty streets.

At home, Celia pounced on him before they'd fully entered the apartment. After a lovely round in the living room, she kissed Victor goodnight, did her nightly rituals, and climbed into bed. Despite her anticipation, she fell asleep right away.

Friday morning, Celia woke up alone, naturally. As she glanced around her sunny room, that excited energy came rushing back. She let out a squeal. Literally jumping out of bed, she rushed to the bathroom to shower. Their flight was scheduled to leave at 6:10 p.m. They'd be pushing it a little with the time, but she figured they'd be okay. It was November; the sun began setting at 4:30 this time of year. They would just have to cross their fingers for a smooth sail through security.

She focused on the day ahead. She needed to clean her fridge, since she had some leftovers that probably wouldn't last the week. She had laundry to do; that way she could come home to fresh linen. She also wanted to straighten up. She just loved to come home to a clean house. It was one of those naggy tidbits that had stuck in the back of her brain, thanks to her Aunt Meg's tutelage.

After showering and dressing, Celia went to her aunt and uncle's house in Lower Mills. No one was home, of course. She raided the fridge and watched daytime television while doing her laundry.

When she returned home, she changed her bedding, swept the entire apartment, cleaned and disinfected the kitchen and bathroom, and dusted the living room. Satisfied, she went to her room. There, she rechecked her bags to make sure she had everything. She checked her Ziploc bag too, to be certain all of the little bottles were three ounces.

Glancing at her alarm clock, she saw that it was just before 3:00. She stood there, not sure of what to do. When her stomach grumbled, she made a sandwich that she ate over the sink.

Her cellphone rang. She found it on the coffee table and smiled at the display.

"Hey there."

"Well, *someone's* in a good mood," Jay said warmly.

"Looks like I'm not the only one. What's up?"

"I'll probably be back in your neck of the woods next week."

"Oh?"

Celia hadn't laid eyes on the hunky hunter, avenger of the undead, since September, before he'd had to return home to Dallas. A drunk driver had plowed through the living room of his parents' house. He'd had to deal with the arrangements to fix it, which was taking time.

"Yeah, I've been tracking this bloodsucker and he might be in New Hampshire." She gritted her teeth at his word choice. "At least, that's what his brother thinks."

"His brother?"

"Yup," Jay said, with a sigh. "It's this whole complicated thing, but the brother knows he's among the undead and wants him gone. The brother believes he wouldn't want to live like that."

Celia frowned, unsettled. "But what if he does? What if he's adjusted? What if he doesn't want to die?"

In a sort of deadpan way, Jay informed her, "He's already dead, Celia."

"You know what I mean. How's that the brother's or your decision to make?"

"Look, he's a newly-turned vamp, out there on his own. That in itself is enough for me to go after him. He's a danger."

She wanted to protest more, to defend the unknown vampire, but she chewed her lip to keep from speaking. It wasn't her place. And it wasn't like Jay was the easiest person to disabuse of his convictions.

"Well, I hope you're getting paid well for this," she muttered. So, okay, she wasn't the best at holding her tongue.

Jay was quiet for a second. Then he snapped, "You bet your ass." His tone was harsh, but didn't quite disguise the pause laden with guilt and surprise.

"So, will you actually be in Boston?" Celia asked, unruffled. Jay was a hunter. It was his job to kill vampires. Luckily, he no longer had his sights set on Victor.

"I'll probably be there mid-week," Jay grumbled.

"Oh, okay, I'll be back then. We can have dinner."

"Where're you going?"

She sighed happily. "Vegas. It's for our anniversary on Tuesday. We fly out tonight."

Jay was quiet again. She didn't know what to make of his silence.

"What?" she finally asked.

"Have fun," he replied.

She might've been less shocked if Jay had insulted Victor in some way. She couldn't quite read his tone. He *did* sound like he had meant it.

"Thanks," she said softly.

They hung up soon after that.

Jay remained on her mind when she set about making oatmeal raisin cookies. She put the baked goods inside one of those blue cookie tins you could buy around the holidays. Out in the hallway, she knocked on her neighbor's door.

The door opened a crack. Carrie's son Kenny, peeked out, his brows furrowed. After making sure it was Celia, Kenny smiled. She held up the tin.

"Here you go," she said. "Some cookies."

"Thanks!" The door widened and he took the container. She rubbed the top of his curly head, and went back to her apartment.

Around 4:00, the sky began to turn purple with the setting sun. Victor showed up at 4:30, red suitcase in hand. His skin was very pale, making his dark eyes stand out like glass beads.

"Are you ready, Seal?" His voice was steady, not showing any of the weariness he might have been experiencing with his hunger.

She couldn't help a grin at the sight of him, as the anticipation erupted inside of her. She hopped up from the sofa and kissed him.

"Hey," he said, feigning like he was miffed by her passionate kiss. "What're you doing to me?"

"Sorry."

She wasn't.

Victor went to her room. He reemerged dragging her orange suitcase to the front door, along with her matching carry-on bag. He made an effort of grunting under the weight of the bags. She chose to ignore him.

Celia checked her purse for her wallet, iPod, magazines and books, her fuzzy sleep mask, and cellphone and charger. She would normally bring snacks and water, but all the strict regulations at Logan Airport forbade bringing outside food through security. Hey, at least she'd have Victor's snacks on the plane as well.

Victor checked the time on the cable box. "The cab should be here any minute," he announced. His gaze shifted back to her bags. "Do you really need so much?"

They'd only ever been on day and weekend trips where a duffel bag was suitable. This was different.

"We'll be gone for a week. So, shut up."

Victor's mouth curved up in a grin. His comment sank in and she nearly giggled. It was such a *guy* thing to say, even for someone over a hundred years old. He'd thank her once he got a gander at the lacy things she had tucked in the bottom.

A horn beeped from the street. As Victor hefted the three bags and Celia's purse, Celia took a last look around the apartment. Giddiness made butterflies attack her stomach. It had been so long since she'd flown somewhere.

Celia closed and locked her door, then headed down the stairs. She caught a flash of her heavy suitcase as the chubby cabbie struggled to lift it into the trunk. Victor stood to the side, watching the display. He was amused—she felt it as if it were her own emotion through their bond. She shook her head while grinning to herself. Her boyfriend could be an ass when he wanted.

The temperature outside had dropped with the sun. Victor held the door open, and Celia hurried down the stairs for the warm backseat. The ride to the airport took fifteen minutes. With their luggage piled onto one of those wheelie things, Victor led the way inside, with Celia holding the crook of his elbow. Her smile had returned, widening when they approached the JetBlue ticket counter.

The woman behind the desk looked exhausted. You could see it in her weary eyes; plus, she stifled a yawn. She had a lot of neck and it jiggled when she yawned. Celia hoped her shift was almost over because she was obviously ready for her pillow.

"Hello, welcome to JetBlue," the woman said. "Where are you flying today?"

"Vegas!" Celia squealed with a bounce. She couldn't help it. The woman raised her thin eyebrows in slight surprise. Victor smiled as he handed her the tickets. They were actual tickets instead of email printouts. Victor must've bought them in person. Who did that?

"Okay," the woman mumbled. Celia's glee was lost on her. The woman clicked away at her keyboard with dull eyes directed to the monitor. "Checking any bags?"

"Yes, two," Victor answered. He placed her large bag and his own on the conveyor belt to the woman's left. She weighed them, told Victor he'd have to pay more since Celia's was ten pounds over—Celia gave him a sheepish grin and reddened cheeks when he glared at her—then tagged the bags.

"Oh, come on," Celia said. "Do you know how nice it is to go five days without wearing all black?"

The woman handed Victor the boarding passes. "You're going to Gate

30. After security, head to the left. Have a great flight."

The farewell would've been more effective if she had injected even the tiniest of emotion into her leaden voice.

A few people were queued at the security checkpoint. Celia and Victor fell into line and started the process. The middle-aged man in front of them had a hole in his brown sock. The young security guard was so thin that his uniform hung on his frame. His hand trembled when he waved the man through the gate. He seemed new, the way he kept glancing to his coworkers. The man went through without any incident and the guard actually sighed in relief.

Celia stood before the gate, eyeing the young guy. After the man cleared, the guard motioned for her to pass. As she went to collect her things on the other side, the alarm beeped. She swung around, thinking that maybe she had tripped it.

The young guy looked scared. He peeked over at the other guards who had been watching the conveyor belt. They glanced up at the alarm. Victor stood just outside of the detector. His face was impassive, but Celia knew he was irritated.

One of the other guards sighed and trudged out from behind the computer monitor to where the young one stood. His nametag read "Miller."

"Jason," Miller said. "You gotta take him out of line." He looked at Victor. "Step over here, please."

Celia opened her mouth to protest when she noticed Victor staring intently into the older guard's eyes. Miller stood there, frozen, metal detector poised in mid-air.

She cleared her throat loudly. Victor broke contact, and then looked at her. She pursed her lips in rebuke.

The guard blinked. He shook his head a few times, as if ridding himself of confusion. Jason looked concerned. He had been observing Miller's every move and had noted his sudden faraway expression.

"Uh, right," Miller said. "Um, stand over here please. And lift your arms out."

He ran the wand over Victor's arms, chest, and down each leg. It didn't beep. As he waved it up Victor's back, two more security guards emerged from a door behind them that Celia hadn't noticed. Fear prickled the back of her neck at the sight of them. The men spoke in hushed tones; she couldn't catch their words. Next thing she knew, they directed Victor to that back door.

"Hey!" Celia called. Miller put his hand up, stopping her.

"Sorry, ma'am," he said. "You can't go with him."

"Don't call me 'ma'am.'"

Miller frowned. "Excuse me?"

"Don't call me 'ma'am.' Do I *look* like a 'ma'am'? What's going on?"

"Random screening," he answered cautiously, as if uncertain about his words now.

She stared at him, not comprehending his last statement. "What?"

"They do random searches," Jason explained.

"But . . ."

That was all she could say. There was really nothing she could do and causing a scene would only make matters worse. As it was, the line had backed up, with passengers glaring daggers at them.

"Where can I wait?" she asked, deflated.

Jason pointed to an area past the checkpoint. Celia gathered her carry-on bag and purse—one of the guards had taken Victor's wallet, shoes, and belt when she hadn't seen—and trudged away.

After standing next to a newsstand for five long minutes, not registering the passing faces, she went to sit in one of the chairs at Gate 20. The area was empty of passengers at the moment, since the plane had already boarded for Chicago. A man dressed in blue coveralls swept under the chairs. A small child ran past her, headed for the giant window. He tripped, but his father caught him in enough time to avoid a face-to-face with the Berber carpet. The little boy shrieked in delight, sticking his arms out like Superman.

Celia sighed, then cupped her chin in her hand, tapping her foot. A cool hand touched her neck, making her jump.

"Shit," she muttered. "You're cold."

"Sorry."

She looked up. Victor's mouth was a pinched line. His eyes seemed blacker, his skin nearly white as paper. Celia figured it was a good thing his skin was so cold because, not that he would, but that meant he hadn't gone off on the security guards.

"Fucking airports," he griped. "Fucking security. I had to pay to check the fucking bags and then I have to deal with fucking random searches? They went through every piece of clothing."

Celia was surprised by his words. She squeezed his hand, opting not to speak since she was technically part of the reason for his grousing.

"Fuck!"

A family of five passing by gave them odd looks.

Victor took her bag. "Well, to be fair," she said, standing, "you have to pay for checked bags on most airlines now."

Victor glowered at her. She did the right thing by refraining from giggling.

They walked to their gate in silence. Then Celia was distracted by the smell of coffee and doughnuts. Her eyes lit up as her stomach grumbled. Without a word, she made a beeline to the Dunkin Donuts counter.

"What can I get you?" the man asked. He was considerably more awake than the woman at the ticket counter. Maybe he took advantage of the coffee on hand.

"Um," Celia said, "can I have one of those chicken flatbread sandwiches and a Pepsi?"

The man left to prepare her food. Victor appeared at her shoulder, extracting his wallet. Since the guy was preoccupied and the woman behind them was busy fixing her little girl's hair ribbons, Celia leaned over to whisper to Victor.

"Do you need anything?"

He looked at the clock over the bagels. It was almost 5:30. He then looked back down at her. She saw his answer in his eyes: a big, resounding *yes*.

The man returned and Victor paid. Celia realized she had asked him if he needed something without the thought of how they would do this. Victor couldn't just latch onto her neck in a semi-busy terminal.

Right before their gate, she spotted a family restroom, one of the single-occupant ones where parents could change their kids in private. She took Victor's hand and pulled him inside. No one seemed to notice. The people around them wandered by in their own bubbles, trying to figure out where they were going and making sure they had everything and everyone.

In the bathroom, Celia placed her food on the sink, though she did so wistfully. The smell of the chicken made her stomach ache.

Victor dropped the bag on the floor. He was on her mouth in an instant. He moved fast, kissing her, squeezing her. She didn't know what to do and she was no match for his speed. One second she stood in front of him, the next he had her pants off and her perched on the edge of the sink.

He stooped down in front of her, his face between her legs, making her gasp and moan. He hit the good spot with each lick and she shuddered already. She lost her balance when her elbow jerked with an involuntary spasm. She was able to grab hold of the faucet to steady herself. The automated spigot kicked on, splashing droplets against her bare thigh.

He bit her inner thigh, which was new. She cried out in pleasure, perhaps a little too loudly. Someone passing by surely would've heard. But she didn't care because her whole body was on fire and she loved it. Victor grunted into her thigh and she dug her nails in his back. He moaned even more.

After taking his fill, he stood. His belt buckle clinked as he opened his pants. Biting her lower lip, Celia helped him. She took hold of his swollen member and directed him inside her. With his hands on her hips, Victor pushed and pulled as another ball of tension built up between their warm bodies. Their eyes connected just as the ball exploded, leaving them both quivering with ecstasy.

When he pulled away, color filled his cheeks. His eyes were gray again. He moved as if to cut his wrist for her, but she shook her head. She jumped down and put her pants back on, stumbling because she was lightheaded.

She then snatched up her sandwich and took a large bite. She moaned even louder than she had when Victor's expert tongue was inside her.

She was smiling again as they left the bathroom, holding the sandwich in both hands. A custodian glanced up when they exited. He frowned at first, since they weren't toting an infant, and then shook his head with a smirk.

A woman's voice came over the loudspeaker.

"Good evening, passengers. Flight number eight thirty-seven to Las Vegas will now start boarding." She then called for people with children and those requiring assistance to make their way to the front.

Celia and Victor's row was called five minutes later. Celia settled in next to the window. She pulled out her iPod and *Entertainment Weekly*, and then tucked her purse away.

Victor placed her bag in the overhead bin and sat next to her. He let out a sigh, but it sounded hard.

"What's wrong?" Celia asked.

He stared straight ahead, his hands gripping the armrests. A groaning sound followed. Celia grasped his hand to make him stop. Her touch brought him from his trance. He turned his head toward her. She was nearly blown away. He looked . . . *scared.* His distress made her heart speed up.

"Victor? What is it?"

"I'm, uh," he began. He licked his lips. "I'm not the best flier."

Her face softened as her own panic lessened. "Aw, honey." She rubbed his hand. "You should've just zipped over there."

"I wanted to go with you."

She smiled. "I would've understood."

He shook his head in disagreement but didn't say anything.

The number of people moving down the aisle began to taper off. The flight attendants passed by, checking on passengers and closing overhead bins. The attendants *had* to be used to shell-shocked fliers, but Celia's concern centered on Victor doing something that would be hard to explain. Like breaking the armrest.

"Hey," she whispered, as the groaning of the metal increased. "You gotta ease up." She indicated his hands.

Victor released the armrests and clasped his hands together in his lap. He glanced around the plane and bounced his knee. She'd never seen him like this. She thought it was cute. To comfort him, she rubbed his back. His muscles were tense and hard, and no amount of caressing helped.

The pilot's deep voice sounded over the intercom, welcoming them to JetBlue, and informing them that tonight's flight would take five hours and fifty minutes. "We'll arrive in Las Vegas at eleven o'clock, local time. Sit back, relax, and enjoy our presentation. It could save your life," he added with a warm chuckle.

The flight attendants started the safety demonstrations as the plane rolled down the tarmac. Celia watched Victor. He'd gone into that trance again, only his eyes were eerily vacant.

The woman sitting across the aisle looked around for her seatbelt. When she found the end dangling over her seat, she looked to Victor with an amused grin, to find someone with whom to be self-deprecating.

At Victor's strange, statue-like posture, her grin disappeared. Her mouth opened as if to say something, maybe to ask if he was okay.

Celia forced a smile like it was no big deal. She pulled the blanket from the pocket of the seat in front of Victor and wrapped it around his chest to disguise the fact that he wasn't breathing. Then she took out her fuzzy sleep mask and put it on his face. It was a soft pink and the little feathers got everywhere, but he'd have to deal with looking foolish if he was going to fall into himself the entire flight.

She didn't meet the woman's eye again as she slunk into her seat. The cabin lights shut off and the attendants went to their own seats. Celia kept their overhead lights off for the duration of the flight. To entertain herself, she watched music videos and episodes of *Lost* and *Heroes* on her iPod.

She drifted off around 10:00.

Celia was awakened by a hand on her shoulder.

"Miss? Miss, are you awake?"

"Hmm?" Celia shifted in her seat. She blinked a few times to remember where she was. One of the flight attendants—a thin woman, with black hair and severe bangs—leaned cautiously over Victor.

"What is it? Did we land?"

"Yes," the attendant said, and then glanced to Victor. Celia looked too. He was just as she had left him: blanket across his shoulders, fuzzy sleep mask, as still as a rock. "Um, we've been trying to wake him but he won't budge."

A spasm of fear seized Celia and she sat there a moment, frozen and blanking. He looked so peculiar; she could only imagine what the others thought. Then she shook herself, because inaction wasn't helping one bit.

"Oh, um, he's a *very* heavy sleeper," Celia replied, as casually as she could manage. "He took a pill, you know, to help him. I'll get him up." She said it with a big dose of intimation. The woman's green eyes went from Celia to Victor, dubiously. Then she moved away.

The woman across the aisle pulled down her bag. She stood in the middle of the aisle, holding up the procession. Celia waited until the line started moving before she eyed Victor again. She had no idea how to wake him. She tried shaking him, pinching him; she even stomped on his foot. Nothing, except she did manage to scuff his shoe.

She peeked around, and spotted the flight attendant making her way back up the aisle. "Shit," she muttered, then shook him some more.

The attendant was closer now, about ten rows away. She scanned the seats, checking for lost items and such.

"Victor," Celia hissed at him. *"Get up!"*

That wasn't working either, and the woman was now eight rows away. Through her panic, she had an idea. She searched around for something pointy but found nothing, which, of course she wouldn't on a plane.

"Shit!"

She looked back once again. The woman was four rows behind them. Out of any other options, Celia brought her thumb to her mouth and bit down hard before she could think about it. A shooting pain worked its way through her thumb and down to her wrist. She tasted blood and nail polish. Ignoring the throbbing, she waved her thumb under Victor's nose like a vial of smelling salts.

She eyed the bubble of blood on the pad of her thumb and felt ridiculous. Victor's lips parted, twisting into a snarl. His incisors sharpened. He growled, which she hadn't expected and did not like. The flight attendant halted at the unnatural sound. She looked at them in concern.

Celia jerked her thumb away. Victor's hands reached out for her, the blindfold not serving as any hindrance. She wanted to laugh at how silly he looked coming at her with that sleep mask on, if only she weren't so alarmed.

She used her right hand to snatch off the mask. All signs of mirth vanished. His eyes were black and savage, making her gulp. His fury and hunger and overwhelming *need* for her warmth pulsed through her at that moment, as if every molecule of her body had just started banging into each other at hyper-speed. Her own teeth trembled in anticipation of sinking into warm flesh, of filling her belly with delicious blood, of draining every last drop.

His nature was so powerful, so jolting that she nearly lost her breath. She wanted to shrink away because he was scaring her, except she needed to be strong or else the predator in him, the one whose face she stupidly stared into, might jump at the chance of seizing something weak.

"Victor, snap out of it!"

He froze. Slowly, recognition cleared his eyes. They didn't change back to gray, but he saw Celia now, which was good. His fangs retracted and his face softened. He took a deep breath, and then smirked.

"Did you enjoy your flight?" he asked.

She could just slap him.

In the terminal, they stood to the side. Celia ran her hands down her thighs, repeatedly smoothing jeans that didn't require the motion. Victor raked a hand through his hair.

He gazed down at her, his brows pulled together in concern. His mouth was a thin line. "I'm sorry that I scared you."

He reached out as if to touch her shoulder. Maybe he felt her sudden, unbidden twinge of fear because he dropped his hand to his side instead.

"I won't do . . . that again. I'll stay present." His tone was simultaneously gloomy and harsh.

Celia told herself to calm down. Told her stupid heart to stop pounding.

Then she smiled in the hopes of lightening the mood. There was no point trying to conceal that bout of fright. She only wanted to fix it now.

"It's sweet that you wanted to travel with me. Come on." She looped her arm around his elbow and turned him toward Baggage Claim.

"Well, look who it is."

A man strolled down the pathway between gates with an air of sophistication. The first thing Celia noticed about him was his amber-colored eyes. They reminded her of a cat. She was struck by how beautiful they were, glittering in the overhead fluorescent lights, half-shaded by thick eyebrows.

He appeared to be in his thirties, husky, with thick brown hair he had tied back at the base of his neck. His skin was smooth as marble and the color of pine. He grinned at Victor.

"Long time, my friend." He held out his hand.

Victor looked at it as if it were foreign. He finally reached out and shook it. The man's stunning eyes switched to Celia. His gaze rubbed across her cheeks as he assessed her.

"Hello. My name is Donald Pescatore."

"Celia," she said. The man's head tilted to the side expectantly. "Wilcox," she added after a second.

Donald's smile widened. "You should be proud of your name, Celia Wilcox. Announce it fully whenever you introduce yourself."

"Um, okay." She leaned closer to Victor.

"Pescatore, it means 'fisherman' in my native tongue. Believe it or not, my father's father was an actual fisherman. Victor knows a little something about that." Donald nudged him. Victor remained silent, his face a mask.

"Names are so important. They tell your heritage without need for further explanation." Donald touched a finger to his chin. "Wilcox. I know that name—"

"There you are."

A woman came up to them, her approach announced by the clicking of her heels. A tight, purple dress wrapped her thin body. Her black hair was long enough to reach her elbows.

"I got you a water, babe," she said to Donald.

Donald sighed. "You know I don't drink water. *Babe*."

"Oh." She blinked at him, her long eyelashes fluttering like a cartoon doe's. "Why?"

Donald placed a hand on her shoulder, right at her neck. His thumb pressed into the hollow of her collarbone. As he stared her in the eye, her face relaxed into a dreamlike stare.

"I don't like water. I only like you."

A flattered smile softened the woman's face even more. Celia's mouth opened to say something, but she didn't know what. She'd never witnessed a vampire enthralling a human. She gaped at the two of them.

Victor shifted beside her. "We're leaving."

Donald glanced their way. He scanned Celia again. "You're upset." He chuckled at her surprise. "Our kind can know what your kind feels and thinks once we've fed on you."

Celia peeked around at all of the people milling past them. None of them paid their little group mind.

"I, on the other hand, can do it without a taste." He shrugged. "Though that's no fun."

"You . . ." Celia's eyes flickered to the woman. "What are you doing to her?"

"Keeping a close watch on my supply."

He pulled the woman nearer. She smiled vacuously. Ignoring Celia's shock, Donald faced Victor. "We didn't see you in Switzerland."

"I don't attend those meetings," Victor answered.

Donald smirked again, without acknowledging Victor's curt tone. He wrapped an arm around the woman's waist. "Times are changing, my friend." They turned toward the exit. "You ought to get in at the ground level, Victor."

Celia and Victor watched them walk away.

"What's he talking about?" Celia asked.

"Some of the area leaders have been meeting to deal with issues. Rogues and property disputes."

She stared up at him. "So you all do have an organized system?"

He shook his head. "We respect boundaries. Usually. And when we can't handle our territories, we sometimes call in help."

He looked at her a moment—her gaze had gone back to Donald and his "supply"—before they followed the signs to retrieve their luggage.

* * *

Victor walked beside Celia, hating himself immensely. She had been genuinely afraid of him on the plane. And what could he do? The damage was already done and there were no takesies backsies.

Outside, the arid night hit them in their faces. Celia whistled as she removed her sweater.

A few cars waited at the curb. Victor scanned them until he saw the familiar black Lincoln MKS. A tall, black man dressed in black linen pants and a white shirt stood in front of the car. He came to attention, his back straightening at the sight of Victor approaching.

He extended his hand. Victor shook it, and experienced the usual prickle up his arm from touching him, like a low-grade jolt warning him not to hold on too long.

"This is Celia," Victor said. "Hastings will serve as our caretaker this week."

"Nice to meet you," Celia said as she shook Hastings's hand. Victor noted slight hesitation when Hastings made contact with Celia. The caretaker recovered quickly, but Victor caught the change.

Hastings opened the back door. Celia slid into the leather interior.

"The house is stocked for you, sir," Hastings said in a low tone. He spoke with a posh English accent. His breath always smelled faintly of sage. Victor knew it was a warding technique. The caretaker's eyes usually skirted Victor's nose and cheeks as well.

Victor thanked him. "Stocked" included towels, food, and blood bags—just in case. Victor got in beside Celia. She beamed at him.

"This is really happening, right? I'm not drooling on my couch with the TV playing in the background?"

Victor chuckled. Then he pinched her arm.

"Hey!" she shouted with a laugh, slapping his thigh.

The ride from McCarron Airport only took fifteen minutes. Celia watched the horizon. There wasn't much to see once they passed the airport. The streetlights illuminated the highway, but not much else. When her hand closed around his, Victor sighed softly in relief at the warmth from her skin.

His gums tingled at her touch; another reaction he couldn't control. It was more than hunger. He just yearned for her, all of her.

When he pried his gaze from her brown skin, Victor's eyes met

Hastings's in the rearview mirror. The man only held Victor's gaze for a few seconds before turning back to the road ahead.

Five minutes later, Hastings turned off the expressway. He traveled down another wide street before turning into a housing complex called Setter's Cove. He took a right at the stop sign, then pulled over at the third house on the right. He got out first to open the door for them.

"Victor?"

A soft light shone down on the woman sitting in a rattan chair on her patio across the street. She had one arm crossed over her stomach, the other bent. The smoke from the cigarette between her fingers drifted toward the night sky in a thin white line. She hadn't spoken loudly; Celia tugged at his shirt when she noticed him staring off.

"What is it?" Celia asked.

She began to turn her head, but Victor stepped in front of her view. "Hastings, please show Celia inside." Victor kissed her temple. "I'll be right there."

She nodded slowly and then followed Hastings.

After they'd gone into the house, Victor crossed the deserted street with his hands in his pockets.

"Viviana, how are you?"

"My name is Mary now." She took a drag from the cigarette. "My name hasn't been 'Viviana' for seven years."

"Is that how long it's been?"

"Yup. A lot has changed, I see." She nodded toward Victor's house. "Keeping company with humans again, are we?"

Victor didn't reply, although the upturning of his lip was plenty response.

Mary chuckled. "God, you're still so sensitive." She waved her hands in front of her, as if deflecting his offense. "Oh, I'm sorry, *protective.* You gotta keep your human lovers from us vamps, you know. We just snatch up anything with a beating heart."

The front door of the house stood wide open. From the dark interior, a voice whined, "Mary."

Mary took another lazy pull of her cigarette as if she hadn't heard.

"Where are you?"

A young woman appeared in the doorway. She wore lace boy shorts and a cropped white top that said "Gangsta" across her tits in black box letters.

"Come back to bed." Her glassy eyes barely registered the other person standing there.

"In a minute. Can't you see I have company?"

The girl glanced to Victor, giving him as much attention as one would bestow on a rock on the ground. She then turned and went back into the house.

Mary took a final drag and extinguished the butt in an ashtray at her feet. She stood and stretched.

"Just so you know, Rita has been causing some issues."

Victor frowned. "Who's Rita?"

Mary's face brightened, making her appear her human age of twenty-five. "Oh, Rita. What can one say about her?"

"Well . . . *something* would be nice."

Mary chuckled as she went inside, closing the door.

* * *

Victor's house was like all the others in the Setter's Cove complex:

shades of beige with rust-colored Spanish tiles on the roofs. All two-story stucco structures, whose shapes and designs repeated every three or four lots. Closed garages, an occasional bike or toy left in the yards or driveways—some faded from the hot sun.

Hastings wheeled Celia's suitcase into the small foyer and held the door for her. Celia stepped inside and smiled.

The kitchen, with its marble counters and shiny black appliances, was to her right. A countertop sectioned the kitchen from the dining area. A high-top dinner table for six was next to it. Beyond that was the living room.

Hastings carried her suitcase to the carpeted staircase, and Celia trailed behind. They passed a full bathroom at the top of the stairs and two bedrooms—one had two twin beds, the other a full-sized bed.

They continued down the hall, crossing the walkway that offered a look down into the living room. A large ceiling fan rotated slowly above their heads, circulating the manufactured cool air.

Around the next corner, they came into the master suite. The king-sized bed was made up with fluffy yellow and gray pillows and a downy yellow-and-white comforter. On the right, the en-suite curved into its own nook. A large walk-in closet stood to the left. A sliding door closed off the bathroom, which had a large shower stall and a Jacuzzi.

"Wow," Celia whispered as she went back into the bedroom. She beamed at Hastings, who placed her bags on the bench at the foot of the bed. He looked to be in his mid-forties and in good shape. His short hair was an attractive salt-and-pepper. A small tattoo sat just below the crook of his elbow. It was a perfect, thick circle, with a smaller circle in the center.

Hastings straightened and met her eyes.

She hesitated. He looked as if something weighed on his mind. His expression was clouded by whatever troubled him. She wanted to ask, but his eyes moved to her left. Victor stood in the doorway. He placed his suitcase on the floor.

Hastings bowed his head and excused himself from the room. The strange feeling from Hastings melted away as her happiness resurfaced. Celia squealed and jumped up and down.

"I'm in fucking Vegas!" she shouted.

Victor laughed. It was such a carefree sound. She rushed to him and threw her arms around his waist.

"Thanks so much, babe," she whispered.

He stroked her hair. Celia looked up slowly. She stared at his lips a moment before rising on her tiptoes. He met her halfway. She was greeted with the familiar tingle from his touch.

See, she told herself. *Everything's okay.*

Victor tightened his grip around her and lifted her, leaving her feet dangling above the floor. They fell into the cloud-like softness of the bed. Whiffs of lavender filled her nose.

"Thank you," she whispered again.

Victor ran his fingers through her hair, releasing her curls from the elastic.

"Anything for you," he whispered. He took a firm handful of her hair.

Her heart raced as she tried to figure out which position to try tonight. Her moaning elicited the usual reaction for Victor. As her tongue caressed his, his sharp fangs slid down. Panic sliced through her like a knife when her tongue grazed one.

She pulled away. Without looking at him, Celia rolled off the bed. She muttered something about needing to use the bathroom. She closed the sliding door behind her. She didn't really need to use the toilet, and she wondered if Victor could hear her not using it. And if he could normally, then gross. Whatever the case, she flushed the toilet after a minute and ran the water in the sink.

"Victor," she called over the water, "I'm kinda pooped."

"It *is* getting late," she heard him say. She couldn't distinguish his tone through the door and over the running faucet. She didn't want to hurt him; she just needed distance, as the memory of his hunger washed over her. She stared at her reflection, waiting for him to say something more. But he remained quiet on the other side of the barrier. She wondered if he was still there. It wasn't like she'd hear him teleport.

Knowing she'd been in there entirely too long, she turned the water off and opened the door. Victor leaned against the doorframe. He had been gazing at the floor, but when Celia appeared, his eyes went to her face. Celia couldn't quite meet his eyes. Her cheeks burned like they were on fire. She didn't want him to leave when it was so awkward, so she stood on her toes, kissed his jaw.

"I'll see you tomorrow?" she asked his chest.

His voice was low. "I'll be here."

She managed a small smile.

Victor vanished before her eyes.

Two

Celia woke to the morning sun slanting into the room through the drawn blinds. Golden steps crept across her lap. She sat up in bed and stretched, taking in the lush room once again. It reminded her of a stylish hotel.

After dressing, she went downstairs. Halfway down, she stopped short. Loud clanging came from the kitchen, metallic surfaces hitting against one another. Celia inched to the railing and peeked over.

A man was bent forward, rummaging through a cabinet next to the dishwasher. He stood with a large skillet in hand. When he turned toward the sink, Celia saw that he was Hastings. He wore an iteration of his outfit from last night—this time his black linen pants were paired with a light blue linen shirt.

Celia released the breath she hadn't realized she'd been holding—she was getting lightheaded—and continued down the stairs.

"Hi," she said.

Hastings nodded his greeting. Celia climbed onto one of the chairs. She watched him take ingredients from the fridge. A saxophone belted a jazz tune from the CD player in the kitchen.

"Is an omelet all right?"

"Sure."

Hastings turned on a flame beneath the skillet.

"Do you live around here?"

"Yes, ma'am."

"Please." She held up a hand. "Call me Celia."

He cracked four eggs into a ceramic bowl.

"So, you're here year-round?"

"Yes."

"Do you take care of other homes?"

"I do."

Celia paused. Was making conversation an additional charge or something? Her true intention was to broach the immediate question: Did he know what Victor was?

Hastings added buttermilk and seasonings to the bowl.

"Do the owners live out of town, too?"

"I only tend to Master Smith's homes."

Celia paused again. *"Homes?"* It hadn't escaped her notice he thought Victor's last name was "Smith."

"Yes. He owns six in this complex and two closer to the Strip."

Celia's jaw dropped. This was like when she'd found out Victor had several bank accounts. She couldn't be too surprised. Victor was a hundred years undead; he was sure to have amassed property all over the country, maybe the world.

"Where is he, anyway?" she asked, with a casual look over her shoulder.

Hastings eyed her before pouring the egg mixture into the hot pan. "The door next to the bathroom" — he tilted his head to the side to indicate the first floor bathroom by the front door — "leads downstairs. But I wouldn't go down there, especially during the day."

He looked at her full-on then, and she understood that he knew. When she didn't exhibit confusion, she confirmed for him that she knew as well.

Hastings turned back to the pan and began adding different fixings. Celia chewed her lip as she tried to think of what to say next. She perked up when he spoke.

"I know we have only just been acquainted," Hastings began, "but I feel it necessary to warn you."

Her interest died away. "About?" she asked archly. She knew what was coming. She'd heard it plenty.

"Associating with vampires is risky—"

"*You* associate with them," she snapped. "You're in one's house right now, cooking his food. I'm sure Victor pays you for your services."

Hastings didn't react to her heated tone. He flipped the omelet. "Yes, but I am a more senior witch than you are."

Again Celia's jaw dropped. She watched speechlessly as Hastings slid the large omelet onto a black plate. He walked around the waist-high counter and placed the food on the table. He also added a bowl of cut fruit, a glass of orange juice, and silverware. It wasn't until Hastings put a cloth napkin next to her plate that Celia found her voice.

"How did you know?"

Hastings placed his palm on her bare forearm. A peculiar coolness spread up to her elbow, as if she had reached into a freezer. With the cool, she also received . . . not flashes . . . but *impressions* from Hastings. He was older, but she couldn't pin down his age. He seemed to have lived a lifetime. He was a father—the joy he had felt while holding a baby was too powerful for him to not have been involved. He also had some past pain, both physical and emotional, that she sensed but could not decipher.

She wanted to dig deeper, but Hastings removed his hand.

"What was that?" she gasped.

"Only Umami can receive energy from supernatural beings in that manner. You were able to read me, no?"

"Sort of, I think." Her brow furrowed as she recalled his "energy," as he called it. The angry, petite witch Corinna had called it that too.

"The more practiced you are, the better able you are to perceive others' energy, which is why I was able to tell what you are, what Master Smith is. Umami can feel that energy, experience it, and reach out to it. As a witch, however, you should be able to do so without touch."

Hastings frowned slightly at that. He probably wondered why she was so inexperienced.

He moved away suddenly. "Once you have eaten, I will take you wherever you would like."

He crossed through the living room to a glass door. A hot tub was visible out back. Hastings closed the door after himself.

The jazz still played from the kitchen, otherwise Celia would've been left sitting in silence. Her gaze dropped to the table, where her breakfast was getting cold. A variety of brochures were fanned out across the wooden surface. Several shows, the Hoover Dam, a spa, shopping centers—all activities were covered. She ate, and read the brochures mechanically.

Hastings reentered when she hopped down from the chair.

"I will take care of that," he said. He took the plate from her hands and cleared her spot. "Have you decided on today's activities?" He rinsed the dishes in the sink. "Might I suggest—?"

He broke off with a sharp intake of breath. Celia had walked up to him without him noticing. She stood right at his elbow, a determined look to her face.

"Are we really not going to talk about this?"

For a moment only the sound of the running water filled the kitchen.

"Do you practice a lot?" she asked.

"Regularly, yes. It's for protection mainly."

"From *Victor*?"

"Master Smith would not harm me, but it is a precaution nonetheless."

Standing this close to him, she detected the scent of sage that radiated from him, though she didn't know the name.

"There are spells for protection or something?" She drew on her movie knowledge now.

Hastings studied her, and then shut off the water. He grabbed a towel to dry his hands then headed for the living room. Celia followed.

Hastings sat on the large ottoman, and motioned for her to sit in front of him on the sofa. When she did, he took hold of her hands. Once again, she experienced his . . . *being*. The heat and life inside of him pulsed through her hands and into her veins.

She stared at him, awestruck. He didn't smile but he seemed pleased.

"I haven't come across an Umami in some time," Hastings commented in a breathy voice. His words resounded in her head before he spoke them.

An image formed in her mind of a young woman with brown skin and bone-straight black hair. Her full cheeks arched up to her eyes when she smiled, only the sinister expression sent a chill down Celia's spine.

Hastings released her hands, breaking the connection.

"I don't quite know what an Umami is," she admitted. "I just know I smell sweet to some vampires."

Hastings sighed at that. "Umami are special witches because of that connection to *all* supernatural beings. Actually, I don't know if they can be called witches. They only have that association because of the magic they can perform."

Celia shook her head. "I can't do magic."

"Have you tried?"

"Well . . . no."

Hastings surveyed her yet again. He then glanced over his shoulder toward the foyer and that door leading downstairs, as if he'd been summoned.

"If you are ready," he said, standing. Celia hopped up too. "I can take you to the Strip."

His tone had changed, along with his posture, becoming guarded now. Celia glanced to the door too and tried not to let her disappointment show.

Hastings let Celia off at the entrance to Caesar's Palace. A pestering, nagging sentiment followed her as she hurried inside the cool hotel. She realized what it was when she walked toward the casino.

She was lonely.

She'd only been in Vegas for a few hours and loneliness clung to her like a stench. She wished Hastings was with her. Or Trixie. Why hadn't she invited Trixie?

Celia sat at a *Wheel of Fortune* slot machine. She pulled out a ten from the hundred Meg had entrusted her with to play for them. She'd played twenty minutes before a woman in a tight romper carrying a tray approached her.

"Can I get you a drink, hun?" she asked with a smile.

"Sure, rum and Coke, please."

Celia pulled the lever again. She didn't want to let herself get excited yet. But after another thirty minutes and two drinks, the ten dollars she had started with was now at about a hundred.

One more pull, she told herself.

Three tries later, she was down twenty-two bucks. She decided to try a different machine.

The perky cocktail waitress sashayed toward her. "Another, sweetie?"

Celia agreed eagerly, even though a slight haziness crept around the edges of her brain.

The waitress came back with her drink. Celia tipped her, grabbed her receipt from the slot, and went off in search of another machine. Her gaze drifted toward the blackjack tables, where four men and one woman stared intently at their cards.

"Have you ever played?"

Celia jumped at the sudden voice. She had stopped on the edge of the footpath. A man stood beside her with his hands on his hips, looking at the tables. He turned his head toward her. His curly black hair had too much gel, making it appear as hard as a shell. His eyebrows were thick, but not too thick, and his dark lashes long. His big, bright eyes were a pretty shade of green, light, almost hazel. She estimated he was at least six-two.

He nodded to the table. “Blackjack? Poker?”

“No,” she said.

He smiled. “It’s fun. Let me teach you.”

“What?”

“Come on.”

Celia coughed out a laugh. “I’m sorry, but I think you have me mistaken for someone you know." She looked around. Maybe there were hidden cameras somewhere.

“I know that you’re cute and that you were rocking that slot machine back there.” He pointed over his shoulder with his thumb. His lips curved to the right in a crooked smile. “I’ve been ditched by my friends. Come on; don’t let me wander around alone.”

“Maybe these ‘friends’ don’t know you either,” she said, with raised brows. She stepped around him.

He skipped into her path, walking backward in front of her. “They’re *real* friends,” he said. “I heard those air quotes.” She smiled, in spite of herself. “They’re at a strip club. It’s eleven in the freaking morning, man!”

“Well, guys are gross.”

He laughed out loud. “Okay, that can be true. So . . .” He wiggled his brows inquiringly.

She shook her head. “Sorry.”

With a quick wave, Celia turned down one of the aisles of slot machines. When she peeked back to make sure he wasn’t following, she saw that he’d stopped on the marbled path. He had dropped his chin to his chest, his bottom lip stuck out in an exaggerated pout. She faced forward, her own lips pulling up into a little smile, and continued on toward the shops.

* * *

Celia was debating gelato when a woman's laugh caught her attention. She looked over at Max Brenner's and crossed to the entrance just as the two women exited.

The red-haired woman wore a cute, floral mini-dress. Her skin was toasty, her long legs stretching down into nude-colored wedges. The other woman, with black hair past her shoulders, wore khaki capris and a blue tank top. Her skin was still very pale, making her collection of tattoos more prominent. Serena and Grace—the Pérez brood's human assistants—had their arms filled with shopping bags.

Serena's gaze landed squarely on Celia. She promptly shrieked. Her voice echoed off the rounded ceiling with its painted white clouds mimicking the sky. Passersby stopped and stared, probably wondering if Celia was some kind of celebrity.

"Holy cow, Celia, what're you doing here?"

Serena threw her bag-laden arms around Celia, jabbing her several times with their sharp edges. Her lips pressed into Celia's cheek.

"It's our anniversary," Celia told her.

"Awww!" Serena sighed, hugging her again. She glanced over her shoulder to Grace. "That's nice, right?"

"He finally took you somewhere," Grace said in her impassive way. "Kudos." Sliding on her black, mosquito-eye sunglasses, she looked off toward the stores.

"We're here for some big-deal conference," Serena replied. "Rafael said we have to show our faces. Come on. We haven't been to the other half yet. I want Inglot," she added hungrily.

She looped her arm in Celia's and pulled her along toward the main lobby. Grace stood back with her arms crossed stubbornly.

"How long are you here?" Serena asked.

"We go back Wednesday night," Celia answered.

"We just got in last night. I hate traveling in the jet. Most of the plane's for the vamps so there's, like, no room. And Grace gets claustrophobic, so she needs to walk around on long trips, and there just isn't enough space."

Celia was intrigued. She had wondered how the vamps without Victor's ability of teleportation got around. Avoiding day travel couldn't always be feasible.

"Rafael has a private jet?"

"Oh, yes. It's the only way we travel. He has a couple of jets, actually. Some of them he rents out to other vamps."

"How does that work, the jets?"

"The vamps fly in these metal trunk things that get sealed up tight. Most of the plane is sectioned off for them, with four or six seats for humans up front. The windows are really tiny, even though the vamp compartment's sealed off and locked to make sure there are no accidents."

That was the nice thing about Serena. She was always so willing to share. She didn't make Celia feel like an idiot for her lack of vampire knowledge.

"Not all vamps do it this way. I've heard of them using trucks and shipping themselves. Hawthorne would do his eye thing on me and then ride in the trunk of his Cadillac. Like I was going to do anything. He should've been embarrassed for riding around in a *trunk* instead of being afraid of me." She shook her head. "I hated that car. I like big, but that was *too* big."

Celia's brow creased. "Why do you do it?"

Serena looked at her. "What, hang with vampires?"

Celia glanced around quickly, but no one had heard.

Serena shrugged. "They're fun." She waved her hand. "Look where we are. I do some errands for them, and in exchange I get to live like a celebrity without the paparazzi, although I guess I wouldn't really mind that part."

She flipped her hair, maybe on the off chance men were hiding around the corner with cameras.

"So, you don't want to be one of them?"

Serena smiled. "Not anytime soon. I like the sun and chocolate and I want to have kids. Maybe when I'm a hot MILF I'll do it."

"Talking about your afterlife plans?"

Grace had caught up with them as they approached the circular escalator. Serena had been walking slowly, switching her hips from side to side.

Serena had a great body, with thighs that moved when she did and a little paunch of a stomach. Celia actually found that comforting. Serena had a real body and she was still sexy as hell, evidenced by the many looks she received.

Serena put an arm around Grace's shoulders. "Are you going to invite me in and let me visit you at night when I'm a vampire?"

Grace grimaced. "No."

Serena gasped in surprise. "Gracie! Stop acting like you don't love me." She pulled Grace closer. "And when I bite you" — she buried her face in Grace's neck — "you'll love me even more."

Grace squeezed out of Serena's embrace and stepped in front of her. Her nose flared under her almond-shaped eyes as she huffed. Her face was free of makeup and her alabaster skin gave her the appearance of a porcelain doll.

"When I'm done with my contract," she said tightly, "none of you will see me again."

She turned and rushed up the escalator.

Celia was stricken. "Her contract?" she whispered.

Serena folded her arms at the chest as they stepped onto the escalator. "She told Rafael she wants out. There was a bad . . . accident . . . and she's tired of it. She originally wanted to be turned, but she's changed her mind. Or at least changed her mind about Rafael doing it. But he won't let her go just yet. So," she said, heaving a huge sigh, "I cherish every moment I have left with her." Her voice was cheerful, but she couldn't hide the pain in her eyes.

Grace was already in the cosmetics store, looking at nail polishes, when Celia and Serena entered. Celia looked at Grace as she followed Serena to the lipstick counter.

"I love it here so much," Serena said. She picked up a peach color. "I think Rafael should buy a hotel here."

"He'll probably look into Switzerland," Grace replied, coming up behind them.

Serena groaned. "All they talk about is skiing. The casinos are fun during the day *and* at night. Who cares about a pile of snow at night?"

Celia tagged along with the two for about an hour. She couldn't complain; Serena was nice company after an hour of sitting by herself at a slot machine. Serena caught her up on their activities over the past month since Celia had first met them at Ramsey's mansion. After visiting the Monte Carlos in Maine, they'd continued up into Canada, visiting

Montreal, Toronto, and Quebec. Serena had complained that it was too cold, so they'd flown to Panama, where Rafael visited with another friend who had just acquired a villa near the ocean.

"We had to cut the trip short once Rafael found out about this meeting thing here," Serena concluded. They were looking around Christian Louboutin. It was the first time Celia had ever seen those shoes up close.

A saleswoman emerged from the backroom carrying three shoeboxes. "You sure you don't wanna try on any?" Serena asked Celia, as she plopped down on the ottoman. She dropped her numerous bags to the ground beside her. Celia only shook her head.

"You don't know what this meeting is about?"

"Nope." Serena slid on a pair of red python platform pumps. "We aren't invited."

"And you're okay with that?"

Serena shrugged. "Yeah, I don't really care. Rafael'll tell me about it, I'm sure. All his business stuff is so boring. I'd rather him be screwing me than telling me about that stuff."

"Right," Celia said, because that was all she *could* say to that. She made herself busy checking out a strappy sandal.

Serena hopped up in the pumps, gaining a good five inches. She walked up the aisle toward Celia, and placed a hand on the shelf. She leaned closer.

"Have you been screwed by a vampire?" she asked. "I mean, *really* screwed? Because Victor is very sexy but he doesn't seem like he lets loose, you know? It's magnificent, Celia. They toss you around and catch you before you fall and when they go at it in that hyper-speed it's like they might break you apart."

She smiled sweetly, because she was Serena and she thought this kind of talk was appropriate or even solicited. Celia had no words.

Serena tested the shoes, walking back and forth a few times, blissfully ignorant. She wound up buying two pairs.

A half hour later, they ended up back at the gelato stand.

"You have to come to our party Monday," Serena declared. The worker behind the counter handed her a cup of chocolate gelato.

"Party?"

Serena nodded grandly. "Yes, Rafael's having company. We're celebrating his new book. Something about aliens," she added with a wave of her hand. Obviously it wasn't her cup of tea. "The party's a little fancy. Drinks and hors d'oeuvres. It's going to be amazing! Very Vegas."

"What does that mean?" Celia accepted her cup of strawberry. Grace had coffee.

"Lights, glitter, music," Serena said, as if that was an explanation. "You two *have* to come!"

"Okay!" Celia cried.

Serena had taken hold of her forearm in a death grip. Her bags jabbed again as she encircled Celia with her arms. She kissed Celia's cheek goodbye, and then she and Grace headed off toward the valet.

Celia's phone chimed from her pocket. She didn't recognize the number.

"Hi, may I speak with Celia, please?" came a pleasant female voice.

"That's me."

"Hi, I'm calling from the Oasis Spa and Salon on the Strip. I have you scheduled for the deluxe package in our spa today. Victor booked you at one o'clock. Is that time still okay?"

Surprised, Celia nodded. "Yes, yes, that's fine."

Celia called Hastings as she went out into the blazing heat, to let him know where she was going. She found the Oasis Spa just off the Strip, after passing the MGM Grand. The stark white building had gold trim around the large windows. The brown venetian blinds obstructed her view inside.

Celia beamed when she pushed the glass door open. Everything was so posh: dark, hardwood floors; plushy white sofas and chairs in the waiting area; exotic plants and golden, abstract statues in strategic locations. Ambient music played in the background.

Employees strutted by in crisp outfits of creased white pants, white sneakers, and silky white jackets with high collars. Celia was impressed.

The woman behind the desk beckoned her forward. She was very beautiful, with a face shaped like a heart, brown eyes that seemed to dance against her glowing bronze skin. She appeared to be Hawaiian. Her thick, dark hair was twisted on the sides to keep it out of her face.

"Hi, there," the woman replied. "Welcome to Oasis. I'm Leilani. Do you have a reservation with us?"

"Yes, my name's Celia Wilcox. My boyfriend, Victor, signed me up."

Leilani clicked on her keyboard, then smiled. "Ah, Celia. If you'll follow me this way."

She stepped from behind the desk in all her stunning glory. She was about four inches taller than Celia, even in sneakers. She placed a hand on Celia's shoulder. Her hand was warm, which for a second reminded Celia of her coworker Michael. He was a shifter, which made his body a few degrees warmer than regular humans. Celia found herself taking in deep breaths. But she didn't detect the Shifter Smell, as she dubbed the astringent scent that only she could recognize, and made herself quit before the woman noticed.

Leilani led her down a hallway lined with closed doors. She stopped at one and reached inside to flick on the light. A masseuse's bed stood in the middle of the room, a sink and cabinets against the right wall, and a rack of towels and sheets in the corner.

Leilani went to the shelf and retrieved a white sheet that she used to cover the bench. She took out another sheet and placed it on the foot of the bed.

"If you would remove all clothing and lie down under this sheet, Keoki will be in shortly." She closed the door behind her.

Celia stepped out of her dress. She had just settled on the bench with the sheet around her body when someone knocked at the door.

The guy who entered was so handsome that she stared, open-mouthed. He grinned, sheepishly, in response. His skin was bronze like Leilani's. Black hair flopped into his face. His entire body was a rock of muscle. His eyes were slits behind his chiseled cheekbones and his mouth small. He could've been a movie star, easily.

"Hello, Celia," he said. "I'm Keoki." His voice was tinged with an accent she didn't recognize.

"Hi, Keoki," she breathed.

Keoki's hands were large. And soft. He kneaded her muscles like dough.

"Celia?"

Some time had passed, she was certain. She just didn't know how long.

"Yes," she whispered.

"Come with me."

"Where?"

She opened her eyes, because he didn't answer. She blinked a few times and found the room empty. She sat up slowly. The music still played from the ceiling, but she couldn't hear anything beyond the room. The door had a frosted panel in the center that didn't allow a view into the corridor. With the sheet wrapped around her body, Celia opened the door and peered out into the hallway.

Though the music tinkled from overhead, there was no movement. The spa seemed deserted. She walked toward the lobby, the pads of her bare feet pressing against the cool wood floor. A group of women—she counted four of them—sat in a circle in the waiting area. They were all dressed differently, and seemed to be of varying ages. Their main similarities were the tanned skin and dark hair.

All of their eyes were closed, their faces upturned. As Celia inched forward, she recognized one as Leilani. They appeared to be meditating. Their breathing was in sync and their expressions were clear and serene.

Celia's mouth opened to speak but a hand touched her lower back. Instead of words, she moaned deeply. There was a low chuckle.

"It's okay," Keoki said, as he rubbed her hips. "Everyone gets into it."

Her eyes sprang open, her senses working overtime to understand what happened. She lay on her stomach on the bed. Keoki's fingers still massaged her muscles.

"People moan, sigh, fall asleep," he was saying. "One guy even farted. That wasn't cool. And it was really awkward the rest of the time."

She made herself laugh. "You probably saved that one for the employees' lounge," she replied distantly. He chuckled again.

She tried to relax, but the vision had been so vivid. Why had she dreamed about the woman at the podium?

Keoki continued to press into Celia's back. After a few minutes, she found herself drifting back under his spell. He worked on her entire body—even her forehead—for sixty glorious minutes. He finished with her left foot, which he set back down on the bed.

"There."

"That was amazing," Celia sighed. She didn't want to move. She was sure she'd just slide to the floor, since her body had turned to Jell-O. She sat up with the sheet over her breasts. Keoki had gone to the sink to wash the oil from his hands.

"How long have you been working magic?" she asked with a besotted smile.

Keoki halted, his back tensing. His head whipped around, his expression suspicious.

Celia's smile slipped away.

"What did you say?" He sounded angry.

"I just wondered how long you've been a masseuse," she said.

Now Keoki seemed confused. He remembered the water and shut off the faucet. He then pulled a paper towel from the dispenser to dry his hands. His face was still clouded when he apologized.

"I'll let you get dressed," he said. "Aria will be out front, for your next service."

He slipped out the door so fast you would have thought the room was on fire.

Celia hopped down from the bed and hastily threw on her clothes. She didn't see Keoki when she went out into the hall. Back at the front, Leilani was gone. A woman Celia's height, with black hair cascading down her back, smiled at her from the desk, creating deep lines in her temples.

"Hi, I'm Aria. Come with me, please."

They walked through the waiting area, where two women thumbed through magazines, and down a short hall into a smaller section. The smell of acetone and polish greeted them. Four raised leather chairs were lined up against the wall in front of foot baths. A couple getting their feet scoured occupied two of the seats.

The woman showed the man a spread in a decorating magazine. The man scrunched his nose at the picture.

Celia sat in the empty chair beside the woman. Aria started up the massage feature, which was like baby toes pressing into her back. Keoki had gotten in deep.

As Aria scrubbed her heels, Celia flipped through a magazine. She had only been barely aware of the couple, who continued to argue.

"You're crazy," the man replied. "I love you. But you're crazy."

"This kitchen is gorgeous," the woman protested. "Excuse me?" She poked Celia in the arm, making her start. "What do you think of this?"

She held the magazine up for Celia to see. The cabinets in the colonial-style kitchen were all a light, sandalwood shade. Even the fridge matched. The yellow wallpaper had beige swirls every few inches and the countertops were white. It was a spacious kitchen, but nothing to which Celia would aspire. Her mouth pulled down in a *well* . . . expression, and the man threw his hands up in triumph.

"See!" he cried. "It's ugly."

The woman shook her head, clearly indicating this wasn't over. Celia smiled at the amicable bickering. She didn't want to let her mind wander, but it did anyway. She imagined herself in their position: newly married, judging by the *very* shiny wedding bands, looking up decorating tips for her new home. Only, she didn't know who sat next to her.

She pushed those thoughts away.

A half hour later, her feet were smooth and her nails a deep red. She practically floated toward the exit.

As Celia was leaving, phone to her ear, she noticed Leilani and Keoki whispering at the podium. They looked at her, which made her pause. They seemed to be examining her.

When they didn't acknowledge her further, she continued out the door.

The black car idled at the curb. "I could get used to this," Celia whispered to herself when Hastings held her door open.

Back at the house, Celia shimmied into one of the bikinis. She then pulled a white, mesh cover-up over the suit, slid her feet into white flip-flops, and headed downstairs with a novel.

Hastings looked up from a notepad he had been writing in when she entered the kitchen. Celia reached out for the fridge. Hastings stepped up immediately.

"What would you like?"

"Oh, I was going to see what there was to drink." Her hand was still poised for the fridge handle, but Hastings stood in the way.

"Wine, juice, pop? Or I could also make coffee or tea."

"Um, I guess wine," she said, a little overwhelmed.

"White or red?"

"White."

With a glass of sauvignon blanc Hastings insisted on pouring for her, Celia slipped into the hot tub. The bubbling water splashed at her shoulders. She took a long sip of the cold wine, then closed her eyes and rested her head on the lip of the tub.

She wasn't aware that she had drifted off. The water bubbled in her ears, creating a soothing hum. Some nearby pigeons cooed happily. But she must've fallen asleep, because the orange glow through her eyelids from the sun had diminished until there was only blackness. After a few seconds, the sounds disappeared too, all but a soft thumping somewhere over her head.

"I am a more senior witch than you are."

Hastings stood outside. Celia could hear insects chirping, feel the stuffy heat. A swath of light fell across the right side of his face. He held a few pieces of mail in one hand and a grocery bag in the other. He stared at a closed door as if steeling himself for what was on the other side.

The image dissolved into darkness. Celia's eyes were open, but she could only see black. She sat up, stood, stretched. Then she reached out in front of her. A deadbolt met her fingers.

The door opened into a dim antechamber. Only a single bulb in the ceiling lit the space. A set of stairs stood just ahead.

At the top, she used a key she retrieved from her pocket to unlock two deadbolts. Once she opened the door, the rhythmic thumping that had been beating in her ears increased in volume. She followed the sound; it had captured her mind entirely.

She walked through a dark house, toward a door that led out back. A muted light shone down across the courtyard. There was a swimming pool, with a connected hot tub. A woman was there, her eyes closed. The thumping pulsed in her chest as well. Celia's gums tingled, but she fought to control it. The all-too-familiar urge to take the woman swelled. She reached out again and touched the woman's shoulder . . .

Celia shot up, catching water in her mouth when she gasped with surprise.

"Hey, sorry," Victor said. "It's just me. You know, falling asleep in a hot tub can be dangerous. Wrinkled skin and all."

Celia wiped the water from her face and stared at him. The porch light shimmered in his dark hair. When he saw she was upset, his smiled went away.

"What? Bad dream?"

"Uh . . . weird dream."

She pulled herself out of the tub.

Victor rubbed her shoulder. "How was your day?"

"Pretty good. I guess I was tired." She touched her cheek and realized just how hot the tub had gotten. "Thank you for my spa treatment."

Without thinking about it, she leaned forward and kissed his lips. His chilly fingers against her waist gave her a shiver. He moved closer. She wrapped her wet arms around his neck, soaking the collar of his shirt.

She realized she was waiting for the appearance of his fangs. He held back—but she was aware of them all the same.

Someone cleared their throat. They pulled apart and looked toward the house. Hastings stood a respectable distance away, his eyes averted.

"Your dinner reservation is in one hour, sir."

"Thank you, Hastings."

He nodded and went back inside the house.

"Where're we going?" Celia asked.

Victor smirked. "I guess you'll have to get dressed to find out."

They took turns showering. Celia dressed in a pretty pink sundress, with her hair up in a ponytail.

"You look nice," she told Victor when she got into the car beside him. He wore a short-sleeved light blue polo, tucked into his black slacks that hugged his thighs perfectly.

He wrapped his arm around her shoulders and kissed her temple.

Hastings drove them to the Palazzo. Celia smiled widely as she and Victor crossed the marbled floor to Lavo.

The restaurant was stunning. The lights had been dimmed, and plush, leather sofas were arranged around a low table in the waiting area to the left of the bar. Just past, the dining area was filled with white-clothed tables and booths.

"Hello," the hostess said. "Welcome to Lavo. How many in your party?"

"Two," Victor answered. "We have a reservation under 'Smith.'"

She gathered the menus, and led them toward the dining area. They passed tables of people eating and drinking merrily. A party of well-built men occupied one large table. Red bruises and cuts marred their faces, contrasting with the suave suits they had donned. Despite the hurting they must've taken earlier, they laughed and joked without a care in the world.

Celia and Victor were seated in a booth under a wall of white candles. Celia squirmed excitedly as she opened her menu. And then she paused. Her eyes popped once she scanned the prices. Without looking, Victor rubbed her knee reassuringly. He was telling her to relax.

"What else did you do today?" Victor asked.

"Um, some gambling. Oh, I saw Serena and Grace, of all people. Serena said they're here for some meeting."

Victor stilled. When he looked at Celia, his expression was puzzled.

"What?" she asked.

"I'm just curious who they're meeting."

"Serena said it was a big deal."

“Rafael wants to move from Florida. He might be courting the leader of this area.”

“What does that entail—?”

“Hello.” Their waiter had stopped at the table. “My name is Adam. Is this your first time at Lavo?” They nodded. “Well, we’re famous for our meatballs. They’re one full pound of Kobe beef *each*. Most people order it as a starter. The appetizer is one giant meatball that will definitely feed four people. And we offer a whipped ricotta on top to give it that extra something. I would definitely recommend that.” He clapped his hands together. “Can I start you folks off with something to drink?”

Victor ordered merlot, and Celia tried the sangria.

“I don’t understand,” Celia said once Adam left. “I thought you all didn’t have a government.”

“There isn’t one government. Different areas have different leaders and different rules.”

Celia shook her head as she turned back to her menu. “You vampires are so complicated,” she said in amazement.

Adam brought their drinks at that moment. He also took their food orders.

“How come you aren’t involved in any of that? I’m sure Ramsey would let you.”

Victor shrugged. “I don’t have an interest in politics.” Celia marveled silently at how formal he could be. He’d probably make an excellent politician. Of course, having vamp mind-control would be a plus as well.

Adam returned with their appetizer. Celia dug into the meatball.

“So, how does Ramsey rule?” she asked as she took a bite.

Victor sipped his wine, his eyes on the table. After a pause, he began.

"Everyone is to join a nest. They have to report to Ramsey about any newcomers, deserters—really, any kind of movements. No deaths or turning people. He has to know about long-term visitors."

"What happens if someone breaks a rule?"

"Milo, Clarice, and Arturo were the first rule breakers, for as long as I've been in Boston. Arturo is gone. Milo and Clarice will be taken care of too. There was one other. She's been exiled."

Dinner was pleasant, even after the mention of Milo and Clarice. Victor kept mum about their itinerary, though. No matter how many ways Celia tried to get information, he would only smile and shake his head.

"Come on, babe! Just a hint!"

"Nope."

For dessert, they ordered beignets. Celia was quite full when they left the restaurant. Out on the Strip, Victor draped his arm across Celia's shoulders. They ambled down the street, gazing at all the lights and sights.

They passed three women in tight miniskirts, fishnets, and sparkly bras. They smiled invitingly to Victor.

"I hope *they* aren't the 'Vegas' Serena talked about for their party," Celia mumbled.

A group of raucous guys stepped out of Harrah's, laughing and jumping around. One of them held up his hand for Celia. She giggled, and gave him five.

This was nice. Being with Victor on a hot night, with the flashing lights and music. They even waited in line a half hour for entry into Jet nightclub, where they danced off the earlier calories.

A few minutes before one, Celia grabbed Victor's shoulders, pulling his head down to her level.

"Let's go home."

At the house, they slowly took off each other's clothes. Victor handled her with a light touch. Soft kisses on her shoulder. Gentle caresses across her hip. Victor lifted her, and she automatically wrapped her legs around his waist. He carried her to the fluffy bed and they fell together. Celia gripped the edge of the bed, her knees up, her moans rolling from her throat. She clasped him closer as her body unfolded for him and he was there to receive her.

His lips brushed her neck. His hair fell forward, tickling her skin. When she forced her eyes open through her mounting bliss, she found him watching her. His hand stroked her neck. She stared at him for a moment before turning her face to the side, exposing her throat.

Victor's hand tightened ever so slightly as he pulled her closer. His fangs sank into the flesh of her neck, piercing her vein. Celia's breath caught in her throat. He pulled her into him through the wound as they both came together.

She was lightheaded when he leaned back. Victor cut his wrist for her and she was flying.

* * *

Celia was tucked into bed, sound asleep. Victor closed the front door behind him. He decided to take a deep breath. The arid air was comforting in his nose and lungs. Celia's blood caused a rosy hue to fill his cheeks.

A chuckle broke the silence of the night.

"See? Hang around humans and you start to think you're one of them."

Mary sat on her porch, smoking a joint. She brought it to her lips. The end blazed orange for a few seconds. She let the smoke drift out her open lips before inhaling it back in through her nostrils.

"It's a delusion, Victor."

Victor waved his hand as if he hadn't heard her words. "Nice night out," he called cheerily.

He walked to the curb, where a black Jaguar XJ was parked. Hastings had neglected to put it in the garage apparently. Or, more likely, he had anticipated Victor needing it.

Victor keyed in the entry code to unlock the door. Mary's gaze rubbed across him. He ignored her, climbed into the car, and started the engine. Hastings had filled the tank.

Without looking across the street, Victor whipped the car around and exited Setter's Cove. He was back on the Strip in twenty minutes.

Outside the Riviera casino, directly to his right, three people were gathered around a table. The outdoor patio had several tables roped off from the traffic of the sidewalk.

They caught Victor's attention because they were vamps. The tallest of the three was a black man with thick locks cornrowed halfway back. His white t-shirt and loose white shorts accentuated his muscular build. The woman was slender and only a few inches shorter than the first. She had lemon-colored, wavy hair that rested over her shoulders. The last man was portly, with very short reddish-blond hair, a goatee, and round glasses on his round face.

The three studied Victor. After a moment, Victor nodded once. The man with the glasses nodded back. Victor carried on.

Celia had pointed out a t-shirt in one of the myriad souvenir shops they had passed. He picked one out for her and one for Trixie. He also picked out a few things for Celia's aunt and uncle. For Trixie, he chose a gold necklace with a "T" pendant, as a thank-you gift for helping him plan the trip. The words "Las Vegas" etched the longer portion of the initial.

He'd noticed the young woman with the rust-colored hair eyeing him since the bell above the door had announced his presence. She wore the same black tee, with the store's name above her left breast, as everyone else working there did.

She arranged shirts on a circular rack. She smiled at Victor when he came closer to look at the shirts.

"These here are on sale this week." She spoke with a Southern twang. "Only six ninety-nine each."

Her smile widened.

"Thanks," Victor said, and he browsed through the rack. She helped him at the register.

"Bye now," she said sweetly. She leaned forward on the counter, offering him a view of her cleavage.

Victor left out the door, the bell ringing after him. He had just imagined the parking garage when the bell dinged again.

"Sir?"

He glanced back to the door.

The woman's flip-flops slapped against her heels as she hurried over to him. She smelled like cinnamon. Brown freckles speckled her cheeks and nose.

She held out a slip of paper to him. "Your receipt, sir."

He let his gaze drop down to the paper. His fingers slowly closed around it. The woman grinned and went back to the store, slower this time, in case he wanted to check out her toned legs in her denim cutoffs.

Victor noticed writing on the other side of the receipt. Turning it over, he discovered that she had jotted her phone number and "5:00", the time her shift ended, no doubt.

There was someone behind him. Victor turned around to find there were actually *four* someones behind him.

All four of them were burly, even the one woman. They all had dark hair of varying lengths and skin that looked like old leather. There weren't many identifying markers to differentiate the four—besides the woman's massive breasts. Either they were related, or the years spent together had simply made them indistinguishable.

They strolled toward Victor purposefully. The way they sort of *floated* across the pavement without a sound showed they were vamps. Of course, Victor had known that before he'd even seen them.

The woman spoke first. "Well, who do we have here?" Her high-pitched voice contrasted with her appearance. She gave Victor an even stare.

One of the men growled ferociously, revealing his fangs. Victor instantly put up his guard.

Growly tried to pass the woman, but she held up a hand to stop him. One of the others had to take hold of his arm to keep him back.

Okay, so Victor had done something wrong. He just needed to figure out what.

The woman's gaze slid to the store's door. Two more women exited.

"Your nose must not be too good," she commented. "That human? She's someone's property."

Growly growled. Victor kept his eyes on the woman. He hadn't detected any scents on the human. Growly tried to stake claim on a human with whom he hadn't connected.

"I didn't know," Victor said diplomatically.

"Stay away from her," Growly snarled.

Victor raised his hands in the air as if surrendering, though he was so casual about it that it was obvious he wasn't serious. People passed by without giving them much notice. It was a wonder if it was because they were vamps, or because they were in Vegas.

Growly spat something at Victor in what sounded like Chinese. The words were too fast and jumbled to understand completely, but he caught the gist. He was calling Victor a fucking, limp-dick son-of-a-bitch, to put it mildly.

Victor tightened his grip on the plastic souvenir bag. The other goons hissed as well. The woman continued to watch him.

"Where are you from?" she asked conversationally, as if her friends weren't readying themselves to pounce.

"New England," Victor answered vaguely.

She paused, thoughtful. "What's your name?"

"Victor."

"Are you here alone?"

"No."

"More vamps?"

He hesitated for a millisecond, knowing she probably noticed. "Why?"

She shrugged, still gazing at him, still calculating. "I like to know who's in my territory."

That gave him pause. "*Your* territory?"

"That's right," the goon on her left snapped.

Victor decided now was not the time to press the subject.

"Who else is with you?" the woman asked again.

"It's only me."

"How long are you staying?"

Victor understood the line of questioning; it was just her stare that caused his misgivings. Like she was evaluating his every word and move. Suddenly, he had a theory he wanted to test.

"Three days."

The woman's brows pulled together, an angry cloud crossing her face. "Three days?" She shook her head. "I don't like liars."

She grabbed hold of the older man who happened to cross in front of her at that moment. Her hand flashed out and wrapped around the base of his neck while her eyes remained on Victor. The man gasped in surprise.

She twisted her wrist. There was a snapping noise. The man's eyes crossed at Victor, and his tongue lolled out of his mouth.

She released him. Goon 2 on her right caught the man before he hit the ground. He settled him on the sidewalk, his back propped up against the brick wall.

Victor stared down at the man. Anger and guilt simmered in his veins.

"I just needed to confirm something for myself," Victor said slowly. He met her gaze. "I'll be here for six days."

The woman's hostility melted as she realized he'd been testing her. She barked with laughter, then looked at Goon 1. He didn't join in.

"You hear that," she cried. "He was *confirming* something." She faced Victor again. "You're quicker than most. I'm Rita, by the way." She didn't introduce her companions.

"Nice to meet you, Rita," Victor said, politely enough. The man's motionless legs were visible in his periphery. "I'll try to stay out of your way while I'm here."

He took a few steps without turning his back to them.

"He can't get away with this," Growly snapped, breaking free of his restraint. He jumped at Victor, his anger and fangs distorting his face into something unrecognizable, certainly not human.

Victor hit the ground hard, the colossal vamp on top of him. As Growly raised his fist to punch Victor's face, the vamp stumbled because he was unbalanced.

Victor swung with his elbow and caught him in the nose. Growly screeched in pain and fell over, holding his bleeding face.

Victor shoved him away and got to his feet. The other goons approached. He looked to Rita to see if she would stop this. She smirked, enjoying the show.

Victor ran around the nearest corner, the two at his heels, and teleported once he was out of sight.

Celia was still fast asleep when he appeared in the room. Victor climbed into bed beside her, grateful for her warmth and the melody of her body: light, even breathing; gentle sighing; rhythmic pulse. All of it helped to alleviate the adrenaline firing through him.

He eased her to him and held her until it was time to leave.

Three

Celia woke to the sun warming her face. The alarm clock on the nightstand said that it was nearly noon. She stretched, scratched her scalp, and then took a shower. Like yesterday, when she went downstairs, she found Hastings preparing breakfast.

"Good morning," she called as she sat at the table. "Well, I guess, afternoon." The brochures still lay on the table. She picked up one for a comedy club.

A different jazz CD played from the kitchen. She liked this one too. She peeked over her shoulder. Flour, baking soda, and spices were arranged around a bowl on the counter. Hastings stirred the batter a few times. She watched him pour some into a waiting waffle griddle. He then went to the fridge, where he pulled out a bowl of cut fruit.

He was silent as he set a space on the table for her.

"This looks delicious, thank you," she said when he placed the steaming waffle in front of her.

She smiled up at him. His shoulders were rigid, and his brows were pinched in the center.

"What?" she asked.

Hastings's gaze rested on her.

"What?" she said again.

He didn't say anything. Instead, he headed for the back door.

"You don't have to leave," she said quickly. "Have something to eat."

"I'm not hungry."

"Well, keep me company then." He paused in his exit. "Please."

Hastings sat across from her, not quite looking at her. She tried a few times to spark a conversation.

"How long have you been—?"

"Where would you like to go today?" Hastings interrupted. Today, his tone wasn't professional. He sounded . . . angry.

Celia halted, her mouth still open. She frowned. "What's with you? I mean, you tell me you're a witch. You know I am one—well, if you can actually call me one. And now when I try to ask questions, you're short with me. So, what's with you?"

He didn't immediately answer. She waited.

"You've," he finally began, "had his blood."

Celia's heart sped up to a normal rate. Her cheeks warmed.

"You contaminate your body with that poison."

She sat in silence, mostly because she didn't know whether to deny or justify. "That's really none of your business," she said at last, as a sense of *déjà vu* settled under her skin.

"You are correct. But I would be remiss if I didn't warn you."

Her cheeks flamed even more. "Do I have a fucking sign up telling people to warn me? That I don't know what I'm doing?"

Hastings sighed. "You don't know."

Her eyes narrowed. "This coming from the ultimate hypocrite."

"Lash out all you must. You don't understand the power you give him. Sharing blood with a vampire is dangerous and nonsensical. That goes for regular humans. The blood from witches is more potent. An Umami is even more so. I'm rather surprised he has had enough self-control to not drain you dry."

"Because he loves me, you asshole. Victor's my boyfriend; he wouldn't hurt me." As the words left her mouth, the memory from the plane popped into her head.

Hastings didn't say anything. A clock somewhere ticked off the seconds.

"Where would you like to go today?" he finally asked. "I will drive you."

"What I would really like is for you to explain."

"There's not much else to say, Miss Wilcox. Witches know not to associate with vampires."

"But *you* do! You clean his fucking house! You cook his food!"

Hastings sighed again, never shifting from his aloof posture. "Only because I owe a debt."

She was shocked. "To Victor? What kind of debt?"

"That's personal."

Celia had to laugh, even though she found no humor in that protestation. "Oh, and blurting out that I shouldn't be with him isn't?"

Hastings paused as he considered her. "All right. He helped me, a long while ago, when I escaped from London. I had nothing when I started here in the U.S. He offered me a job."

"So, you're in hiding?"

"In a manner of speaking, yes. No one would look for me here in this . . . this breeding ground of vampires. And Master Smith makes sure of that."

"So, okay, there you go," Celia said, pointing at him. "Victor *helps* you, so why do you condemn him?"

"Because I have more extensive experience with vampires."

"I think my experience with them has been plenty extensive."

"This extensive?" Hastings rolled up his right sleeve. Five scars cut across the flesh of his bicep. They had puffed up into long, bumpy keloids.

"How about this?" He pulled down the collar of his polo, giving Celia a view of more scars on his chest.

She stared at them. The scars had healed in lighter shades than his brown skin. Markings from bygone stitches were visible as well.

"Is that why you left London?"

He straightened his shirt. "Partly. The other part was family. That Umami I spoke about . . . she was my sister."

"'Was?' Is she . . . ?"

Hastings shook his head. "As far as I know, she is still alive. And I will stay as far away from her as possible." Seeing Celia's confusion, he continued. "She fell in line with a group of vampires and turned on our coven. The vampires wanted control of London. We tried to stop her and killed many of her vampire conspirators, so now she seeks revenge. Most of us were able to flee."

"A whole *group* of you couldn't control her?" Celia asked in awe. She remembered the face she'd seen when she had touched him, the shiver she'd received at that icy smile.

"She'd become a Delmi. A witch who uses black magic," he clarified at her blank stare. "She is no longer the sister I used to know."

Celia took a deep breath. "I'm sorry your family was ripped apart. And I understand what you're saying. But I haven't changed. And I don't even know magic."

"Precisely my point. You're doing things blindly."

She leaned back in her seat. "Well, that's your opinion. We're all entitled to one."

"That would be the opinion of anyone with two eyes."

"Two biased eyes. I'm fine, thank you." She jumped down from her seat and went upstairs.

As Celia fixed her hair, a phone rang. She looked toward the source, but it was silenced. A second later, Hastings's voice sounded through an intercom next to the door.

"Miss Wilcox, you have a phone call."

Celia picked up the handset on the nightstand.

"Hi, Celia!" Serena sang into her ear. "Do you have a dress for tomorrow?"

"What?" How had Serena gotten this number? "Um, no."

"Good. We're going shopping. Tell that British man that we will *arrange your travel and accommodations,"* she said with a flawless accent that surprised Celia. Serena giggled. "I'll be there in thirty."

Serena drove up in a midnight blue Cadillac SRX. The scent of fresh leather greeted Celia when she climbed into the backseat.

"Hi," Serena said. Grace gazed out the window. "Buckle up."

Serena turned up the Kings of Leon CD playing from the speakers. They all hopped out when she pulled in front of Caesar's.

"These are my favorite stores," Serena explained. She handed the car keys to a young valet, who passed her a blue ticket. She then looped her arms with Celia and Grace's, and they headed inside the hotel. Celia stopped off to get a coffee. She didn't drink it often but she had a feeling she would need it today.

"Hi, there."

Celia glanced over her shoulder. The man from the casino yesterday stood behind her. His hands were in the pockets of his khaki shorts, his shoulders hunched up and forward. He had a sheepish, hopeful grin.

"So, this is fate, right?" he asked. "You were meant to save me from boredom."

"Are your friends still in that strip club?"

"Actually, a different one this time."

"You might want to get new friends."

"Not all of them are there today," he amended. "Besides, it *is* Vegas, and most of them are married or with girlfriends, so they're trying to make that Vegas slogan mean something, you know?"

"Sure."

It was her turn at the counter. She stepped up and ordered an iced vanilla coffee. He ordered a mocha frappe.

"My name's Alec," he said when they stepped aside.

"Celia."

"Nice meeting you." Alec stuck his hand out.

She shook it. "Am I going to regret this?"

He feigned shock. "I'm a great guy. It's just that naked boobies trump great personalities sometimes. Which means I have to befriend cute strangers."

Her mind lingered on "cute."

"Are you here for business or pleasure, Celia?"

She hesitated. He was nice, but his friendliness was too close to flirtatious.

"Pleasure. My boyfriend and I are celebrating our anniversary."

"Nice," he said, without missing a beat. A man placed their drinks on the counter. "You should go to the wax museum. Oh, and make sure you see the fountains at the Bellagio."

"Are you a tour guide or something?"

"I could be. I've been here so many times." He pointed behind them. Two guys sat on a bench. They were both busy with their cellphones. "These guys and I come here about three times a year. For business," he added with a raised hand, as if she might object. "Our other friends are here for a birthday."

"Where are you from?"

"ATL. Have you been?"

"Only once, when I was younger."

"Oh, you have to go now. I could tell you where to go."

"I bet."

He smiled.

She held up her cup. "Well, it's nice meeting you, Alec, officially."

She turned toward Serena and Grace. When she glanced back, Alec was still watching her.

"Ready?" Serena asked, looking up from her purse.

"Sure," Celia replied, although she didn't know if her wallet was ready. It definitely wasn't on Serena's level, that was for sure.

They had made it through six stores by 3:00.

"Nothing?" Serena asked with a pout.

Celia only shook her head. Truthfully, she'd seen plenty. There was the sexy leopard print pencil skirt, and the flowy LBD with the low collar, and the royal purple strapless dress—although *that* was a stretch with her boobs.

Serena had collected five bags. Many of the items were for the Pérezes for the party—shoes, jewelry, perfume. She'd also arranged for ten dresses to be sent to their home.

At the next store they entered, a blue dress immediately caught Celia's eye. She walked up to it as if she'd just been reeled in. The sapphire evening gown showcased a low back and shimmering sequins along the bodice. She flipped the price tag over and cringed.

"Is that the one?" Serena asked with a huge smile. She'd caught Celia fingering the material for the twentieth time.

Celia snatched her hand away. "Um, maybe," she replied, her cheeks afire.

Serena took the dress from the rack and held it up. She nodded her approval. "Well, let's get this on you."

In the fitting room, Celia carefully slid the dress on. The satin material was soft against her skin. She modeled it for Serena, who beamed. When Celia came out of the dressing room in her own clothes, Serena took the dress from her.

"Gracie, come on, let's go."

Celia began to protest, but Serena strutted to the register with the gown draped over her arms. Celia rushed up behind her.

Serena handed the dress to the woman, who rang it up so quickly, you'd think she was afraid they would run from the store once they got a look at the highway robbery their prices were.

Celia sighed, accepting that she was buying this dress. She figured if she could avoid spilling or sweating on it, she could return it the next day. Hopefully Victor wouldn't notice the charge; he'd left her some spending money. She reached in her pocket for his credit card. Serena whipped her Black Card from her wallet and handed it to the cashier.

"Serena, you don't have to—"

"Don't be silly. You're coming tomorrow. The least I can do is buy your dress."

Celia gaped at her. That wouldn't have been the first conclusion regular people would come to if they'd invited someone to a party, but Celia was touched by her generosity. She hugged her. Serena's eyes welled up in surprise.

The cashier finished the transaction and put a plastic dress bag around the gown. She happily agreed to hold the dress until they finished shopping.

Celia found a pair of strappy silver sandals in Jimmy Choo and a clutch in Michael Kors. She was *so* not used to this. Her shopping sprees typically encompassed Old Navy, Forever 21, and H&M. And if she wanted to be lavish: Express, Guess, and J. Crew. But all of the charges, even the earrings Grace picked up at Tiffany and the chocolates from Vosges for shopping fuel and the cologne from Armani, went on Serena's—well, Rafael's—Black Card.

They stopped at a Korean BBQ restaurant on the way back to Setter's Cove. Celia was exhausted from the shopping and the heavy food when Serena parked the car in front of the house.

"Now, remember," Serena told her, "the party starts at ten. That's to give the vamps time to get ready, you know?" She handed Celia a sheet of paper. "That's my phone number, just in case."

"Thank you again," Celia said, for the tenth time.

She went inside and upstairs, where she tried on the dress again. She really did love it. She'd never owned anything so formal. She quickly took it off and hung it up in the closet. She then put on one of the other bikinis and went for a dip in the pool. The water was very warm, but her full stomach prevented any real swimming.

When she went back inside an hour later, she found Hastings sitting at the dinner table. From his stance, he appeared to have been waiting for her.

"Have a seat, please."

The water dripped down Celia's shoulders. Goosebumps crawled across her arms as anticipation and a little fear washed over her. She approached the table.

A thick, wooden chopping block sat in front of Hastings. Piles of fresh herbs were next to that, and a mason jar of a clear liquid beside them. There were also two ceramic bowls in front of the block.

Celia sat in the opposite chair, leaning forward, her damp hands wrapped around the edge. Hastings picked up a green, leafy herb.

"This is thyme." He broke off a few twigs and dropped them in each bowl. "This is rosemary."

He listed off the rest of the herbs—lavender, chamomile, aloe—before tearing pieces or chopping leaves. His fingers worked effortlessly as he added them into the bowls. He held up the mason jar last.

"This is distilled white vinegar."

He unscrewed the cap and poured about a tablespoon's worth into the bowls. He then stirred the mixture with a wooden spoon.

"Wood works best. Metal spoons might interact with the ingredients."

Hastings tapped the spoon on the edge of the second bowl and placed it on the table. He then placed a hand over each bowl and closed his eyes. After a few seconds, with Celia watching his every move, a white light glowed between his fingers. She gasped, the air knocking her back in her seat.

The light shone for five seconds and then died away. Hastings removed his hands and pushed a bowl toward Celia. She looked down at an amber-colored liquid. There was no trace of the herbs.

"What is this?"

"A standard cleansing potion. It'll also protect you from any dangers."

"What kind of dangers?"

"From anyone wishing to do you harm. It shields you. Takes you off their radar, so to speak."

She shook her head. "No one even knows me here. Why do I need a shield?"

"Everyone needs a shield. Trust me. Simply walking down the street alone can inspire dangerous ideas in some."

Celia stared down at the potion. "Sounds paranoid." But he did have a point, she mused, as she thought back to the most recent events in her life.

She lifted the bowl.

"Cheers," Hastings said, and they drank. The potion was warm as it went down her throat. It had a light, minty flavor, like tea.

Hastings stood and began to clear the table. "Master Smith has requested that you are ready to leave at sundown. That is in an hour or so."

She nodded.

Celia did see Madame Tussauds'. They took plenty of pictures with the celebrity figures. Victor bought her a Madame Tussauds' frame for their picture with The Rock that had been snapped before they entered the museum. He also bought her a plushy teddy bear.

After, they went to the casino so Celia could play more of Meg and Max's money. "I might have to take a service fee," Celia replied when her winnings jumped up to $236.

Victor nuzzled her neck. She giggled. She definitely didn't condone PDA—Victor neither—but she didn't push him away.

He sat back suddenly. "Did you change your shampoo?"

She pulled the lever. She'd lost five dollars. "I used that stuff in the bathroom." She pulled again. Another five dollars. "Shit. I think my luck's a'changing, babe." She finished her drink and turned to him. "Where to?"

Victor shook his head as if clearing it, and then took her hand. It was another nice, easy night. Celia was nearly floating. She was just happy they were back on track after the incident on the plane.

The next stop was the famous Bellagio fountains. They squeezed in between a group of five women buying beer from a man selling from his backpack, and a couple completely engrossed in their make-out session. Victor wrapped his arm around Celia's shoulders as they watched the water dance to "Billie Jean." She felt like a giddy little kid as her eyes followed the dancing jets spraying a fine mist at the crowd.

Afterward, they stopped at a bar inside New York, New York. Loud bass pumped from the club upstairs. Celia ordered a frozen strawberry daiquiri. Victor leaned his elbow on the bar with his head propped up in his palm. He watched her drink the daiquiri.

"Our anniversary's almost here," he said lightly.

"Can you believe it?" She grinned. She'd only had one other relationship reach an anniversary. That had been in high school. Her boyfriend had helped her cope with the loss of her mother. He'd ended up going away to Florida for college. The relationship had dwindled.

She wondered how many anniversaries Victor had had over his lifetime. She tried to imagine the women, what they'd been like, what they'd looked like. Images of women decked out in lavish petticoats and hair swept up in fancy, intricate up-dos popped in her head. Had he dated any royalty? Or anybody famous? She'd never asked him any questions like that, and he wasn't very forthcoming with his past.

Victor's hand squeezing her thigh brought her back to the present. She reached out to stroke his hair. The memory from the plane flashed so vividly before her that it was almost as if they were there again.

Victor's snarl was loud enough to capture the attention of the flight attendant.

Feral hunger pulsed from him.

Hunger for her blood. Every last drop of it.

Celia gasped and snatched her hand back.

"What is it?" Victor asked immediately. He reached out for her, but she flinched and he pulled back.

"I . . ." Her hand touched her chest. Her fingers grazed the heart pendant. "I'm sorry. I . . . don't know where that came from . . ."

She looked away from his worried face and focused on calming her pulse. What the hell was that? Everything had been going great. She didn't want to be scared again. She'd never been scared of him before. When Victor first told her he was a vampire, when she should've been terrified, she hadn't believed him. In fact, he had to prove it to her.

It was a cool March night. Celia stood at her stove, making popcorn in a pot, while Victor set up the DVD player.

He stepped into the kitchen with his hands in his pockets.

"About lunch tomorrow . . ." he said slowly.

Celia glanced over her shoulder as she swirled the pot over the burner. "My aunt's going to make Indian food for the first time," she said with a wince. "Don't make any plans afterwards."

"That's the thing . . ." He trailed off again. His eyes finally met hers. She noticed they were black tonight. It had been fascinating to her, how his eyes darkened and lightened with his moods.

The kernels clinked against the pan. "What's wrong?"

"Unless we have it after sunset, I won't be able to attend."

She shook her head. "I don't understand."

Victor crossed the room. "I can't come out in the sun because it will kill me."

The kernels came to life, rattling the pot. Celia jumped, and tightened her grip on the cover.

"What the hell are you talking about?" she demanded.

Victor waited for the popcorn to finish. She placed it aside and faced him. They'd been dating for three months—she hadn't expected him to play a joke like this.

Victor sighed. "I've been debating about telling you this for a while. Now that I see we have something here, and that I want to continue to see you, I thought I should tell you the truth, before you started to become suspicious and angry."

She stared at him for a long time. Her boyfriend was a fucking nut job. Great. And she really liked him.

"Hadn't you noticed I could never come to your job during the day?"

"Because you were at work."

"That I rarely eat anymore?"

Celia frowned at the counter. "Yeah, that was weird."

"And how my eyes change color?"

"I thought it had to do with your mood."

"Or how cold my touch can be?"

"But you're warm, too."

She grabbed his forearm. His skin was like a block of ice. She jerked her hands away and clasped them together at her chest. She shook her head a few times, fighting what he was telling her. It couldn't be true. Which meant he was crazy. And he was in her house. Wait . . .

"That's why you couldn't come into my apartment the first time. That's why you had me invite you in."

Celia remembered that night clearly. She'd invited him upstairs, but when he'd stopped short at her door, she thought maybe she had made a mistake. Maybe he didn't want to be with her.

Victor nodded once in response. Except a crazy person would have done that too. Because he would believe it was true.

"Okay," he said, after another stretch of silence. He opened his mouth.

Her gaze dropped to his white teeth. The two canines lengthened into two sharp points.

"Holy shit," Celia exclaimed, jumping back. Her hands came to her own mouth, covering her lips. Victor's fangs retracted and he closed his mouth.

"Now do you see?" he asked.

"Holy shit," she repeated.

She had kicked him out and avoided his phone calls for a week. But she couldn't stop thinking about him, how he made her feel sexy and happy. She'd stopped by his apartment during the day. The doorman had said he must've been out of town again. That he was bicoastal with his job.

The phone calls had stopped—she'd noticed they were only at night. He'd given her space to accept the unthinkable.

After another week, Celia had called him. She'd asked a ton of questions over the phone; she hadn't been ready to see him in person yet. Victor had had to dispel a lot of myths.

Vampires could see their reflections, for the most part. Those that could no longer see them were very old and had long since parted with their humanity.

Vampires could survive without drinking human blood. It was a harder existence; they needed to partake more often. They were weaker, lethargic.

Vampires could only enter a place of residence with permission—permission that could be revoked.

"How many of you are there?"

"Maybe seventy or eighty in Boston."

Celia laughed humorlessly. "In Boston," she repeated. Victor didn't respond.

"Are you going to drink my blood?" she asked abruptly. Her cheeks reddened. She found she was afraid to hear the answer.

"Do you want me to? Before you answer," he added, "I must tell you that I've found that humans can easily become addicted to the high they receive if they drink our blood. That's usually how it works. We give our blood so that the human doesn't become sick from blood loss."

Her eyes flooded in disbelief. Was she really having this conversation? Was she really trying to accept that he was a . . .

"So, this is common?"

"Only when a human is bound to a vampire. Humans can't know that we exist. We have to be careful with whom we share."

She chewed her bottom lip. She had to admit she was flattered. The only thing giving her pause was the bound *part. She'd only known Victor for three months, and look at this bomb he had dropped on her. What the fuck would it look like "binding" herself to him so soon?*

This was completely fucked up.

"So where do you get . . . um, you know . . . blood from?" She looked around the apartment as if someone would overhear.

"Strangers," Victor admitted. "I have to erase their memories afterward."

"And you've never . . ." How could she say it? She couldn't even believe she thought it.

"Drunk from you? No."

"Why not?"

He was quiet for a moment. "I don't know, to tell you the truth. I wanted to, that night we met. I was going to send Trixie back inside and then take you somewhere secluded."

Celia gulped, her skin prickling.

"But there was something in your eyes. I was intrigued. I thought maybe it was possible to have a normal interaction with a woman again, and I was intrigued."

She began to relax, but she was still a bit troubled by his aborted plans. She'd been his prey at one point. What if that urge resurfaced one night?

"I just want you to know that I don't endanger anyone. It took me a while to build up the willpower necessary to ensure I don't hurt anyone. It's just nourishment. I take what I need and then I leave them alone."

"This is all so crazy."

Even then, even after she'd found out what he really was and was able to sort out her thoughts, Celia hadn't truly been afraid of him. She'd been in shock for a while—and it had taken a couple more weeks for them to settle back into their comfortable groove—but then she'd been excited. Here was a secret no one would ever in their lifetime come close to guessing. She'd felt like a teenager again, silly grin included.

She didn't like this new feeling. Experiencing and witnessing the darker side of the man she loved, actually seeing it with her own two eyes, was unbearable.

Victor was staring at the crowd. He didn't seem to really see the people around them.

Okay, she thought. *Okay*.

"What're you thinking about?" He didn't look at her when he spoke.

"When you first told me."

"That was the worst two weeks of my life."

"I'm sure that's an exaggeration."

He shook his head in disagreement.

Celia studied him for a moment. "I guess technically our anniversary is in December."

His jaw clenched. She took in a breath. She didn't think it was funny either.

"Have you had other anniversaries?"

"Three." Victor's gaze remained on the crowd.

She was surprised. "Only three?"

"Yes."

Celia looked at the wooden surface of the bar. "Malik was my boyfriend in high school. No one else had really . . . captured my attention long enough." She took another sip of her drink and peeked at Victor.

A soft smile touched his face. He turned to her. Hope glimmered in his eyes.

Celia brushed her hair behind her ear. "Have you ever dated anybody famous?"

His smile widened. "Sure. They're gone now."

"Who were your three?"

His voice was steady. "I was with my maker for ten years. Then there was Rose Hollingberry. I met her in the spring of nineteen twenty-three when I had just returned to England. I couldn't go back to London."

"Too many memories?" Victor had been turned in London.

"Good and bad. So I tried a town called Durham, which was far north. I met Rose on my second night. It was obvious from the start that she could serve as a distraction. And I needed a place to live.

"I had to keep her enthralled to ensure my secret. I worked the docks. The town didn't question why I slept during the day. However, I could only stay there for three years. Rose's brother came to visit in the summer of 'twenty-six. He was suspicious of Rose's behavior in regards to me. And I can't be certain, but I think he saw me kill. I didn't want to kill him, because Rose adored him, so I left."

Victor paused. He had been staring at Celia's shoulder as he spoke. Celia waited.

"The last was Ingrid Rawlings. I met her in nineteen fifty-eight. She was an actress in a town called Juliette, in Georgia. I watched her perform as Lady Macbeth and knew I had to meet her. She had encompassed the role completely, and I was mesmerized. My only regret today is that I had to enthrall her as well. Nevertheless, back then I was convinced I had the real Ingrid. Somewhere in there was the real woman." He paused for a second. "But I could never know for certain. I still don't. Enthrallment makes humans pliable. My guilt made me end the relationship after a year.

"There were also stories of humans killing vampires in the area. A group of hunters working together to rid Georgia of vampires. I didn't have any allies. I had to leave. We had expensive champagne and chocolate cake, and then I erased myself from her life."

Victor paused again. Celia reached out and squeezed his hand. He didn't seem to notice. He hadn't blinked since he started.

"After Ingrid I decided to forgo putting down roots. It was too difficult, the guilt. Knowing that I couldn't experience a genuine relationship with a human. They could never know what I am. And I couldn't stay in their lives for too long."

He smiled sardonically. "Despite that logic, I did try again, in nineteen eighty-one. I'd met a woman while attending Duke. We were both taking the ancient folklore seminar. She had a lot of questions about vampire and werewolf mythology. I thought she believed."

He sighed. "After our fifth date, I told her the truth. From our conversations, she seemed to understand." He chuckled. "She did not take it well."

"Worse than me?"

Victor laughed. "That's an understatement. She screamed and threw things. I thought someone would call the police. I had to erase her memory."

Celia stared at him in wonder. He'd lived so many lives before she was even born: college student, dance instructor, Spanish teacher, chef, fisherman.

"I thought for sure after her," he continued, "that I could never have a normal life." His eyes finally met hers. She could swim in those dark pools. "Until a year ago."

Celia smiled and tightened her grip on his hand. "The supernatural just seems to find me."

"And I am so grateful for that."

They headed back to the Strip. After a few quiet minutes, Victor tensed, his hand gripping hers harder. He looked over Celia's head, across the street. Celia looked as well, but nothing seemed out of the ordinary. People milled about, going in and out of M&M's World. Cars honked, taxis pulled over to pick up passengers.

A low but fierce growl pierced the air. Celia was confused, because it hadn't come from Victor. When she looked again, she noticed a group of four had stopped in the middle of the sidewalk. They were too far off for Celia to make out features, except that they were all males.

"Let's go," Victor said abruptly.

He marched up the street. Celia was running to keep up.

"Victor, slow down. What's going on?"

She glanced back. The men still stood like human statues, obstructing the sidewalk, glaring at their retreating backs. The flashing lights all around reflected off their eyes, like cat eyes when the angle was just right.

Celia gasped at the impossible sight. She nearly tripped over a discarded soda bottle in her path. She turned forward to keep from falling on her face. Victor slowed just enough to ensure she had her footing.

When she looked back, the men were gone, just . . . *gone*. A shiver ran up her spine.

Victor didn't stop until they were back in the car.

"What was that all about?" Celia asked, rubbing her hand where he had been gripping her.

"Wolves," he said simply.

No elaboration was needed. There had been a group of them, and it would have been a hard task fighting them off if they had decided to attack.

Victor started the car. When the headlights automatically flared on, they flooded across a man standing in front of them. Celia yelped.

The man's dark hair rested against his ears. His hands were balled into tight fists. The muscles of his arms pulsed and bulged quite literally under his skin. His pupils, which had been brown, brightened to a molten gold, as if a light was slowly coming to life behind his eyes.

"What the—?"

Victor slammed the car in gear. The Jag flew forward.

The man jumped out of the way as Victor accelerated from the spot. Celia looked back through the rear windshield. The man watched them go.

"What the hell was that?" Celia gasped. She clutched the seatbelt.

Victor had to stop short at the garage exit. A line of cars waiting for the green light blocked their path. He glanced at the mirrors.

"A message."

The light changed. Victor nosed his way into traffic, ignoring the honk from the car now behind them.

"I don't want you going out on the Strip," he said, once they hit the expressway.

Celia gawked at him. "Am I supposed to stay cooped up in the house all day and night?"

"We'll do things together."

"Yeah, at night."

Victor's exasperated sigh was low. "Fine. Bring Hastings."

"Oh, how fun! I can go shopping with my dad! Or maybe everyone will think he's my sugar daddy. That's even better!"

Victor glared at her. "You don't think that man was alone, do you? I thought we would've lost them in the casinos. They surely know your scent now."

Celia rolled her eyes at her window. "Ugh."

"And . . ." he said softly, "I can't be there to protect you."

She just shook her head. She understood there were werewolves all over. She just hadn't expected to encounter any here. Didn't the supernatural world know she was on freaking vacation?

"Why would he try to attack us anyway?"

Victor's voice hardened. "I'm going to find out."

Celia stared at him. "But they might hurt you. You said yourself that was a threat. And you trying to run him over doesn't exactly say, hey, let's be friends."

Victor pulled into Setter's Cove. He stopped the car at the curb in front of his house. "Please," he said. "Just go inside, okay? We'll figure out tomorrow."

She wasn't thrilled but she said fine. He leaned over and kissed her lips. This time when the plane memory came to her, she was able to hold back her wince. She got out of the car. After closing the door, she turned for the house.

A woman appeared in front of her. The tailwind of her approach in signature lightning speed blew Celia's hair off her shoulders.

"I thought I would introduce myself," the woman said. Her flowered maxi skirt and white tank top hung from her bony frame. Her fluffy black hair was shaped in a wavy bob just past her chin. Her waxen cheeks were round like marbles, and looked just as unyielding.

She extended her hand. "I'm Mary. I knew Victor from way back."

Victor got out of the car. "Don't you have some pot to smoke?"

Mary *tsked.* "That's so rude," she said to him. She looked back to Celia. "Just because a girl was an addict in a past life doesn't mean everyone should hold it against her."

Her hand was still proffered.

Celia glanced to Victor. The car stood between them; he must've known Mary wasn't going to hurt her.

She reached out and shook her hand.

When they made contact, Mary's face crumpled in pain, and she let out a cry. When she tried to pull her hand free, she seemed to be stuck. She jerked her elbow frantically, whimpering as she did so. Celia released her and skipped back in surprise.

"What the fuck?" Mary shouted. She held her wrist.

Victor had flitted over to Celia's side. "What happened?" he demanded of Mary.

"She fucking—I don't know what she fucking did. God, that's worse than silver."

"I didn't do anything!" Celia cried.

They all looked at Mary's hand. In the streetlights, it was bright red and swollen. Tiny blisters were forming on her fingertips and palm.

"Shit." Mary tucked her sore hand to her side. Glowering at them, she crossed the street and retreated to her house.

They stared, Celia's mouth hanging open. She looked up at Victor. "I don't know what just happened."

Victor took her hand—she noticed he did ever so carefully. He let her in the house. "Stay inside," he instructed. She continued into the living room, dazed. He flicked on the front light for her.

The door closed and locked behind her.

* * *

Victor's first stop was M&M's World. He smelled wolf, but the scent was so mixed up with all the humans he couldn't trace where they had gone. As he strolled down the Strip, he pulled out his phone. Rafael was in town and would know how he could contact the leaders. He didn't believe for a second that Rita had a territory here.

He was about to dial when he noticed the black vampire he'd seen last night. He stood to the side, flipping through a brochure.

"Hello," he replied when Victor approached him. Tonight, he wore white cargo shorts and a white t-shirt. His thick locks were held back by a white sweatband. When he looked up at Victor, he smiled with straight, white teeth.

"We haven't met before, no?" he asked. "I'm Akeem Umaru. Well, this month anyway. How is my accent?" He meant the Nigerian inflection to his words.

"I haven't been here in a while," Victor admitted. "I guess I've been out of the loop. Has there been a change recently?"

Akeem laughed. "You're talking about Rita and her flock? She's been talking a lot lately. Ava and Wesley know she's been claiming territory. Come. Sit with me for a bit."

They went up the street to the Luxor casino. Akeem settled down at a gold mine slot machine. "Too bad I can't control computers as a super power," he commented when he immediately lost all of the ten dollars he had inserted into the machine. He rifled through his wallet with a dejected shake of his head.

"What kind do you have?" Victor asked.

Akeem peeked up at him, studying him a second. "Super powers" weren't things vampires talked about freely. Back in the days of leaders like Nathan, they were often exploited.

"I can control the wind." He shrugged. "Having witches' blood in your human lineage has its perks."

"Is that how it works?"

"You didn't know that?"

"No."

"Oh, yeah. That's how we vamps get our extra powers. The change triggers that magic in your bloodline, so even if you didn't have any powers when you were a human, it'll show up somehow in your vampire life." Akeem shrugged again. "My grandmother never made it a secret she was a witch. My parents called her crazy, but I guess I believed her. And now" — he looked at his hands— "I *definitely* believe her."

He inserted another ten into the machine. "So, where are you from?"

"I live in Boston currently."

"Ah. Never been. I just came from Mozambique. I missed city life too much though. You know, crowds and car horns and pollution. I think I'll look into L.A. or New York somewhere. Maybe Paris with Amaryllis. She's always looking for more vamps in her area. Then I can work on my French. *J'aime femmes méchantes."* He grinned at Victor, who was polite enough not to correct him.

A cocktail waitress came around a corner. "Hey, sweetheart," Akeem called. She hurried over, a large, eager grin on her face.

"What can I get you, sugar?"

Akeem locked eyes with her. Her gaze clouded in a familiar way. He had positioned her between them so that she blocked the aisle behind her.

He took an empty glass from her tray.

"Hold out your wrist."

She did as he instructed. Akeem pulled out a knife, cut her wrist, and put the knife away in a quick three seconds. She winced but didn't pull back.

He tilted her bleeding wrist over his glass. When he was satisfied, he leaned forward and, in the guise of kissing her, he cleaned and healed her wound. He then placed a twenty on her tray. She smiled happily.

"Thanks, babe."

"You're welcome." She skipped off.

Akeem brought the glass to his lips but paused. “Aww, shit, man. Where are my manners? Did you want some?”

Victor had been sitting silently throughout that exchange. There wasn’t much to say. “No, I’m fine.”

Akeem sipped. “So, anyways, I’d steer clear of Rita.”

“What do you know about wolves in the area?”

“Stay away from them too. Man, Vegas is all about territory right now. That’s why I keep my damn head down whenever I’m here. I let Ava and Wesley know I’m here and then I hang out, get some money and women, and then I leave.”

Victor watched the passersby as Akeem spoke. A few caught his eye for various reasons. If a vampire’s stomach could growl, his must’ve screamed. Akeem noticed. He downed his blood and stood.

“Come. Let’s see what the night has in store for us.”

* * *

After five minutes of sitting on the sofa in dark silence, Celia looked around. When her gaze happened upon the dinner table, it struck her.

As if zapped by a jolt of electricity, Celia raced to the kitchen. On the fridge, someone had written phone numbers for different delivery services—from food to laundry. At the top, she found Hastings’s number.

She didn’t realize how late it was until Hastings answered, his voice thick with sleep.

“Something happened,” she said. “This lady—she was a . . . a, you know. She touched me and her hand burned.”

“Where was this?” Hastings asked immediately, the grogginess disappearing.

“Outside the house.”

"Why were you outside? Where is Master Smith?"

"He was with me. Wait, why can't I be outside?" Celia sucked in a breath. "You know about that vampire? You know that she lives across the street? Is that why you gave me that potion? Why didn't you tell me?"

"Okay, slow down, please." The bed creaked across the line as he sat up. "I do know about the one across the street. She is in a relationship with the woman who owns the house."

"She's holding her captive?" Celia twigged.

"Not quite."

"Why don't you do something then?" He was quiet. "Hastings? Are you still there?"

"I am. I'm just curious why that is upsetting you."

She frowned. "Why wouldn't it? If that woman is doing something against her will, then that's wrong. Duh!"

Maybe he was still asleep.

"Why is her situation any different from yours?"

Celia snorted in disbelief. "Are you serious? I'm not being brainwashed or used." She waved her free hand in the air in the classic timeout fashion. "Hey, that's not why I called. What did you do to me? Why did I burn that vampire?"

"She wanted to harm you," he answered simply.

"And why do I keep seeing—?"

She stopped herself. Hastings already thought Victor wasn't right for her. Would confessing that she kept seeing the time he'd scared the shit out of her whenever he touched her help matters? It was probably an effect of that stupid potion.

"Seeing what?" He sounded curious.

"Nothing. Goodnight."

She hung up and leaned against the fridge. This definitely had to be the stupidest thing she'd ever done.

* * *

Victor was a bit reluctant, but Akeem seemed harmless, despite using the waitress's vein in public. They had gone to Flight bar at Akeem's behest. He told Victor more about Rita while they sipped bourbon at the bar.

"She and her friends came here from a Pueblo in Texas about six or seven months ago," Akeem was saying. Victor could hear him perfectly fine, even over the house music pounding the floor. "I hear the leaders over there kicked them out for the same shit she's pulling here. So you say she's a freaking lie detector? That explains so much."

He took a sip. "I love bourbon. Another thing I miss about cities. Dark bars, good music, anonymous encounters. Even this sub-par stuff is better than the swill in the village I was living in. Oops. Ha, 'swill.' I'm losing my accent already. Anyway, they had good Sambuca. The best I've had."

Victor only nodded. His drink was just for show. Akeem, however, savored his very much.

"About these wolves . . ."

"They giving you trouble?" Akeem asked. "Just ignore them. They're all bark." He chuckled at his own pun. "There're too many vamps around to really try something. I knew some shifters in Africa. It must be cool changing into an animal. They turned into foxes. But I still outran them," he added, raising his glass in a salute.

"One of them was about to change right in front of us."

"'Us?' You have a girl here with you? Or guy? I don't mean to assume."

Victor just stared at him. Akeem smiled. "Chill out, man. I'm not going to try and find her. She's human, huh? Is that why all the secrecy?"

Victor didn't answer.

"All right." Akeem lifted his hands in surrender.

A woman fought her way out of the crowd. Either she threw herself at the bar or tripped into it. Either way, she landed between them. Akeem grabbed her arm to help.

"Are you okay, there?"

"Yes," she breathed, and then giggled. She leaned over the bar, waving at the bartender. Akeem nodded to the woman, wordlessly telling Victor to take advantage. Victor shrugged, thinking, *why not?*

Akeem moved closer and whispered in the woman's ear. She looked at him, then at Victor. She didn't appear to be under his vamp hoodoo. She smiled at Victor and nodded, then whispered something back to Akeem and walked away from the bar without ordering. Akeem, smirking, gestured after her.

Outside, they waited for the lady and her friend, who finally emerged from the club ten minutes later. They introduced themselves as Betsy and Stella. Betsy, the one from the bar, had a light brown pixie cut, while Stella's long brown hair was loose and wavy.

Akeem extended his hand to them. "I'm Adewale."

"Wow, nice name," Stella remarked.

"Pleasure to meet you." He shook her hand while peering deeply into her brown eyes. No spell passed between them; he was just showing interest, you know, the normal way.

"This is my boy." He paused a second. "Michel. He's from Paris."

The women were visibly awed by that.

"Shall we, ladies?" Akeem asked, extending his elbows for them to hold. "You're at the Four Seasons, right?"

When Victor didn't follow, Akeem glanced back.

"What, you want to do this on the street?" Akeem asked without much regard for who could hear him, including the women. "Maybe in the toilets? Come on, man. These girls are cute. You don't have to go all the way," he needled, with an obsequious grin twisting his lips.

Victor looked in the opposite direction. He was so not in the mood for this.

"You coming, Michel?" Akeem called. They had started to walk away.

"Yeah, you coming?" Betsy asked. She then burst into laughter. "Coming."

Stella laughed, too. "Let's hope so," she whispered, but of course his vamp ears heard. The women laughed harder.

Akeem had an eyebrow raised. Victor sighed, and hoped he wasn't going to regret this.

Their suite was very roomy; the expanse of windows in the main room offered a panorama of the passing cars on the Strip, and Mandalay Bay next door. Betsy explained how this trip to Vegas was her husband's attempt to make up with her for his recent infidelity.

"I told that bastard I wanted a huge room and a fucking per diem before I even *considered* forgiving his lying ass."

Stella rubbed her arm. "I think you can get a Beemer out of this."

Akeem shook his head to Victor, as if to say *these heifers* . . .

"Anyway!" Stella clapped her hands together. "Who wants a drink?"

After receiving their glasses of wine, Victor and Betsy sat on the sofa. Victor placed his glass on the end table. Akeem and Stella took the loveseat.

They didn't wait for small talk; their macking commenced as soon as they sat. Betsy watched with a tense, sad expression. She glanced over to Victor and then quickly looked away, focusing on something on the carpet.

Victor really didn't want to be here. The longer he sat there, the more convinced he became this was a stupid idea. He looked over at Akeem. Stella had her legs across his lap. One of his hands was up her skirt; the other held her throat. His face was pressed into the crook of her neck. On the outside, it appeared he was in the process of giving her a prodigious hickey. But Victor knew he was drinking from her vein. Stella's eyes had closed, her face slack with ecstasy, her hand slowly stroking his locks.

Victor stood. Betsy, misinterpreting his movement, hopped up too. "Wait, I know, I'm—just give me a second."

"That's not—" he started, but she rushed off to the bathroom.

He turned back to Akeem. In just the few seconds he had looked away, Stella no longer appeared to be in bliss. Her skin was terribly pale and she looked to be asleep. Her hand dropped to her lap.

Victor crossed the room in vamp speed. "Akeem!" he shouted, shaking his shoulder.

Akeem pulled away. His chin and lips were wet with blood. A lazy stream of blood leaked from the puncture wounds in her neck. When he moved, Stella's head flopped to his shoulder.

"Oh, shit. I wasn't paying attention, man." He wiped his mouth sluggishly. His gaze was a bit unfocused.

They both looked to the closed bathroom door. Betsy ran water in the sink and muttered to herself to get it together.

"So, I'll give her my blood," Akeem replied, with a puerile shrug.

Victor's uneasiness morphed into anger. He glared at Akeem, which seemed to be enough to impart how much he hated this situation. He used to play these games, sure. When he was single. Blood and sex. Those were the advantages of being a vampire. Erase yourself from their memories if you wanted, but why would you? Leave those humans with memories of the best sex they'd ever have.

Times had changed, though, and Victor no longer enjoyed seducing strangers. And now the vamp he had thought was possibly trustworthy, if not useful for the information he could convey, had gone and nearly drained someone. And then he had suggested giving her blood, which could turn her. He was so casual about it all.

"I didn't hold you captive," Akeem spat. The blurriness from Stella's alcohol-tinted blood was leaving his features. "I'm capable of dealing with this. This isn't my first rodeo."

"Fine." Victor turned to leave.

Betsy stepped out of the bathroom. "You know, guys, maybe this isn't such a good idea."

Her gaze stopped on her friend. Akeem was cleaning her wound with his tongue. Stella's heartbeat was faint.

Betsy watched in silence as Akeem laid Stella on the chair. Her arms dangled as if made of rubber.

"She's not going to make it to a hospital," Akeem commented.

"Wh-what's wrong with her?" Betsy hurried over to the loveseat. She picked up Stella's hand, but, feeling how cold and limp it was, she released it with a gasp. Stumbling backward, she couldn't stop staring.

"She's dead!" she shrieked suddenly. Her voice seemed to echo throughout the room. "She's *dead!* She's—"

Akeem flitted to her and slapped a hand over her mouth. He caught her gaze. She immediately relaxed.

"Go have a seat and don't say a word while we figure this out."

He removed his hand, leaving behind a red smear across her cheek. She walked over to the sofa and sat. Her eyes were wide enough to show the whites all around. Her skin had blanched after touching her friend. Back as straight as a board, she wrung her hands over and over again.

Akeem turned to Victor. When Victor didn't speak, he said, "So we put her in the tub. She said she was sad about losing her job. We'll make it look like . . ."

Victor raised his hand, maybe to silence him, maybe to stop him from going down that route. Akeem didn't speak again. He gathered Stella in his arms and carried her to the bathroom. Five minutes later, the water ran in the tub. He came out, knelt in front of Betsy.

He used his thumb to clean the blood from her face.

"I'm so sorry for your loss, Betsy. You and Stella . . . you had a lot of fun tonight. You got so drunk and then came back here. You all never met us. Only the two of you came back to her room. Betsy, you fell asleep on the sofa. When you wake up in the morning, you'll find Stella. You hadn't known just how upset she was about losing her job."

Betsy's eyes widened with each of Akeem's words. She pointed to her mouth.

"Yes, speak."

"She lost her job?"

Akeem considered for a second. "Yes, she told you after your fourth drinks. You both cried, and then you said fuck that company, and she said fuck your philandering husband."

Her eyes brimmed with tears. "'Philandering?'"

“Cheating, sweetheart.”

“He’s a bastard.”

“That’s right.”

“He hit on Stella once, at a party. I didn’t tell them I knew. Stella slapped him. She wanted to tell me but she never did.” Betsy’s shoulders shuddered and she began to sob. “I love her! Why did she do that? Who else do I have?”

Akeem squeezed her knee with a grimace. “I’m sorry,” he said softly. The remorse rang true in his voice. He then laid her down on the cushion. “Go to sleep now.”

Betsy nodded, her crying immediately subsiding into sniffles. Her eyes closed and her breath slowed to an even rhythm.

Once she dropped off, Akeem stood. He nodded grimly to Victor and they headed out.

“Heavy,” was all Akeem said in the elevator.

Victor left him in the lobby.

When Victor went back to the house, he was surprised to find Celia asleep on the sofa, curled up in the corner. If he hadn’t heard her breathing, he might’ve missed her altogether. The light from out back was on, and it poured in through the blinds, stretching across her body.

Gently, Victor lifted her in his arms and carried her upstairs. She stirred when he placed her on the bed.

“Victor?” she murmured.

“Right here.”

Her eyes blinked open. “Did you find out anything?”

“Yeah, stay away from them.” He had a wry smile.

"Well, duh," Celia said with a soft chuckle. Her eyes closed again. "I'll be okay, Victor."

He took her hand in his. Her warmth seemed to burn his flesh like fire. His mind wandered to Viviana, Mary—whatever she called herself today. Were Celia's abilities still manifesting themselves? He'd only had a cursory lesson on Umami from Elizabeth. They were able to connect with supernatural beings. Did that include protecting themselves from them as well?

He couldn't help feeling pleased that her abilities weren't reacting to him in such a way. He knew he had really scared her on the plane. It appeared she still trusted him.

He watched as she drifted back to sleep.

Four

Hastings wasn't around when Celia got up at 8:00. He'd left her a sandwich and a note saying he was called away to one of the other properties. Celia had just sat down to eat when the house phone rang.

She hesitated, but then thought maybe it was Hastings, checking in. When she answered, however, a woman's voice came over the line.

"May I speak with Celia Wilcox?"

"This is she."

"Great! This is Leilani from the Oasis Spa. We met yesterday."

"Oh. Hi."

"We have promotions from time to time and like to extend them to select patrons as a way of showing our appreciation. I would like to offer you a package this afternoon. Either the same one you had yesterday or another of the same price."

"Oh. Wow. Okay."

“Excellent. I’ll book you at ten. See you soon.”

Celia hung up, feeling excited. She’d never been to a spa, and here would be her second time in a row. She called Hastings. He said he’d pick her up in time, so she ate, then dressed.

When she went outside at 9:30, Hastings got out of the black Lincoln to open the door for her. She waited until he drove off.

“So what else can I expect from that potion?” she demanded.

“It appears you’ve already witnessed its power. We’ll want to repeat it in a day or two.”

“I don’t know . . .”

Hastings looked at her in the mirror. “Why not?”

“Because I don’t know anything about this stuff!” If she sounded mopey, well, that couldn’t be helped. “How do I know I won’t grow an extra arm or something?”

“I’ve never heard of that happening.” He actually sounded serious.

Celia groaned. “I really hate this. I don’t know anything.”

“Not true. You know that you are protected from those that mean you harm. You know we used herbs and imbued them with magic to perform the spell. You know that you are a witch because this particular potion only works for witches.”

She just stared at him.

“Okay,” he said. “I will teach you the spell when we perform it.”

“We’ll see about that.”

She climbed out when he stopped in front of the spa.

Leilani had smiled when she entered. It seemed to brighten when Celia came closer to the podium.

“Hi, Celia. I’m glad you made it.”

"Free massage? I'm there."

Leilani laughed as she led her to a room. Keoki wasn't in to work his magic, but it was still a pleasurable experience.

Leilani was still at the podium when Celia dragged her gooey muscles to the front afterward.

"Did you enjoy?"

"That was amazing. Now I see why people do this all the time."

"So, um, Celia?" Leilani looked around the foyer. They were alone. "I'm having a few friends of mine over today and I would love for you to join us."

Celia blinked. "Me?"

"I think you would find it beneficial." She frowned down at Celia, and tilted her head to the side when she saw she didn't understand. "You . . . do know, don't you? What you are?"

Understanding dawned on Celia. "Oh, the witch thing."

"So, you do know. Oh, good. Your energy is different today, so I thought you just had to know. Anyways," she said with a wave of her hand, "meet me outside at one. That's when my shift ends."

Celia glanced at her watch. That was in two hours.

"There's this great restaurant just down the street called Lenny's. Tell the girl at the front—Makala—that I sent you and she'll set you up."

Celia nodded vaguely and headed out into the blazing heat.

Hastings was quiet after she told him about Leilani's offer.

"What is her last name?"

"I don't know."

His expression was blank, but the cogs turned behind his eyes.

"Should I not go?" Celia asked.

They stood on the curb next to the car. The engine was running, giving the AC a chance to cool the interior. Celia had put her sunglasses on and was watching his face. Hastings looked from her to the pavement, then down the street toward the traffic on the Boulevard.

"I do not know this witch personally," he finally said, his words leaving him in careful intervals. His gaze returned to hers. "The decision is ultimately up to you."

"I know that, but I wanted your opinion."

"If you received a genuine, pleasant vibe from her, then trust your instinct."

She nodded. Leilani was incredibly friendly. Too bad she didn't know how inexperienced Celia was. She might not have been so eager to bring her into her group.

"And you still have the protection from the potion."

True.

After relieving Hastings, Celia entered Lenny's. It was a small, shack of a restaurant. There wasn't much to the outside; it could've been a converted bungalow. All of the design aesthetic had been used up on the interior. Brightly colored round tables that sat groups of two and four were placed within inches of each other. You were going to get to know your neighbor whether you wanted to or not.

A small bar had been erected at the back of the place, next to a swinging door for the kitchen and restrooms. A podium was placed at the front door for patrons to wait for seats.

The hostess was a few years younger than Celia. She had the same tanned skin as Leilani. Her dark hair stopped just below her ears. She wore a white blouse with the sleeves rolled up to her elbows, revealing an extensive collection of black rubber bracelets covering both wrists.

"Hi, welcome to Lenny's."

"Are you Makala?"

"Yes?" She leaned back from the podium, putting more space between them.

"I was sent by Leilani. She said you would set me up while I waited for her shift to end."

Her eyes scanned Celia. Then she smiled. "Sure thing. Follow me."

The upper level was smaller, but it had a terrace with five two-top tables. Only three of the tables were occupied, and Celia assumed those patrons were crazy for eating outside in this weather.

She was seated by a window that offered a limited view of the MGM Grand. The other buildings on this side of the street obstructed most of the Strip. Every few minutes, people ambled in and out of the entrances of the hotel.

"Order whatever you like," Makala replied as she set the menu on the table. "It's on the house."

She bounced away before Celia could question her.

Her waiter was a friendly boy with a white apron, acne, and red lips, like he just had a few gulps of Hawaiian Punch before coming over. He brought her a glass of water and a newspaper.

She wasn't very hungry, so she ordered fries and a beer. She was so absorbed in her food and the paper that she didn't notice her company at first. He had to clear his throat.

Celia peeked up from the paper. Alec stood in front of her table, smiling down at her.

"What do you know about this place?" he asked. "Only locals know this exists."

He sat across from her and plucked a fry from her basket.

"It was recommended."

"Is this your appetizer or something? Tell me you ordered a burger. They use bison meat here. I'm no Top Chef, but it just tastes better than regular old cow meat."

Celia was surprised to find that she wasn't annoyed or perturbed by his presence. It was nice to sit with someone.

"I had a late breakfast."

"Have you been to the museum? Or the fountains?"

"Both. The fountains were fun."

"Won lots of money?"

She snorted. "For my aunt and uncle. I haven't played with my own money yet."

"We should go to Circus Circus. See, my friends—"

He pointed to a group of five guys clustered around a table in the middle of the room. Two tables had been pushed together to accommodate their party. The guys laughed and shouted as they pored over their menus, as if they were the only ones in the joint.

"—they're going to this burlesque show thing."

Celia couldn't help but chuckle. "You're kidding, right?"

"I know! But I told you—"

"Yeah, yeah—"

"Naked boobies trump personality," they said in unison.

She laughed. "And you're not into that?"

He waved his hand. "Seen one topless show, you've seen 'em all, know what I mean?"

"Some of us only need to look in the mirror."

He laughed. "See," he said, pointing at her. "Great personalities. So you'll take me away from these terrible influences?" He clasped his hands together in front of him in a prayer-like manner.

Her mouth opened slowly as she tried to come up with an excuse.

"Finish up," he said before she could hedge. "I'll meet you outside in ten."

Alec got up from the chair and hurried over to his friends. They each glanced over to Celia, looking her over, then back to Alec as he spoke. The friends didn't seem too happy. The restaurant was suddenly very quiet.

Celia waved down her waiter to let him know she was done. She tried to pay her bill, but he refused to give it to her. He didn't speak much English, but in his heavy Spanish accent he kept saying, "Makala say no. Makala say no."

She stopped fighting. After drinking the last of her beer, Celia left a tip and then made a beeline for the door.

Makala glanced up when she reached the foyer. "I'll see you in a bit," she said with a knowing smile.

On the sidewalk, Celia adjusted her outfit while waiting. The sun was warm on her back, making her wish she had slathered on suntan lotion. Alec came out with a huge grin.

"Whoo!" he exclaimed. "It's hotter than a French whore out here." He waved his hand in front of Celia like a fan. She giggled.

They strolled toward the Strip.

"Where are you from, Celia?"

"Boston."

"Beantown!" he exclaimed with a snap of his fingers.

"Uh, right," she said, chuckling. He was definitely . . . enthusiastic.

"That's, like, one of the only major cities I haven't been to yet."

"So you can't tell me where to go?" she asked in a deadpan. "You're so fired."

He smiled. "Don't worry. It's on my list."

"Do you travel to all these places for work?"

"Uh-huh. I'm a consultant for Apple. I'm on a team of folks who go around making sure everyone's doing what they need to be doing. And when they're slacking, we give ideas on how to improve."

That sounded so grown-up.

"That's pretty awesome."

They had made it to Planet Hollywood. A shuttle the size of a coach van boarded at the curb. They got into the queue behind two round women dressed in Hawaiian shirts and straw hats for some reason.

"It's okay for now," Alec went on. "I'm actually an architect. Well, I've just gotten my degree." He shrugged modestly. "I'm going to start job-hunting in January. My sister knows some people."

"That's really cool too."

He grinned. "You?"

"I'm a bartender." She found her voice had just the slightest edge to it, as if daring him to say something disparaging.

Alec didn't seem to notice. "Oh, nice," he said, and he seemed genuinely impressed. "Let's have some Boiler Makers after this."

She laughed.

They climbed aboard the van. The driver pulled off with a start, making

Celia lurch into Alec, her hand grabbing his knee to steady herself. He smiled down at her. She chuckled nervously as she adjusted in the seat. The ride was bumpy; their voices shook whenever they spoke.

"Is there only one sister?" Celia asked.

"No, my youngest one just started high school. Ah, youth," he said with a cheesy smile. "I wouldn't mind going back there. How about you?"

"No siblings."

He frowned. "Are you sure you're not vacationing alone?"

"My boyfriend has a stomachache. I was just getting some air and food when you absconded with me."

Alec glanced out the window to see where they were. "Don't you mean 'absconded me'?"

"No, I said it right." She remembered the SAT lessons in school.

"I'm pretty sure you didn't."

Celia shook her head. "Look it up sometime."

"Five dollars says you're wrong!" He pulled out his phone. She caught a glimpse of his phone's wallpaper before he opened a browser: a photo of a fluffy brown dog.

After a minute, Alec's brow rose. He put the phone away, pulled out his wallet, riffled through, then handed Celia a crisp five-dollar bill without a word. She fought hard to hide her smile.

The van came to a stop in front of the Circus Circus hotel. Celia and Alec disembarked, leaving the cool.

"I love this heat!" Alec stretched his hands up to the sky. His shirt inched up, revealing a light covering of soft brown hair across his torso. She remembered that dream she had after the experiment with the vamps . . . Of Ramsey's downy hair leading toward his . . .

"It's funny," Alec replied, and Celia shook away the memory as fast as she could. "I wanted to work with animals."

He was looking at a small white dog at the intersection. Two women stood beside it, bickering about something. The dog peered up at them with a look that implored them to hurry up.

"When I was younger, I wanted to be a vet."

"I think I did too," Celia replied. "My best friend had five dogs, all kinds of mutts. I loved playing with them when I went to her house."

He spread his arms out. "Just call us Dr. Dolittle!"

Twenty minutes later, they were inside the amusement park and waiting in line for the Disk-O ride that would spin them into nausea after eating not so long ago. They spent an hour and a half trying out most of the rides.

When they got off the Sling Shot, Celia glanced at her phone for the time. She was completely spent when she plopped down on the shuttle bus headed back toward Lenny's.

Alec was a bit corny at times, but still nice. He had told her about his travels and working while going to school, and she had told him about working at Cage's.

"How long are you here?" he asked. The van had just jerked to a stop where they'd first picked it up.

"Two more days."

Alec followed behind her as they got off.

"So, can I see you again, Celia?" He gave her a dazzling smile. The sun shone off his over-gelled hair. His eyes seemed a lighter shade of green.

She put her hands in her pockets. "I don't know. I have to check with my boyfriend. He made all the plans."

Alec nodded. There was a flicker of disappointment in the crease of his lips.

"I'm sure I'll see you in the casinos." She rubbed his arm. The sun had baked into his skin and radiated from him against her palm. He nodded again and threw on a smile.

Back at Lenny's, Celia waved goodbye to Alec. At 1:10, she stood outside the day spa. The door swung open two minutes later, and Leilani and Makala stepped out. Celia managed a small smile.

Leilani seemed surprised. "You came."

Celia nodded, and tried not to fidget. Leilani gave her a quick hug. She then straightened her purse strap and headed down the street with Celia and Makala in tow.

"So, where are we going?"

"My house. It's not too far. Have you done any spells?"

"Uh, no. I'm really new to . . . all of this."

They went around a corner to a gated parking lot. Leilani's red Volkswagen Cabriolet had seen better days. The front bumper was missing a piece; a long scrape cut across the back quarter panel; and the antenna was bent backward.

They climbed in, the doors squealing at them. Leilani put on her sunglasses and drove out onto the main road. Celia enjoyed the wind in her face.

They rode in relative quiet, aside from Leilani singing along with the music from the radio. Makala would chuckle every once in a while as she played with her phone. About ten minutes later, Leilani pulled into a driveway and stopped under a slab of freestanding concrete that served as her garage. She lived in a group of homes like Setter's Cove, only her neighborhood was one long line of rectangular houses.

"This is my house," she announced. Her box home was dark blue with a tin roof. A silver gate sectioned her land from her neighbors'. The yellowed grass was patchy, with two plastic flamingos standing guard near the front door. Their backs had been bleached nearly white from the sun.

The three of them got out of the car and walked along a path to the front door. Leilani tripped on a crack in the pavement and muttered a curse. It sounded like she tripped on that crack often. She had arranged succulents around the porch in pots of various sizes. A large wreath of dried flowers on the door must have been enchanted, because it still smelled sweet.

They stepped into the bare living room. The furnishings consisted of a blue sofa and a black leather chair, a black coffee table, and an entertainment center against the wall. Behind the sofa was the kitchen. Past that, a hallway led to the back of the house.

Two women were already inside, chatting and drinking wine. They offered warm smiles when Leilani let them in.

"Girls, this is Celia," Leilani announced. Celia waved shyly.

Leilani pointed around the room. "That's Thomasina and Kiele."

Thomasina was the oldest. Her long hair in a braid over her shoulder was streaked with gray. Wrinkles appeared at the corners of her dark eyes when she smiled. She wore a loose tunic over loose pants and many turquoise rings.

Kiele was probably Victor's age. Like the others, she had bronze skin and dark hair tied up into a bun. She wore a dark gray business suit, minus the jacket, and a light pink top. Her feet were bare, and she seemed to be enjoying the wine the most.

"Have a seat," Leilani offered, and then disappeared into the hallway. Makala dropped down on the sofa, leaving the armchair open. Celia sat there.

Leilani returned in a green terrycloth robe, carrying three glasses of red wine. She handed them out to Celia and Makala then sat on the arm of the sofa, with her legs crossed modestly.

"So, Celia hasn't done any magic," Leilani informed the others. They nodded wisely.

"I can see it too," Thomasina replied.

"I knew right away she was a witch," Leilani said.

What the fuck, Celia thought as she drank her wine. *Who the hell says that?* Witches were in movies. They had green faces and pointy hats and giant moles. They gathered in wooded areas and chanted around boiling cauldrons. They didn't sit in an unassuming apartment with glasses of wine like your typical book club.

"I've been practicing since I turned six," Makala said proudly. "My mother's a witch too."

"I'm new too," Kiele said with a shrug of her shoulder. She had a raspy voice that made her words sound like velvet. "Don't worry; it gets easier the more you practice."

"Do you have anyone at home who could help you?" Leilani asked.

Celia opened her mouth to respond . . . only, no words came out. The room tilted to one side, like she was back on the Disk-O ride. She looked around in surprise.

When her eyes met Leilani's, the witch smiled.

"I think we're ready." Leilani finished her own glass and stood. "Let's go out back."

She took Celia's hand. Celia followed without realizing. When she looked back, she saw herself sitting on the chair, laughing hysterically.

Outside, the air was still hot, only somehow not as oppressive. Leilani's backyard was an open field, surrounded by high trees to afford them privacy. It was an impossible sight. This lush backyard, with thick, dark green grass, butterflies and bees bouncing off blooming flowers, and a hammock attached to two trees, didn't belong in the desert.

In the center of the yard, a circle of torches burned. Five mason jars containing a clear liquid sat nestled in the grass.

Leilani released Celia's hand and shrugged off her robe. As she undressed, the sun turning her naked skin golden, so did the others.

"What . . . what's going . . . on?" Celia managed to utter. Her tongue tasted like copper.

The women were humming as one. The four of them began skipping around the open space. Kiele had freed her hair from its bun, and it fell loose around her neck.

"Join us, Celia!" Leilani called.

Celia took a step forward, but that was as far as she could go. Her legs didn't seem able to work.

The women danced and hummed as they made circles around the torches. Leilani was first to pick up a mason jar. Once the others had one in hand, she held her jar to the sky.

"We take of the ocean, to give back to the earth."

The others repeated in unison, *"We take of the ocean, to give back to the earth."*

After drinking all of the liquid, they opened their circle and traced between the torches. Celia stood in her spot, swaying in an invisible wind. The women suddenly slowed to a crawl, though they still laughed and frolicked. Large bursts of orange and blue shot up from the torches. Celia's palms were becoming slick with sweat.

A golden haze began to surround each of them. Leilani had the brightest glow.

This wasn't right. Celia looked down at the glass she still held in her hand. It slipped from her grip. The red liquid splashed on the grass. The soaked green blades turned their faces to her.

"We take of the ocean, to give back to the earth."

What the fuck had they done to her?

"Psst!"

A vision of herself stood to her right. The light breeze swished the vision's hair around her shoulders. Her hand was stretched out to Celia, her palm to the sky. A round, golden ball rotated slowly. It was brilliant and beautiful and Celia didn't understand.

She looked to the women. Did they see the vision? Instead of the slow pace, however, their movements had sped up to warp speed. She could barely keep up with them.

"We take of the ocean, to give back to the earth."

Celia realized these were the women from her dream at the spa. The serenity in their faces matched the dream versions.

She wiped at the sweat leaking from her temples. Suddenly, she wasn't watching the naked witches. Everything had gone black. She thought maybe she had gone blind.

Just as the panic began to rise and overtake her, the darkness vanished. The women had stopped, and now stared at her curiously.

"Did you see something?" Thomasina asked. The others approached Celia with excitement in their eyes.

"She saw something," Makala cried breathlessly. "Did you see that burst of her energy?"

"What did you see?" Leilani asked.

They were too close, asking too many questions at once. Celia shook her head and tried to step back, but she stumbled in the grass. Four sets of hands reached for her to make sure she didn't fall. She had to get away.

"Take me home," she mumbled. She swallowed hard, and then said more forcefully, "Take me home *now*."

The others looked at each other.

Celia turned and staggered back inside the house. The room swayed in front of her eyes and she thought she would vomit. She had to stop a few times to steady herself.

By the time she made it to the front door, Leilani was there, fully clothed and grabbing her keys.

"It's okay," Leilani said as they went out to the car. "It'll wear off soon."

The suffocating heat made it hard to breathe. Celia sat heavily in the passenger side. "What . . . What did you do to me?"

Leilani smiled sadly beside her. "Sorry." She pulled off. "You get a little woozy after the first couple of times, before you understand how it reinforces your Inner Eye."

"My what? What was in that drink?"

Leilani's voice deepened, like a record that had been slowed down. "Vamp blood and LSD."

"What?"

Celia's scream made Leilani jump. The car swerved, nearly hitting the curb.

"You fucking drugged me?" She had to grasp her forehead because the road had just tilted upside down. The world went black again for a minute.

". . . how we harness our powers. Vamp blood makes you stronger and the LSD just helps when doing spells. If you had a vision, that's great! Thomasina gets them sometimes but we can never interpret them."

Celia couldn't quite concentrate on what she was saying. The wind in her face was making her nauseous. Or maybe it was the fucking LSD. Leilani, seeing her discomfort, rolled up the windows, lessening the wind.

A half hour later, she pulled up in front of the house. Celia couldn't move just yet.

"If you're up for it," Leilani said after a moment, "we're doing a ritual tonight. I don't know the exact time yet."

"You're doing *another* ritual?"

"That was just a cleansing ceremony. We do those every other week. No, we're doing a Memory Spell. Kiele needs someone to forget a spell he saw her do. Some spells require more people to make them work the best."

"I don't think so." She clutched her slick forehead.

"Are you sure? You seem to have a lot of energy."

Celia could only shake her head. Leilani's voice was still sluggish to her ears. She leaned forward and her mouth began to fill with saliva.

"I'm really sorry," Leilani continued. "But if I had told you what was in the wine, would you have taken it?"

"Hell no."

"Exactly. It's like learning to swim, right? Sometimes you need a push."

Celia's eyes watered. "Whose blood did you give me?"

"A friend's," she said softly.

There was another flash—that same stifling darkness. Celia finally understood. Leilani's friend was dead to the world. Blackness was all she could see.

Celia groaned. She had betrayed Victor without her knowledge.

Leilani had been waiting her out. "Celia," she said. "It's important to have other witches help you. We're able to channel each other's energy. It makes us stronger."

"I don't care." Celia rubbed her temple.

"But you have visions—"

"I'm not a fucking witch!" she shouted. "I don't have whatever energy you think I have! I'm not . . ." She shook her head. "Strong."

She turned from the shock and sadness in Leilani's eyes, fumbled with the door and stumbled out onto the sidewalk. Leilani stared after her.

Celia shuffled to the bedroom. She crashed down on the bed and tried to sleep.

Five

Celia awoke at 5:30 that night. The aftereffects of the blood and LSD were minimal, with only slight dizziness left. She sat up, rubbing her eyes, her hair disheveled. The room was dark. Music played somewhere outside the bedroom door.

She followed the sound downstairs, where she was met with the aroma of herbs and fish. The lamp in the living room glowed in the corner. The other light above the dinner table was on, illuminating the setting for two with candles flickering.

Victor came around the counter from the kitchen with a tray of salmon. "Did you have a busy day?" he asked as he set the plate down, obviously noting her nap. He smiled, his face brightening.

She rubbed her head. A wave of guilt hit her when she saw that smile. She rushed over, throwing her arms around him.

"I had someone's blood today." She couldn't look at him. "I didn't mean to, I swear. I was being stupid. I didn't know . . ." She tried sniffling back the tears, but they flowed freely. "I didn't . . . I'm so stupid."

Victor wrapped his arms around her. He stroked her hair as he waited for her to calm.

"That explains the change," he murmured.

She started to cry again. "Our connection?"

He was quiet for a moment. "What happened?"

She told him about the witches. She stepped back, her gaze averted, unable to meet his eyes.

Victor rubbed her cheek. "You're not stupid," he said. "You didn't know."

"Isn't that the definition of stupid? Doing things when you don't have all of the details?"

"That's more naïve than stupid. Stupid is when you lack the ability to learn and understand."

"What're you, Webster's?" She chewed her lip.

Suddenly, she wasn't looking at Victor. She was peering down. A pair of shiny men's shoes adorned her feet. A small brown dog, with a wet pink nose directed up at her, wagged his little tail hard enough to make him lose his balance a few times.

Celia shook her head, clearing the vision. Victor had grasped her shoulders when the vision erased all emotion from her face.

"Are you okay?"

"No," she groaned. She wiggled free of his hands and paced the room in the hopes of releasing some of her anxiety.

She stopped after a minute, next to the sofa. Her fingers twisted at the dart on the edge of the cushion. "We have to fix this."

Victor approached her slowly. A pleasurable tickle started in her lower abdomen at the heat in his eyes. She always loved to witness the lust she could evoke in him. His desire eased her nerves.

Victor's cool hands cupped her jaw. His lips pressed onto hers. She kissed him hungrily.

They made it to the sofa, pawing at each other's pants. Celia pulled his shirt over his head. Victor pulled her close. When he made a trail of kisses toward her neck, that memory from the plane appeared before her eyes again. The same fear and panic from that day swelled in her chest.

She pushed him away harder that she had intended. Victor sat back, surprised. Through the small gap between his lips the points of his fangs were visible.

She hopped up from the sofa. Shaking her hands out, she backed away from him.

"That fucking potion," she muttered under her breath.

"What potion?"

Victor stayed seated, kept the space between them. The farther away from him Celia found herself, the more her panic receded. She was finally able to steady her flustered heart, her shaky breath. There was grief and confusion in Victor's eyes when she brought herself to look.

"I keep seeing the plane," she admitted. "And it's freaking me out."

"Celia, I would never hurt—"

"I know," she said quickly.

"I didn't mean—"

"Victor," she interrupted again, her hand raised for him to stop. "I know. But it happened and I felt it and I was scared. Hastings gave me this potion for protection—that's why I burned that lady's hand. And as some sick side effect, I keep having these reminders. In my head and heart, I know you would never hurt me, but my body isn't cooperating."

His shoulders slumped as his gaze fell from hers to the floor. She crossed over and sat beside him, wrapping her arms around him. Thankfully, the memory didn't resurface this time.

"I'm sorry," he said quietly.

"I know. Me too."

"It is a challenge being around you sometimes."

"Because I'm short?"

She had rested her chin on his arm and blinked up at him in faux innocence. His smile brought some life back into his expression. She grinned back.

He shifted, putting his arm around her. "Because sometimes I don't want to stop. Fighting my nature has become perfunctory by now but it's still a challenge at times."

The smile was gone but he didn't seem as depressed. Celia lifted her hand, showing him her wrist. He took hold of it. His thumb rubbed the veins pressing forward. He then brought her wrist to his mouth.

His fangs penetrated her. She winced, but once he began to drink, the pain died away into pleasure. She grabbed his leg with her free hand, her nails digging into the meat of his thigh. He groaned.

After a minute, he licked his wounds, sealing them. The nail on his index finger extended to a sharp point. He cut a line across his own wrist for her.

His tart blood filled her with lovely warmth. She released him and sat back in the sofa. Her eyes opened to tiny sunbursts. Her body seemed to lift a few inches from the cushions.

"The food is getting cold," Victor replied.

"Huh?"

The bursts melted away, and everything sharpened to crystal clarity. She floated to the table. Victor had made salmon, jasmine rice, and asparagus. It had been a few weeks since he had cooked for her. The meal was delicious, as usual.

They ate in silence, each digesting the other's confessions. She knew it had to be hard for Victor to suppress his hunger, but she had never heard him admit it.

She glanced his way a few times. He ate his rice impassively, his eyes on his plate. Was he being modest about how much of a challenge it was around her? She'd never thought about how distracting or overwhelming her beating heart must be. His cool façade had never betrayed that.

She opened her mouth to speak—what she would say was anybody's guess—but he spoke first.

"We have tickets for a seven-thirty show." Victor turned his head, and the light above cast a warm glow across his rosy skin. The clock in the kitchen said it was just after 6:00. "Hastings will be here at quarter to seven."

Her instinct was to take his hand . . . but would that set him on edge? She nodded, and then continued to eat.

"So," Celia eventually said, to end the silence, "do you have something to wear to Serena's party?"

"I do. But we're not still going, are we? Are you up for that?"

She sighed. "Serena's really excited about it. Of course, she seems excited about everything."

"There will be other parties."

"I know, but she bought me a dress." She shrugged.

He looked at her for a long moment. "Not all vampire parties are like the one at Ramsey's."

"What does that mean?"

"They're not always tame."

She shook her head. "Serena wouldn't invite me to a kegger. Look at the dress she bought!"

Victor glanced down to his plate.

"We have to stop by for a little bit."

When Hastings arrived at 6:45 on the dot, Celia left the bedroom in cuffed gray shorts and a pink- and white-striped peasant shirt. She draped her gray sweater over her purse as she approached the stairs.

"She's coming." Celia's steps faltered. Victor had spoken softly, but there was a taut thread to his words that drifted up the staircase. "Don't do that again, not without proper guidance. What were you thinking?"

"You are right, sir," Hastings replied just as tightly. She noticed he didn't apologize, unless he had done so before she heard.

Celia descended the stairs. The two men stood in the foyer. Victor looked at her, while Hastings stared steadfastly ahead at the wall behind Victor's head.

"Ready?" Victor asked. His lips were pursed slightly in displeasure, but he held his hand out for her.

He wanted to make the most of the night, so she did too. She nodded in response and slipped her hand into his palm. The three of them headed out, back to Caesar's Palace for the Celine Dion concert.

* * *

Celia was exhilarated after the show. She was still humming to herself as she pulled on the gown.

Victor wore gray pants and a dark blue shirt that nearly matched Celia's dress, as if it were kismet. His tie was the same shade. He had brushed his hair back, giving it a nice sheen.

It was almost 11:00 when they went downstairs. The doorbell had rung a few minutes before. Celia peeked out the window. The Cadillac SUV waited for them at the curb. A man jumped out when he saw them approach.

The driver, dressed in a black short-sleeved shirt and shorts, came around to open the back door.

"Celia? Victor?" he asked. Celia nodded. "Serena sent me to bring you to their home."

The Pérezes were staying in a gated hub just off the east side of the Strip. The driver bypassed the Las Vegas Boulevard, opting to come down by way of the freeway.

A tall brick wall shielded the condominium complex from prying eyes. The driver pulled up to the massive wrought iron gate that guarded the entrance. A modest sign hung on the barrier wall with the complex's name in gold cursive: Tower Heights.

He reached out his window and keyed in a number in a pin pad extended forward on a gray pole. There was a beep, and then the gate opened with a whine. They rode for a few yards before the first mansion appeared on their left. It was a beige stucco structure set far from the path. Dark green grass had been planted in the yard. A narrow walkway led from the car path up to the wide porch, illuminated by old-fashioned, pewter lampposts. Two small spotlights shone up toward the house, their beams pointing at the space above the front door where the house number was nailed.

They moved on, passing others just as prodigious, until the road curved into a cul-de-sac. A massive fountain the color of steel shot water high up into the air from its place in the middle of the rotary. The last house sat directly ahead.

The driver circled around the fountain and came to a stop at the walkway. The water fountain created a peaceful symphony as they stepped down from the car.

"Wow," Celia whispered when she took in the house.

It was a giant square with a stone porch. Strategically placed spotlights lit up the perimeter. A two-seater wooden chair hung from the ceiling of the porch. Four tall palm trees swayed in the night breeze on either side of the staircase.

Victor placed a hand on the small of her back and they walked toward the house. Silver, gold, and black confetti covered the stone path. They were shaped like party hats and masquerade masks and noisemakers. The light from the lampposts glinted off their shiny surfaces. Gold streamers and more of the confetti decorated the porch.

Celia looked to the right at the sound of quiet laughter. Two men and a woman in dressy clothes stood in a shaded section of the driveway, smoking cigarettes. The woman smiled at Celia.

Victor rang the bell. A minute passed before the door opened. Jazzy, upbeat music poured out. Grace stood in the doorway in a black, strapless empire-waist dress that grazed her ankles. Her black hair was pulled to the side in a ponytail below her ear, the big curls resting on her shoulder.

She didn't smile. "Hello, Celia, Victor."

"Hi, Grace," Celia said. The infinity tattoo behind Grace's ear, the same one Serena had on her inner wrist, was visible when she stepped aside.

"You may come in for tonight only," she instructed to Victor. Celia thought that was interesting. Could you put stipulations on how you invited a vampire into your home? She assumed Grace said that to all the vamps coming tonight, and wasn't only picking on Victor, which she would have no cause to do.

Her musing was interrupted, however, by the interior. They stood in a large foyer with a wide staircase and high ceiling. A beautiful chandelier containing about a million crystals reflecting the light hung from the gold-plated ceiling. Italian marble stretched beneath their feet. Massive art prints hung on the wall, and candles flickered in impressive, Tiffany-style sconces. The other lights were low, making the rainbow refractions from the chandelier visible across the walls and floor.

More confetti and streamers littered the side tables. Gold and black ribbons looped through the banisters of the staircase. Two women crossed to the stairs, dressed in sequined mini-dresses and high-heeled sandals. They laughed and clutched each other's hands, their cheeks bright red from giddiness.

They passed a small wooden podium at the base of the staircase. Bottles of liqueur were displayed on a table that served as the back bar. A large tub of ice was to the left of the podium. Two men in all black stood behind the bar mixing drinks and gabbing with the people waiting.

The bar seemed a bit out of place. They must've erected it for the night.

"This way," Grace said.

The kitchen was on the left, with its frosted cabinets and marble counters and blue accent lights along the cabinets. The island in the center looked about the size of Celia's entire kitchen at home.

Now *that* was a kitchen for which to aspire.

The hallway opened into the sitting room. Although the music was louder in here, the people mostly stood around talking. A few would break out into a shimmy, but no one was really dancing. They were all dressed in pressed pants, handsome ties, shiny shoes; gowns and short skirts with exposed thighs and backs. They laughed, they clinked glasses, but their glances repeatedly returned to the center of the room.

Celia immediately recognized the Pérezes. The three women were as lovely as ever. Like at Ramsey's, they all wore dark dresses, chosen from the ones Serena had selected. They stood in the center of the room, looking very much like models or socialites. People flocked around the women, mesmerized.

Celia's attention went to the far wall, which was made completely of glass. It looked out onto a wide patio that spanned the length of the window, and just beyond, the dark yard.

The sitting room was pretty bare for its size. There were three eggshell-colored sofas that would hold four people each and a few black leather chairs. The furniture looked more like art deco sculptures than comfortable seating, with its harsh corners and symmetrical lines. End tables held lamps and burning candles that made the room smell like vanilla. The candles seemed a precarious choice, what with the balloons bouncing around every once in a while. Someone had spent a lot of money at iParty, because the confetti was strewn across almost every surface in the room. One woman in a black dress had a few clinging to her backside.

With the dim lighting, the jazzy music, the beautiful people, Celia was immediately put into the mind frame of a twenties' speakeasy.

Rafael smiled at Celia and Victor as they entered. The Pérez patriarch wore black pants and a turquoise shirt under a vest with black and turquoise checkers. He spoke to two men. Celia couldn't tell if they were vamps or otherwise.

Looking around, she surmised almost thirty people were dispersed around the room, and five or six out on the patio smoking. Most of them drank wine, although a few held martini and lowball glasses. They stayed in groups of three or four, with a few people floating around like satellites amongst the clusters. About ten of them didn't have any kind of drink. She noticed they were the nuclei of the larger groups.

Celia was usually okay in crowds, but mingling made her nervous. Trying to come up with small talk, joining groups that were already in conversation; it wasn't her favorite thing. That's why at work she preferred tending the bar, where conversations were usually quick, and one-on-one.

Victor's hand on her back was comforting. She wasn't alone.

"Celia!"

They turned at Serena's voice, as did a few others. The guests glanced at Celia, sparks of envy in their eyes that one of the hosts knew her name.

Serena bounced down the hallway. Once again she stood out in the fashion department. Her vintage, buttercream dress had a ruched bodice and an uneven hem that billowed around her calves. A sheer, gold organza layered the dress. Her hair was curled like Grace's, and pulled back so that the red hair flowed down her back. A few tendrils framed her face. She looked like a ballerina.

"Wow, great dress," Celia said, looking her over.

"Thanks," Serena gushed, then kissed each of them on the cheek. She smelled like roses. "I'm glad you guys came. Here." She stopped a waiter who had just emerged from the kitchen with a tray of glasses. She handed Celia white wine.

Celia glanced to Victor out of habit.

"Don't worry," Serena replied with a smirk. "He'll be taken care of."

Celia tried to make sense of that.

Serena sipped her red wine while she eyed Victor, then Celia. There was something strange about her look. She was assessing them, but Celia didn't know why.

Victor spoke for the first time. "We should say hello to Rafael."

His hand on Celia's back steered her to the patio door. He must've received the same weird vibe from Serena. When Celia peeked up at him, his face was expressionless, which, at that moment, did nothing to ease her nerves.

"We can leave," he whispered close to her ear. "We don't have to stay."

Her nervousness jumped up a notch. He knew something she didn't.

She glanced around at the faces they passed. Some people smiled hello, some were too engrossed in their conversations to notice the new guests. Serena moved around the groups now, prodding the people into dancing to the Fergie song that played over the speakers. Everyone seemed relaxed, like they were having a good time.

So, why the tremor of anxiety?

"What's going on?" Celia whispered back, but they were too close to Rafael and his companion now.

"Victor," Rafael replied. Two lonely gold streamers were hanging out on his left shoulder. "Serena told me you're here on vacation."

Victor nodded tightly in response. His cold demeanor had a lot to do with the last time they'd been acquainted with Rafael, when he'd propositioned Celia right in front of everyone.

Rafael peered at Celia, inciting a creepy-crawly feeling up her arms. "Are you enjoying your time here?"

"Yes," she answered.

"What have you done so far?"

"Um, we've been to the wax museum and Celine Dion's show. And I went shopping with Serena and Grace. They helped me pick out this dress."

"Well, let's see," he said.

Celia hesitated. She looked to Victor. His face was still blank. Rafael stared at her expectantly.

She turned slowly so he could see the dress. She felt like a child forced to perform in front of her parents' friends. When she faced Rafael again, he grinned with open desire. She took a step closer to Victor.

"Who are your friends?" Rafael's companion asked.

"This is Victor and his human friend, Celia," Rafael introduced. "I met them while traveling through Massachusetts. This is Hector. He is one of my accountants."

"I handle his book sales," Hector expounded.

Rafael shrugged, indifferent. "I have too many people of whom to keep track." He glanced somewhere behind them. "Ah, my realtor is here. Hopefully I can close on this house at week's end." He clapped Victor on the shoulder. "Enjoy, you two."

He walked off. Hector took a long sip of his wine. The silence between them stretched into *awkward*.

"So, Rafael's pretty popular, huh?" Celia asked.

Hector nodded. "Yes, very much. And he writes in a lot of different genres, so he appeals to many audiences."

"What's his newest? I'd like to pick it up."

Hector gave her a playful smirk. "Sorry, can't say."

A server wandered by with a tray of grilled chicken. Celia flagged him down and took a toothpick holding a large piece. It was delicious, laced with lime and cilantro. She took another. The other humans ate as well, she noticed. She wondered why the vamps weren't drinking from glasses, like at Ramsey's. Surely all the warm bodies were enticing.

A tall woman sidled up beside Celia. She wore a long white dress with a very low neckline. A thick gold necklace rested against her chest. Her dark hair was brushed back into a complicated chignon at the base of her neck.

Her dark pink lips parted as she smiled at Celia and Victor. "Are you two exclusive?"

Celia heard her words, but for some reason they didn't make sense. "Exclusive?"

"Yes," Victor snapped.

The woman pouted. Celia still didn't understand.

"Too bad," the woman said. "I'm very flexible. Like contortionist shit." Her gaze moved from Victor to Celia. "Look, I just wanted to get my place in line, you know? I won't be able to get near enough to Rafael or the sisters."

"But they're right there." Celia's arm felt heavy when she pointed across the room.

Victor squeezed her shoulder. "Celia—"

The woman giggled. "Wow. You must be new. Too bad you all don't share." She leaned in closer. "I could show you a thing or two."

Celia stared as she sauntered away. "What a weirdo."

Hector moved on with a nod.

A short man struck up a conversation with Victor. They spoke about someone they both knew in France. Celia pointed to the bar. Victor seemed unwilling to let her go, but she wandered out into the foyer.

"Celia!"

Serena stepped away from the two men with whom she was speaking. "I want you to meet someone. Naomi," she called.

A woman stood in the foyer, checking her phone. Her long, black braids were pinned back from her face. Her dress stopped just above her knees. It was a light gray color and backless.

She looked up when Serena called her name. Her skin was a pretty shade of milk chocolate. She watched them curiously as they approached.

Serena placed a hand on the woman's arm. "Celia, this is Naomi. Celia's from Boston."

"Oh," Naomi replied. "I went to college there, Northeastern. It's a nice city."

Celia shrugged. "It can be."

Naomi smiled. "We had a lot of parties in our rooms since the clubs closed so early."

"Yeah, what's up with that?"

A man had stepped up to them silently. He stood taller than the women, with dark, smooth skin like brown porcelain. His black hair was styled in a neat afro, and his charcoal gray suit was paired with a burgundy shirt and tie. He wrapped an arm around Naomi's waist.

"I don't know how people stand that," he said. "I'm Clay."

"Celia."

"Clay owns a bar in Long Beach," Serena said. "They have this peach mojito drink that's so yummy."

"I'm thinking of changing the name to Serena's Peach. You like that?" He chuckled, nudging Serena with his elbow.

"Yes!" Serena exclaimed blissfully. "You *have* to do that!"

"Clay." Naomi wasn't as amused. He gave her a wide smile.

"Oh, wait!" Serena headed to the kitchen, waving her hands. A server was placing champagne flutes on a tray. "It's not time for champagne yet."

"If you're ever in Long Beach, Celia, you must come by the bar," Clay replied. He shifted his hand and rubbed Naomi's back.

Naomi stiffened noticeably when his hand touched her skin. She looked at Clay, her brown eyes examining him. Celia recognized the radiance in his skin. A light danced in his eyes, and he seemed to visibly restrain a frenetic energy trying to erupt from him. Like he might burst into song and dance at any second, he was so energized.

Naomi's jaw clenched.

Oblivious, Clay kissed Naomi's cheek then walked away to talk to someone in the living room. Naomi's eyes brimmed with tears, her face tightening with anger.

The shift confused Celia. She didn't know what to say. After contemplating for a second, she pointed over her shoulder with her thumb. "I was going to get a drink. Do you want something?"

Naomi marched over to the bar by the stairs without a word. The bartender stopped arranging glasses when they approached.

"Scotch, neat," Naomi said gloomily. Celia ordered another glass of wine, even though she felt a little loose already, which was strange. That didn't usually happen until she was on her third drink.

She followed Naomi when she stepped away. The two of them stood under a beautiful tapestry hanging on the wall. Gold thread intertwined with red thread, forming an abstract, dreamy design. A window next to the tapestry looked out onto a desert garden. Another wing jutted out from the right of the house. There were no windows on what had to be the second story. Beside the extra wing, the blue water of an in-ground swimming pool lapped against the edges. A tennis court sat farther out.

"Are you okay?" Celia asked.

Naomi sighed, staring out the window. "I'm in Vegas. I should be ecstatic." She took a gulp of her drink. "I used to hate hard liquor. Now it's all I drink."

Celia waited for her to clarify. Naomi looked at her with a sad sort of smile.

"I'm turning thirty-two in" – she looked at her watch – "thirty minutes."

"Happy birthday," Celia said brightly.

"It would be if I wasn't aging."

Celia's smile fell away.

Naomi chuckled but there was no humor in her tone. "Clay won't turn me. I've asked every birthday for the past four years. He refuses. He says he's safeguarding my soul. That's the way he talks sometimes. 'Safeguarding your soul.'" She snorted and sipped her drink. "Who cares about a soul when I'm going to die and he won't?"

She lowered her voice now and stepped closer to Celia. Premature lines had begun to take root at the corner of her oval eyes. Her scotch smelled sweet on her breath.

"Half the time I wish I'd never met him. Half the time, I want to demand he erase himself from my head. Then I could get on track with my life's plan. I could get married and buy a house and have children like I've always wanted.

"But I love him. And I don't want to be without him. So, every year I ask him to turn me. At least then I'd no longer have a half-life."

Celia's mouth went dry.

"What about you?" Naomi asked after another sip.

"I . . . I don't know," Celia said lamely. She could feel her nose reddening.

Naomi nodded slowly. "Well, this is the last year I'm asking."

She finished her drink in one large gulp and placed the glass on an end table. Without meeting Celia's eye, she said goodnight and disappeared into the crowd in the living room.

Celia walked back to the bar on stilted legs. She asked the bartender for the nearest restroom, since the main floor powder room was occupied. He directed her to the stairs. There was one located right at the top of the staircase.

The woman waiting smiled at Celia. "I do hate these formalities," she replied with a French accent. "Why can't we just get on with the party?"

The door opened. The man presented them each with a beguiling grin as he headed toward the stairs. That nervous feeling started up again.

The woman came out two minutes later. She ran a finger down Celia's arm when she passed. *Okay*, Celia thought.

She took a moment to check her hair and makeup in the mirror. Naomi's words swamped her mind.

Half-life.

Was that what Celia had? It sounded so . . . pathetic. Was that the reason Serena wanted her to meet Naomi? What was the point? She shook the questions away and rushed out of the bathroom.

Downstairs, she found Victor speaking with the Pérez sisters. Isabel, the youngest, stared at Celia the whole time, giving her the creeps. At least she didn't sniff her this time. The girl wore a dark green baby doll dress. An ivory flower design wrapped around the straps and across the chest. She had a black leather jacket on over it with the sleeves rolled up to her elbows. Clunky black boots were on her feet.

The other sisters spoke about their upcoming venture to Thailand. Or something like that. Celia drifted away mentally. She thought about Alec and how much he enjoyed surfing. He went to San Francisco every summer to "catch the waves." He loved it. How you used every muscle in your body. How once you caught that wave, it was like you were flying.

She felt like she was flying.

A server appeared at her side with wine. Suddenly, Victor's hand darted in front of Celia in a blur of whiteness. When she glanced down, it didn't register immediately that he had covered her glass. The poor server looked so startled by his sudden movement. The wine bottle in her hand was still tilted over Celia's glass.

"That's enough," Victor said harshly. The woman nodded and hurried away.

Celia frowned. She finally noticed her glass was never empty. She had no idea how much she had drunk; she didn't even remember drinking. It was out of pure habit—glass in hand, down the hatch. After Leilani's stunt, you would think she'd stay far away from alcohol she hadn't poured herself.

They'd only been there forty minutes and she was lightheaded. She forced herself to focus.

"Relax, Victor."

Celia glanced to the middle sister, whose name she couldn't recall. This was the first time she'd been in the vampire's company. Her full, wavy hair rested over her bare shoulders. Her black dress was a flowing satin that swished around her thighs, with an intricate, beaded bodice.

She didn't look at Celia when she spoke. "It's a party," she replied. "We're celebrating."

"I gather that, Elena," Victor said. "Unfortunately, I don't think we'll be staying much longer."

Elena's lighthearted smile disappeared. A sudden tension surrounded the group as the two stared at each other; even the awestruck humans seemed uncomfortable. Celia wanted to be concerned, but couldn't muster the correct emotions. At least no multi-colored sparks shot from anyone's eye sockets. Thus, she was only drunk.

"Leaving before the fun starts?" Elena shook her head, her lips pursing in a disappointed fashion. "You've changed a lot."

"Change isn't a bad thing."

Elena shrugged. "Not how I see it. If you enjoy something, why compromise?"

"Because there are more important things in life than your idea of fun."

"Hmm. It used to be *your* idea too. Or have you forgotten?"

Victor just glared at her. She smirked. Point: Elena.

Celia saw this interaction; it just didn't penetrate her clouded head.

Esperanza rolled her eyes. She looked elegant in a black column dress that hung from her like a sheath. A sheer panel with crystals and gold beads covered her chest and shoulders.

"Don't start, you two," she chided. "Victor, at least stay for the toast."

He didn't answer. Instead, he turned Celia away from the group. She went along, concentrating hard on not tripping. People had really gotten into dancing, swinging their arms, shaking their hips. They could've been navigating through Cage's on a Friday night.

They passed one of the sofas where two people were snuggled together. Celia glanced at them, then made herself stop, wobbling a little on her thin heels.

She turned back to the couple. A strange glow surrounded them, like their skin radiated light from the inside. Celia couldn't tell if it was real or if her wine-drenched mind was playing tricks on her.

"Do you see that?" she asked Victor, motioning to the couple. "Hey," she said before he could answer. She tried not to giggle at how slowly she spoke. "I know you."

The man moved aside and Celia got a better view of the long dark hair, the bronze skin, the stunning beauty. Leilani gasped.

"Celia? What're you doing here? How're you feeling?"

"I don't know," Celia said. She'd given up on keeping in her giggles. "How do you know Rafael?"

"I don't, actually. This is the first time I've met him. I know Mason, here. He's in town for the week."

Leilani placed a hand on the man's shoulder. He was long and slender like her, with a thin face and light brown hair pulled into a ponytail. He smiled, but the expression was peculiar. It didn't look very natural. Maybe he sensed that, because he frowned and then tried again. The expression appeared a little more genuine this time around, but he still looked like someone who wasn't accustomed to using his facial muscles in such a manner.

Celia chuckled at his attempts. "It's nice to meet you, Mason," she said with a wave. Victor was pulling her away again. Normally she would've protested, but she was too loopy at the moment to mind.

"Where are we going?"

"Back to the house," Victor said softly. He took the half-full wine glass from her hand and placed it on the tray of a passing server on his way back to the kitchen.

"We should say goodbye to Serena and Grace." She glanced around and caught sight of Serena making her way to the center of the room, where Rafael and Grace waited. Celia took a step in that direction, but Victor caught hold of her elbow.

The music faded out. The clinking of silver against glass hushed the crowd. Serena stood in the middle of the room now, with a champagne flute in her hand. She smiled to the server beside her and handed her the knife she had used to grab the room's attention.

"Hello, everyone," Serena replied with a huge smile. She winked at Celia. Again, a flare of envy was lobbed in Celia's direction. "I'm so happy you all made it out tonight for our celebration of Rafael's success. He's a bestselling author around the world," she went on. Rafael grinned modestly as he massaged the back of her neck, like she was a cat. Celia wondered if he was truly humble or if it was an act for the guests in his home.

Her eyes drifted to his middle-aged belly. She knew that vampires stayed the way they were changed. It must've been annoying lacking the ability to shed those extra pounds; to see that paunch whenever he looked in the mirror. Did Serena rub it like he was a Buddha?

Okay, she had drifted into dangerous territory. Celia shook her head hard, yelling at herself to focus.

"I promised Rafael that I wouldn't speak too long," Serena said with a laugh. "You may or may not know but I can go on and on for days about him." She looked at him, then rubbed his cheek. "You're the best, babe."

The group cooed in admiration. Serena giggled, then kissed Rafael on the lips. Somehow, their kiss acted as a cue. The music rose again. Celia glanced around to see what was next. Perhaps a performance?

Leilani and Mason had gone back to their smooching. The glow returned as well. Others began to pair up. On a sofa, a woman kissed a man's chin while unbuttoning his shirt. The woman on his other side stroked between his thighs. In a corner, two women were making out, the blonde one's fingers searching for the zipper of the other's dress.

Most of the humans moved closer to the vamps. Isabel included, which was disturbing because even if she was a couple hundred years undead, she looked sixteen.

A man passed in front of them, towing a woman along behind him. They wended their way to a small group on another sofa.

Elena was there. The five or so humans pushed against each other, vying for space beside her. A lean man and a pretty blonde woman won. They both beamed as they settled on either side of the vampire. Elena seemed amused at their competition. Her slender hand stroked each of their cheeks before she bestowed them with kisses.

When she pulled away from Blondie, Elena threw Victor a haughty smirk. The humans didn't seem to notice or care that her attention was elsewhere. They were too busy undressing and snuggling closer to her. The two in front of her dropped to their knees and the last man went around the back of the sofa. His hands slid from Elena's thin shoulders down to her breasts.

Elena's eyes, which had been focused on Victor, closed. Her lips spread into a satisfied smile, serenity washing over her, which probably had more to do with Victor's annoyance than the man's prowess.

Celia blinked a few times. She couldn't quite comprehend the scene in front of her. Everything happened at once and in a blinding speed.

Suddenly, a strange shiver rustled in the pit of her stomach. She frowned, confused because she was pretty sure that was arousal she felt. But she wasn't aroused. She didn't even know what the hell was going on.

She looked to Victor, as if he would have an answer for this odd sensation. Victor's jaw was set as he glowered at the display on the sofa. She looked again, took in all the exposed skin, saw Elena's fangs, saw her caress and stroke the humans before her as if soothing them, as if promising them that their patience was about to pay off, and gasped.

The turn in the evening finally sunk in. Celia's jaw dropped as she realized where this *party* had headed. All the moaning and gyrating helped make it clear, as well. Serena's words about Victor being "taken care of" came back to her in a rush.

"What the fuck's going on here?" Celia hissed at Victor.

He glanced down at her, his face harsh and angry, and then shook his head. He took her hand and led her to the door. His mouth was weird, like his jaw couldn't close behind his lips.

They were out in the hallway, but not before Celia glimpsed Serena. She was still in the center of the room. Rafael stood behind her, gently kissing her neck. Her pretty gold dress slid from her chest and dropped to the floor. Her breasts were amazing. Rafael would agree since they were cupped in his beefy hands.

Victor had Celia at the door in a matter of seconds. She didn't feel bad about their hasty departure; she was sure Serena wouldn't notice. And what the hell had Serena been thinking? Yeah, she dated a vampire, but did Celia look like she partook in fucking *orgies*?

She shook her head over and over again, completely astonished.

Not as tame as Ramsey's, my ass, she snapped internally.

Sorry. Victor's voice responded in her head.

It was the second time he'd been able to speak directly to her through their bond. She hadn't expected him to hear her musing. Was that another common occurrence for vampire-human bonds, or a side effect of her status as an Umami? On rare occasions, outside of the flashes, when she had control over her side of the bond, she could sense his emotions. That was the norm; that was as complex as it would usually get.

The front door stood ajar. Victor had paused but she didn't notice.

"Something's wrong," he said. At the same time, the unmistakable sound of crying drifted inside the house. Celia pulled the door open.

"Help me," someone whispered.

Celia immediately went out on the porch. Only a single, dim bulb just above the door illuminated the porch. A man waited at the far end, where the swinging chair hung, his back to them. In front of him, Naomi stood with her arms outstretched. She used her forearm to wipe the tears from her eyes. Her wrists were slick with dark blood.

Alarmed, Celia's mouth opened. Victor placed a hand on her shoulder, stopping her.

"Why are you doing this, Naomi?" the man asked. "And here, of all places."

Clay's voice was strained. Naomi only stared at him. She didn't seem to notice Celia and Victor.

Her tears dripped from her jaw. Her eyes held fierce determination, almost hypnotic in their resolve.

"I . . . can't, Naomi."

"Why not?"

"Because I love you, dammit. You deserve to live. You deserve to go on to heaven."

"I don't believe in heaven."

"Don't lie."

We shouldn't be here, Celia thought. They were intruding. But she couldn't seem to move.

"We'll be together," Naomi said.

"We're together *now*."

She shook her head. "It's not enough, Clay. I need *all* of you. Then you won't have to shield me from things, because I'll be right there with you."

"You're asking me to *kill* you. And for what?" His anger, desperation rose. "Me? I'm just a shadow, on the outside always looking in but only when the damn sun's away. That's not a life. That's a curse. I only do it because I have to. Not because I want to."

"We'll be together." Her voice was losing its vigor.

"Naomi . . ."

The silver dress trembled around her knees. Her legs gave out. Clay stepped forward, caught her in his arms before she touched the stone ground. Naomi's gaze came to Celia and Victor without acknowledgement. The resolve slipped from her eyes as they lost focus.

"Then I'll die."

"Naomi," Clay groaned, dropping to his knees, his arms cradling her to his chest. He bit into his wrist and held it over her lips. She opened her mouth. He hesitated. His head tilted as if he were looking at her chest.

"Dammit, Naomi."

So much pain and anger filled those two words. Celia could feel him reaching for her, wanting her back. Clay moved his wrist before his blood could reach Naomi's mouth. He held her again and began to rock her back and forth. Her braids swept across the porch, into the puddle of blood there.

Victor's hand tightened on Celia's shoulder. He wanted her to look away. She had to blink a few times because tears had blurred her sight, but she didn't turn away.

"Leave us," Clay said, his back to them still. His voice sounded ground up, deflated.

"What can we do?" Victor asked him.

Naomi's eyelids drooped until they closed. "I love you," she whispered. Her right hand twitched, her blood staining Clay's jacket, as she tried to touch him, perhaps. The effort proved to be too much. Her fingers stretched out, then dropped.

"Leave us!" Clay thundered. His head whipped around. Celia stepped back from the ferocity in his dark eyes. His fangs showed as he scowled at them.

"Hold your breath," Victor said, then wrapped his arm around Celia's shoulders. His icy tidal wave of magic washed over her, and they teleported to the house.

Celia gasped a few times. Traveling like that didn't do much for her lightheadedness. Her knees felt wobbly. She sank to the bed.

"Are you okay?" Victor asked her.

She pressed her palm to her forehead and sighed. "Yeah, I guess."

His hand touched her back. She glanced up and saw the same

indecipherable questions in his eyes. She took a deep breath, stood, and crossed over to the closet to find her pajamas. Carefully, she eased out of the dress—the same dress that no longer incited the same ardor as before—and hung it up in the closet. She peeled off the pasties she had used since the low-cut back hadn't allowed for a bra, and then pulled on her shorts and t-shirt. Before getting in bed, she cleaned her face and teeth and ran a brush through her hair.

She had to focus on every step to actually perform them.

When she checked her cellphone, it was two minutes to midnight. She smiled and glanced over to Victor, who gazed out the window. He tensed, somewhat confused. He frowned over to Celia.

"What?" she asked, her own brows furrowing.

"Well . . . you were happy. What were you thinking about?"

She smiled again. "We have two—no, make that one minute until it's officially our anniversary."

He came to her side of the bed and kissed her warmly, then looked down at the time on her phone. It was midnight.

"Happy anniversary, Seal."

She took his cheeks in her hands and brought his face to hers.

Okay, she thought. *This is good. This is nice*. She pushed away the last hour and contented herself with Victor's lips. The familiarity and pleasure. When he pulled away, she saw his eyes were black.

"Let's go somewhere. Are you tired?"

Celia shook her head. She wanted to have fun on her vacation, dammit. She could sleep when she got home.

She threw on clothes, checked her hair in the mirror, then followed Victor downstairs.

The air was warm outside, of course. Laughter and the smell of burning wood greeted them; the neighbors had gathered around a fire pit in their yard.

She couldn't help a glance across the street. Mary's house was dark. With only the streetlights, it appeared quite forbidding.

Victor took her hand. They were mostly quiet as they walked toward the entrance of Setter's Cove. Neither wanted to—or couldn't—talk about what had happened.

A band played somewhere. The cheery tempo carried over the rhythm of tires on the road.

They followed the music across the wide street until they came upon an outdoor bar. It was located on a strip of concrete that it shared with a few restaurants, a laundry mat, and a Wal-Mart. The lot was bare, aside from the spots in front of the bar.

The band played on a wooden platform behind the building. A small, but lively group of patrons swayed to the beat. They also laughed and talked amongst themselves at tables and on the dance floor.

Celia and Victor went inside the bar proper, which was the only way to access the outdoor section. Celia ordered a soda and they found an empty table outside.

The band was just finishing their set as they sat. Before Celia had time to be disappointed, another group climbed on stage. The area was quiet save for the din from the patrons. The band tuned their instruments. After the female singer introduced them as the Tumble Weeds, they started an upbeat ditty with a bit of a rumba flare.

"Can we join you?"

Celia had been sipping from her glass when the voice seemingly came out of nowhere. She slurped her drink, startled, and then looked up.

The two people standing in front of the table were both dressed in jeans, dark t-shirts, and sneakers. The woman smiled at Victor before her eyes went to Celia.

There were plenty of empty tables. Celia thought it odd these strangers would ask to sit with them. She glanced to Victor and saw the strain in his expression.

The two pulled out the empty seats and sat without waiting for acceptance. The man was on Celia's right side, prompting a glare from Victor. The man sneered and leaned a little closer to Celia.

"Do you all know each other?" Celia asked. She wasn't tipsy enough to miss the tension.

"I'm Rita," the woman said, placing a hand on her ample chest. "We met Victor yesterday. You are . . . ?"

"Celia."

"Nice to meet you, Celia."

Rita looked to the stage. Her friend—Growly—took the moment to move even more toward Celia. She noticed how close he had gotten and peeked at him. His eyes were closed as he smiled and inhaled.

Vampire, Celia thought. She shifted in her chair then eyed Rita for vampy signs. She was breathing and blinking. That was about all Celia had to go by. Rita was as husky as her companion, her only distinction being her breasts that encompassed the entirety of her chest.

Rita sighed contentedly and faced the table again. "I think I love this band," she replied. "This is my first time here."

"Was there something you needed?" Victor asked. He had uncrossed his legs and now leaned back from the table. "Celia and I were looking to be alone tonight."

Rita looked Celia over again. "Where are you from?" she asked her, ignoring Victor.

Celia hesitated, since Victor was so on guard. "Boston."

"What brings you to our neck of the woods?"

Celia glanced to Victor. "It's our anniversary."

Rita paused only a second before smiling. "That's wonderful!" She beamed at Growly, who, surprise surprise, growled. "Isn't that sweet?"

"I'll tell you what's sweet . . ." he mumbled. As he spoke, he grazed his finger along Celia's forearm, tickling the hairs to stand on end as electric currents passed through his skin.

She jerked her arm away. He grabbed her forearm so quickly it made a slapping sound. Her teeth gritted together as the electric currents became painful, shooting from where he touched her, into her bones, up her elbow and to her shoulder.

Only a split second passed before Victor was on his feet and leaning across the table, his hand clamping around Growly's wide neck. Growly sputtered in surprise at Victor's speed. Or perhaps he hadn't thought Victor would attack. He wasn't a good fighter apparently; his size was misleading.

This was a bizarre display: Growly grasping Celia, Victor choking him.

"Get off me," Growly growled, though his grimace weakened his hostility. The electric jolts did rescind slightly. Celia only needed to choke back a small cry. Victor's hand tightened and Growly could no longer speak.

"Let him go," Rita snapped. She slammed her fist on the table, shaking up the silverware in the process.

"Let her go first," Victor hissed.

Growly released Celia's arm, taking away the agonizing shocks crippling her. Celia rubbed her shoulder and jumped to her feet. She snatched up her glass and tossed the remainder of her cola in Growly's face. It splashed on Victor as well, because he still had Growly's neck.

Victor let go and stepped back, shaking the liquid from his arm.

A man in a light gray suit rushed over to their table. "Is everything okay here?" he asked sternly.

Three sets of enraged gazes caught him at once. He was so startled that he jumped, and then froze in a cartoonish manner with his shoulders at his ears and his hands splayed out at his sides. He was bombarded by angry vamp magic from different angles and his poor little brain didn't know how to compute. He finally spun on his heel and marched back the way he came. That's when Celia realized all the eyes staring at them. She had almost forgotten where they were. Even the woman on stage watched them as she belted another upbeat song.

Celia tugged on Victor's shirt. "Let's get out of here." She examined her aching arm as they made their way to the exit. A dark purple bruise circled her forearm where Growly had gripped her. Tears burned her eyes but she blinked them back, determined to keep her cool.

All on its own, her mind shifted back a year, to before she had met Victor. She didn't have bruises or sore bones then, nor had she been felt up under a bridge. She didn't want to, but she found herself blaming him for all the troubles she'd had over the last few months. If he had never told her what he was . . . if he had never come up to light her cigarette . . .

She stopped that train of thought right there. Yes, she felt miserable and she wished she could yank her arm off if that would stop the pain, but she would not let herself regret having met Victor. She loved him, they had fun together, she could talk to him about anything, and she enjoyed his mystique. She hated justifying her relationship to others, but defending it to herself was disturbing.

And why hadn't Hastings's potion worked this time?

They had only gone a few feet from the front steps of the bar when Victor grasped Celia's good arm and tugged her aside. She was surprised and confused but that cleared up real quick when Growly whisked past her. Of course Victor would hear them approach.

Growly lost his balance. He skidded to a stop and fell on his side. Victor's head whipped around, looking behind him where Rita no doubt brought up the rear.

Growly scrambled into a crouch. "Give her to me."

"Fuck off," Victor responded.

Growly's neck disappeared as he tucked his shoulders to his ears. He lurched forward. Rita snarled from behind as she stormed at them as well. Victor's hand tightened on Celia's elbow and they vanished. Celia hoped the vamps rammed into each other, hard.

They appeared in the dark living room. As soon as they materialized, Victor dropped to his knee with a groan. He clutched his head in both hands. Celia rushed over to turn on the lamp, and then stooped down beside him, rubbing his back.

"Are you okay?" she asked, even though it was obvious he wasn't. His face pulled together in an agonized knot. She felt horrible that he was in such pain. Tentatively, she held out her arm.

His eyes found hers. Something made him hesitate.

He sank to his haunches, shaking his head. "No," he mumbled, "it'll pass in a minute."

It was more like ten. Celia didn't insist he take her blood, but she did sit with him until his grimace went away. Growly's attack had cleared her head of the alcohol.

She picked at her nail, with Naomi's face on an endless loop in her head, when Victor sighed. She glanced up. "Better?"

He nodded, and then licked his lips. He was very, very pale and his eyes midnight black. His lips, dry and white around the edges, seemed unnaturally thin, as if they would disappear right into his face.

She frowned, concerned. Why did he look so haggard? Maybe he was teleporting too much.

"What was that about back there?"

He didn't look at her. "Rita is marking her territory."

Celia snorted. "Like a dog?"

"Like any other predator," Victor said sharply.

"Why did he want me? Did you do something to them?"

His head jerked to her in anger and surprise. "I didn't do shit. They're a bunch of assholes trying to claim territory."

"So, they're just picking on you? For no damn reason?" Her doubt screamed volumes. She was still rubbing her arm.

"What're you saying?" he snapped, facing her.

She shook her head. She wasn't even sure of what she meant. "Forget it."

Victor was quiet for a moment as he surveyed her. "It's late," he whispered. "You should get some sleep."

She was not tired, but she didn't protest. She watched as he pulled himself to his feet and trudged out the door.

* * *

Victor walked up the Strip while keeping an ear out for Rita and her mooks. He knew their scents now, which was useful. He dragged his feet as he wandered around, waiting for the sun to rise. The multiple teleports had drained him. He knew he looked worn, gaunt. A few people gave him double takes as he passed. He didn't care.

Celia had retreated again. He didn't need their bond to feel it.

He'd never had this problem before, this roller coaster of emotions. Aside from the women he'd told Celia about, plus a few others, he had mostly been with other vampires. Those relationships faded quickly for him because being intimate with another vampire made it too easy to slip back to his old self. He had been controlled by his bloodlust and his maker had indulged the consuming compulsion. Most of the vamps he'd encountered in the last century had little interest in concealing their nature.

Human companions were a different cup of tea. They were immature. They wanted kids. They wanted to be married. They died.

The coed from Duke had been the only other human to whom Victor had revealed his true nature. She had not taken the news well, which was why he had been so hesitant about telling others. But something about Celia had made him confident she would handle the news, maybe not with aplomb, but at least in stride. And she had.

But now . . . something was different. Just like after the incident on the plane, something had changed between them. Celia basically blamed him for Rita. Perhaps she had every right to. The vamps were messing with them because of him.

He didn't like the distance he had just witnessed in her eyes. He was at a lost. Ups and downs were commonplace in any relationship, he knew that. She'd never asked about his past, and he wasn't used to sharing it. She had seemed interested in hearing his story. She had been open. And then she had witnessed another ugly vampire confrontation. He never could seem to properly shield her from them. And watching Naomi's death hadn't helped.

Damn, he wished she hadn't seen that. They'd always danced around the discussion of the future. Mainly because it had always been a non-discussion: he would never turn her.

After witnessing Naomi's death, however, Victor wasn't so sure anymore that if they, themselves, were in the same situation he would let Celia die.

He sighed wretchedly and took a look around. He'd recognized a scent. Akeem waited on the curb outside of the Riviera hotel. He nodded at Victor.

Victor nodded back and continued on his way.

"Aw, come on, man," Akeem called. "You still mad?"

Victor turned back slowly. How could he be? He understood now that he couldn't allow himself to be in that position again. He knew better anyway. That's why he didn't feed with other vamps.

A beat-up Jeep, the kind with the canvas roof, pulled up in front of Akeem.

"Wanna take a ride?"

Akeem was fiddling with the radio dial when Victor got in beside him. He found a hip-hop station and drove off. Victor slouched in his chair, letting the night air wash over him.

Fifteen minutes later, they stopped in front of a house with two mountain bikes tossed onto the trimmed grass. Two flamingos stood in front of the porch.

Victor glanced to Akeem quizzically.

"Come on." Akeem already had a leg out the door. "I'm just visiting my boy. Don't worry—" He patted his stomach with a simpering smirk. "Already fed."

After another pause, Victor climbed from the Jeep and followed him down the path to the house. Akeem opened the door.

"Yo, Key," he said as he entered. "Let him in. He's cool."

"You can come in," a male voice said from the depths of the house.

"Victor. His name is Victor."

"Victor," the guy said, and you could actually hear him roll his eyes. He put on a noble accent, as if he were a king: "You may enter."

Akeem chuckled. Victor noticed that Akeem had dropped the Nigerian accent for a Northeast American one.

Victor stepped into the sparse living room, with the blue sofa and leather armchair. The human perched on the sofa wore khaki shorts and a wrinkled peach shirt.

"Aw, come on!" the man shouted. "No, you dumbass, go to the left. Left! *Your other left!"*

Victor frowned. Just as his concern began to rise, he noticed the headset on the man's ear, connected to a white controller. The muscles of his arms jumped whenever his thumbs jerked across the controller. Akeem stepped behind the sofa for a better view of the television.

"No!" their host shouted again. "You just shot me, you idiot! Hello? Hello?" He snatched the headset off and tossed the controller on the seat beside him in a huff. "Idiots," he muttered, his dark hair flopping into his eyes. "All of them."

"Victor," Akeem said, "you ever play one of these contraptions?"

"Sure," Victor answered. There'd been a stint in 2005, when the Xbox 360 was first released, where all Victor did was play with people around the world. He'd kicked the habit after a couple of months, but still found it easy to figure out the mechanics of new games.

The human looked up at his guests for the first time, his brows pulled together angrily. "Jon? I didn't know you were in town."

"Just got in a couple of days ago," Akeem replied. "You were asleep or out whenever I came a-calling."

"You need a cellphone."

"No, thanks." Akeem jutted his chin at Victor. "Keoki, Victor," he said. "Victor, Keoki."

"Hey," Keoki said. "Where're you staying, Jon?"

"Same as usual."

"Norman's? Dude, I said you can crash here."

Akeem shrugged. "I'm so used to Norman, it's like second nature."

Keoki's gaze drifted back to the television. He was still pretty miffed at being killed by his teammate, if his stiff bottom lip was any indication. Even so, he picked up the controller and began fiddling with the buttons.

"Wanna play, Victor?" Keoki asked.

Playing video games appeared to be a welcomed distraction. Victor sat in the armchair. Keoki attached a second controller and handed it to him. Akeem plopped down beside his friend, his face already pulling down in boredom.

Keoki put on *Call of Duty* as he described which buttons to press and the objective of the game. Three other voices chattered in Victor's ear, along with Keoki's, as they played. Keoki was quite the yeller.

It was easy for Victor to get sucked into the game. They had been playing for a half an hour but it only seemed like a minute.

The front door swung open.

A tall woman strolled in, humming to herself. She stumbled in her heels when she closed the door behind her. Her thick black hair was tousled, her dress wrinkled. Her bleary eyes glanced around the room.

Keoki took a second to see who was coming into his house so late, then froze. "What the hell?" he cried in astonishment. Their team had just entered the enemy's barracks, but Keoki once again snatched off his headset and threw his controller on the sofa.

"What're you doing?" Victor was annoyed. "We need you."

Instead of answering him, Keoki stormed over to the woman. When Victor looked, he recognized her from earlier.

"Hey, Oki," she said happily. She swayed in her spot. Keoki placed a hand on her shoulder to steady her.

"Where were you?" he demanded.

"Out with Mason." She patted his cheek with a silly grin.

"Mason?" Roughly, he pushed her hair off her shoulders. The bites on both sides of her neck were mostly red. He grabbed her arms to examine. Red puncture marks overlapped across her wrists and inner elbows. They should've been a light shade of pink or already healed by now.

Keoki reached for her skirt—probably to check her inner thighs. She was present enough to slap his hands away. "Stop that!"

"What the hell, Leilani? We've talked about this!"

"Blah blah blah," she squawked, shaking her head from shoulder to shoulder. "Mason invited me out, so I said yes. It was a fun party."

"You're crazy. Don't you know how dangerous those parties are? You shouldn't be hanging with—"

His words broke off. Leilani caught when he glanced sideways at his company. She put an indignant hand on her hip.

"Yeah, you can't say it, huh?"

"I only hang with Jon," he hissed at her, like the vampires couldn't hear his undertone. Victor glanced to Akeem. He didn't seem offended in the least as he watched their display.

Keoki still had Leilani's wrists. She yanked them free.

"Hypocrite!"

"Do you see yourself? You look like a pin cushion."

"That's stupid." She tried to push him aside, to leave the room, but he grabbed her shoulders.

"You're gonna kill yourself. Do you hear me? You'll be *dead!"*

"Get off!"

A sudden spark flashed brilliantly, filling the room with white light. At the same time, Keoki yelped in agony.

"I'm sorry!"

As the bright light faded—it had even blinded the vamps—Leilani reached out for Keoki. He clutched his chest. The wrinkled peach material was marred now by a blackened patch in the middle of his chest.

He looked more shocked than hurt.

"You . . . you used a spell on me?"

She looked terrified. "I'm sorry. I—"

She didn't finish that sentence. Her lips suddenly clamped shut. Her eyes widened in surprise. Keoki's jaw was tight, his eyes intense. She emitted muffled sounds as she attempted to speak, but her lips just would not part, no matter how hard she tried.

Keoki stomped out of the room. Leilani looked at Victor and Akeem, noticing them coherently for the first time. Her hands flew to her face to cover her sealed lips, and then she rushed out the room, calling Keoki's name in mumbles.

Victor stared after them. He turned to Akeem, who rolled his eyes. "They go at it all the time," he explained. "But they've never used magic on each other before. That was kinda cool."

Victor glanced to the hallway they had disappeared down. "Maybe we should leave."

Akeem shrugged. "If you want. Yo, Key!" he called out, standing. "We're heading out. I'll see you tomorrow. You better be here."

Keoki didn't answer. Akeem must've received some kind of satisfying confirmation, though, because they headed out the door.

"How long have they been together?" Victor asked.

Akeem chuckled. "Their whole lives. They're brother and sister. Transplants from Hawaii."

"Why?"

"Key said the vamps pushed out all the supes who wouldn't bow down to them. They have total control of the islands."

They climbed into the Jeep and the engine roared to life. Akeem talked about some of the magic he'd seen the siblings perform as he navigated back to the Strip.

"And she can levitate shit. I saw her lift a car once when she was drunk. That girl loves to party, that's for sure. You wouldn't think so, looking at her—well, excluding tonight—but yup. She loves vamps."

"Do you party with her?" Victor just had to ask.

"Nah. I've seen too much shit Keoki can do. I may be a dumbass sometimes, but I'm not stupid."

Akeem stopped the Jeep in front of the Riviera. He looked at the people going inside. "Wanna get a drink? A *real* drink," he added, with a smirk.

"No," Victor said simply, "I better get back."

"To the girlfriend? That's cool."

Akeem watched Victor as he got out. He drove on when he saw Victor waiting for him to leave.

When Victor returned to the house, only an hour remained before sunrise. After checking in on Celia, he went down to his room for the day.

Six

The darkness surrounding Celia obscured the location. Her hands stretched out in front of her, feeling around for something, anything to indicate where she was. But her fingers only grazed the air.

An angry snarl rushed at her. She froze. All the little hairs on her body stood on end as her panic rose. Her head jerked from side to side, but there was only darkness, as if she'd been dropped in a void.

Someone was near, their presence giving her a chill. She saw herself in her mind's eye: standing in the dark, her entire body rigid. She recognized that familiar, overwhelming thirst.

Thirst for blood.

Thirst for her.

Celia spun on her heel to run. The presence was close. Large hands encircled her neck, craning her head to the side. She screamed.

Just then, light swept away the dark. She stood in a room she didn't recognize, with antique furniture and windows covered by thick curtains. Victor's ferociously wild face came closer, his eyes dark orbs lost in his pale flesh. She only had a second before his teeth tore through the flesh of her throat. She was dead; she knew it. She couldn't stop him . . .

Celia woke up gasping for air. A cold sweat dripped down her temples, her heart pounded at her ribcage. Those black eyes; they were all she could see.

Her stomach clenched. She pushed the covers aside and stumbled to the bathroom. Falling to her knees on the hard linoleum floor in front of the toilet, she heaved for all she was worth. The alcohol burned her throat when it came up, and splashed in the water of the toilet bowl.

After a minute, her stomach eased. She sat on her butt, leaning against the wall as she ran a hand through her hair. Dizziness made the room spin. She closed her eyes for a moment, taking deep breaths.

As she sat next to the toilet, she made up her mind about the day. She would live in the present. She wasn't going to think about last night—the argument with Victor, the terrifying vamps, the party, Leilani and her friends. She would gamble the rest of Meg and Max's money. Maybe go for a dip in the pool.

The resolution settled her stomach. Celia pulled herself to her feet to get ready for the day.

Hastings stood at the kitchen sink. He paused when he got a look at her. He didn't seem pleased.

"What? You've never gotten drunk before?" She poured herself a mug of coffee.

"Headache?"

"Not yet." She added cream. "Just icky."

Hastings smiled. It was the first time she'd seen that, she thought. He indicated the small table next to the fridge and she sat. He opened the fridge and peered inside for a minute.

"Lots of grease," he said. "So how about eggs benedict? I have bacon and avocado as well."

"I'll take whatever."

He put two slices of bread in the toaster, then gathered ingredients. When the bread popped up, he placed it in front of her. The toast was one shade lighter than charcoal.

Celia lifted a slice to her mouth, took a small bite.

"I must apologize, Miss Wilcox."

She glanced up. Hastings lit a fire under a pan of water. He didn't look at her.

"I could've better explained the potion."

She swallowed, thinking.

"And I have to admit, on further contemplation, I may not have had the most honorable intentions."

She waited. He separated the yolk from four eggs. He then expertly halved lemons that he juiced into the bowl of yolks. He carried the bowl to the pan.

"The potion," Hastings continued, "was to protect you from threats. I had hoped it would've opened your eyes to the threat right in front of you." The whisk scraped against the metal bowl in a rhythmic tempo as he whipped the yolks.

"That's not fair," she said. Surprisingly, she was calm. She was just tired of this particular conversation.

"Perhaps." He set the bowl aside, and covered it with plastic wrap. He filled a larger pot with water and a dash of white vinegar. He cooked with the same patience as he did with creating potions.

"You don't even know me."

"I know Master Smith."

Celia's brows pulled down low over her eyes. "What does that mean?"

"It means" — the burner clicked a few times and a blue flame licked the bottom of an empty pan he used for the bacon — "that Master Smith is generous and kind, but he is still dangerous."

The way he said that, with an assuredness that left no doubt, she knew Hastings must have witnessed something firsthand.

"You've told me, I heard you, now move on."

He nodded slowly. The bacon had begun to pop and sizzle. He used a spoon to swirl the hot water, then dropped two eggs in the cyclone.

"This man last night," Celia said cautiously, "he was a vampire and he hurt me."

Hastings finally looked at her, his head snapping up, an angry light flashing across his eyes like a spark. Celia sat back, momentarily stunned.

Hastings took a breath and the light disappeared, although the anger remained.

"Um, yeah," she continued, "but I didn't burn him like that lady across the street."

"Are you okay?"

After a bit of hesitation, she lifted the sleeve and showed him the bruise on her right bicep. She hadn't shown Victor after snapping at him. She'd only wanted to go to bed and try to forget.

The bruise was a nasty purple and blue. Dark fingers stretched out from it as if the wound was some kind of alien life form that had grabbed hold of her arm.

Hastings's eyes scanned the bruise. A pocket of grease popped loudly, diverting his attention. He removed the pan from the flame. He remained quiet as he scooped out the eggs. His rhythm was off now. He seemed frazzled as he tried to arrange the eggs but realized he was missing the base.

He held the poached egg, tried to place it on the plate, shook his head. With a hand on his forehead, he dropped an English muffin into the toaster, then cut up an avocado with more vigor than was necessary. After another five minutes of arranging her plate, he sat across from her at the table. His shoulders sagged as if the weight of the world had settled there.

"Having his blood would disrupt the potion's properties," he said in a soft voice. "It should've lasted three days." His eyes were sad, withdrawn.

"You said you would show it to me?"

Celia looked at him plaintively. He nodded once.

The heavy meal did ease her lightheadedness. The sun filtered into the kitchen, slanting across the wooden table where Hastings set out the ingredients for the protection potion. He described each herb again, explaining how they were all essential to personal security.

"My mother created this spell," Hastings replied. "Umami are special. She wanted to protect my sister. I think that is why I have been so concerned for you. Why I had to take matters into my own hands."

He dropped the last of the herbs into the two glasses. He then poured in the vinegar.

"The spell is: *With this potion, I seek protection. From threats, from harm, for safety."* He used the wood spoon to stir.

"That's simple," Celia said.

"Yes."

Hastings placed his hands over the glasses and grew very still. This time she was able to see the light. The herbs lifted from the bottom and began to dance in the liquid as a small glow expanded slowly from the center. It brightened until only the white light was visible. She squinted from its brilliance.

After a second, the light retreated, taking the herbs with it. Hastings passed one of the glasses to her.

"Do you not have to say the spell out loud?" Celia peered down into the glass.

"Once you've mastered your magic, no." He held up his glass. "Cheers."

They clinked rims and drank.

After dressing, Celia asked Hastings to take her to the Strip.

"What do you do all day?"

The Lincoln stopped in front of the Bellagio. A man came forward, his hand out for her door.

"Different things for the properties."

The door opened and a rush of desert heat warmed her side. "Do you want to come in with me?" she asked Hastings sheepishly.

His eyes met hers in the rearview mirror. There was warmth in his gaze that she didn't mind at all. "I have an appointment unfortunately."

She nodded quickly, stuck her leg out the door. "Okay, well, I'll call you."

She'd been sitting at the slot machine for a half hour when someone said, "Hey, Celia."

Recognizing the voice, Celia looked up in dread.

Serena and Grace stood before her. Serena wore a strapless dark green romper. With her red hair, she looked like Poison Ivy out on the town. Grace was more reserved with a black-and-white polka dot tank top and denim capris. Dark sunglasses sat on both their faces.

"Have you been here long?" Serena asked.

Celia couldn't find words. The memory of Serena's naked body in the middle of Rafael's grand living room hit her suddenly. She managed to shake her head.

Serena gestured to Grace, who blew a bubble with her gum. "We just got up and thought we'd try out the casinos. We haven't gambled at all yet."

The woman on Celia's right checked her watch, and then gathered her things. Once she was gone, Serena and Grace sat at the slots. Now that they were closer, Celia noticed how smooth Serena's and Grace's skin was. No marks at all. Well, Serena's knees were a light shade of red.

Celia turned away.

Serena sighed contentedly. She shook the hair off her shoulders and stretched her hands toward the ceiling.

"When did you all leave last night?" She inserted a twenty.

"Um, I'm not sure," Celia said. She fiddled with the lever in front of her.

"Around twelve," Grace answered blandly.

Serena's face whipped from Grace to Celia. "*Twelve?* But you didn't get to the house until after eleven. What happened? Was it the food? The wine?"

Uh, maybe all the fucking, Celia thought. "No, no the food was delicious. And the wine was definitely good."

Serena stared at her. Celia wasn't sure of what she was thinking, mostly because of the shades. She seemed confused, which showed just how different they were. Celia thought it best to be honest. If anything, to avoid these awkward situations if she ever saw them again.

"Listen, Serena," she began. She considered each word as they came out of her mouth. "I'm happy you think of me as, um, a friend. But we don't . . . do . . . those kinds of parties." She paused, trying to think of anything more she could say to get the point across. She had nothing. "Thanks, though," she added, for good measure.

A bell clanged behind them, followed by a yelp of glee. Serena cocked an eyebrow. Grace shook her head, as if she weren't surprised, and inserted her ear buds.

Serena shrugged. "That's cool." She faced the machine again. "Elena was really happy Victor was in town. I thought it would be okay."

"Why? All they did was argue. I think," Celia added with a frown. The night was still a bit hazy.

"I don't know. She's always up to something."

Celia waited to see if she would bring up Naomi and Clay. Finding a dead woman on their porch couldn't be that much of a common occurrence. Right?

The bright lights of the machine flashed across Serena's face, reflecting off her sunglasses. Her lips poked out in a pout when she lost the first round. She didn't seem to be hiding anything. Maybe the vampires had cleaned up before she could see.

Celia faced her game, but her mind was back on Naomi, back to the porch. The heat surrounded them and Naomi's blood dripped into puddles around her feet. She closed her eyes and took a breath.

They were quiet for a while. Celia played more of Meg's money. Grace listened to a rock song from her iPod while she played. Serena seemed to be finally racking up winnings. A waitress came by and they ordered rum and Cokes.

"I'm bored," Serena announced a half hour later. "Let's go shopping." She reached over and pulled out Grace's ear bud. "Come on, Gracie. We're going."

Grace snatched her bud back.

Celia pulled her lever. "Have fun," she murmured, her eyes on the spinning wheels.

A manicured finger pressed the payout button on Celia's machine.

"What the—!"

"You're coming, too," Serena said happily, to Celia's startled expression.

She really didn't want to go shopping. But Serena was picking up Celia's purse. She even downed the last of their drinks for them. Resistance was futile, apparently.

"I stayed here once," Serena said. They were headed toward the foyer. "Our suite had a Jacuzzi. Don't you just love Jacuzzis?"

Celia shrugged. "Sure."

Serena gasped. "Today's your anniversary, right? What're you two doing to celebrate?"

Celia shrugged as she glanced away. "I'm not sure. Victor's been making the plans."

Serena had been watching her curiously. "Is everything okay?" she asked. Celia frowned. That was so unlike Serena to be . . . perceptive.

In truth, everything wasn't okay. It was her anniversary. And what was she doing? *Not* spending the day with her boyfriend.

Celia couldn't look at her. "Yeah," she said to the floor, with a false smile. "Of course."

"You just seem weird."

Celia didn't know how to respond.

They crossed the lobby in the direction of the exit.

"We're not seriously going back to Caesar's." Grace had stopped short and folded her tattooed arms at the chest. Serena and Celia looked back at her. Her midnight-blue eyes glowered at Serena.

Serena chuckled. She then skipped back to Grace and threw her arms and one leg around her. Grace groaned as she struggled out of her embrace.

"Fine, Gracie! Let's see what's in here."

They walked around the stores, but Celia's mind was elsewhere. She wanted Victor to be there with her.

Half-life.

A wave of sadness flooded her. Was Naomi's fate her own? Was that what it would come down to: death or becoming a vampire? Even if she had wanted to, Victor would never turn her. So where did that leave them?

Was this all a delusion? A waste of time? Well, not as much for Victor as it was for her. Yes, she was young and still had time to find that person with whom she would settle down and make a life. But did she want that with someone other than Victor?

No matter how many times she tried to ignore the future, it just kept making its presence known.

Why was this so difficult?

Celia trailed behind Serena and Grace, barely registering the fancy clothes and jewelry. Serena's arms quickly filled with bags—Grace's arms filled with her bags, as well.

"Let's get something to eat," Serena said some time later. "I'm starving."

They approached the bank of elevators. One of the doors opened and a tall guy exited. His two buddies stepped out after him.

"Alec?"

His dark hair swung around his head when he looked up to see who had called him. He beamed. "Hey, Celia."

He slapped the closest friend's shoulder, and then approached them. Once again, his friends weren't thrilled when they surveyed Celia. She wondered what their deal was. Her mouth opened to ask Alec, except his shoulders had gone all tense and his face rigid as he scanned them.

"What's wrong?" Celia asked.

"Uh . . ." His eyes flicked to Serena and Grace once again. He looked over his shoulder at his friends. One of them was average height with a thick build. The other was slightly taller and a lot leaner, with long blond hair pulled back in a low ponytail.

Their expressions seemed to harden even more, if that were at all possible. Were they upset that Alec was talking to girls?

Silent communication passed between the three before Alec faced forward. He shook his head, which cleared the tension. His smile returned.

"Nothing, nothing. How are you, ladies? Doing a little retail therapy?"

Serena took off her glasses for a better look. She hadn't noticed his initial agitation, or else she didn't care. She grinned enticingly, arched her back, and took a step closer.

"Who is this?" she asked Celia, though she stared at Alec.

"Alec, this is Serena and Grace," Celia introduced cautiously. She was not comfortable with his mood swing. She glanced back to his friends, who were talking to each other. She couldn't tell what it was, but something . . . familiar about them struck her at the moment.

"Nice to meet you," Alec replied.

"Pleasure," Serena replied sweetly. "How do you know Celia?"

"We've only just met the other day. She's been my lifesaver, though."

"Really? Did she push you out of the way of a car?"

He chuckled. "Nothing that dramatic. She saved me from boredom."

"Ah. Well, she's leaving soon, but if you're ever in the need for . . . *company*, you should look me up."

Alec grinned politely. His gaze went back to Celia. "Where are you all headed?" he asked her. "Wanna join us for a late lunch? We were going to this Italian place down the street."

"Um." Celia turned her attention from Alec's friends. She looked to Serena, hoping to convey the message that she was uneasy.

"Of course," Serena answered with no hesitation. "We were just heading out to eat too."

She placed a hand on the crook of his arm and guided him back to the elevators. Celia and Grace followed behind them. At some point, Grace had put in her ear buds. Celia could hear the tinny version of a Finger Eleven song.

Celia had no one to talk to, not that Grace would offer any form of conversation. Again, she wished Victor were there. He'd know what to do. She didn't understand this agitation. Alec was always nice. His friends and their attitudes were his business.

They all crowded into the elevator. "Normally we use the valet," Serena replied. She pressed the button for the garage. "But there was a long line."

The doors slid closed, sealing them off from the music and chiming of the casino.

Then it hit Celia. That sharp, astringent scent she'd come to call Shifter Smell surrounded them. She stiffened. As discreetly as she could manage with her panic rising, she peered at Alec and then his friends. She couldn't tell from whom it originated.

Serena told Alec about her plans of seeing Cirque Du Soleil that night. It sounded like she was offering to secure him a ticket if he wanted. Alec peeked back at Celia, his eyes pleading. She tried to keep the alarm from her face, but judging by the shift in Alec's eyes, the way they went flat all of a sudden, she hadn't been all that successful.

Alec glanced to his friends. The doors opened.

"We're over here."

Serena, maddeningly oblivious, pulled Alec along to the Cadillac parked just a few spots from the elevator. His friends stepped off, followed by Grace and then Celia.

"Serena," Celia said slowly.

"Yeah?" Serena called back. She still headed toward the car.

Celia grasped Grace's arm, stopping her. Grace glared at her in indignation.

The friends halted when she spoke. When they turned around, their eyes glowed golden like those of the man who had stood in front of Victor's car.

"Run, Serena!" Celia shouted.

Celia spun around. The elevator had already closed. She hit the Up button, but the doors remained shut.

Serena gave a choking gasp. Celia looked over her shoulder and saw her slump to the ground next to Alec. Celia's heart stopped at the sight of her inert body.

The thinner friend ran at Grace, who kicked out her foot. She had been aiming for his nuts, but her sneaker hit him in the thigh. It still elicited a bark of pain, though it didn't slow him down. She threw the bags when he grabbed at her. He sidestepped them and got hold of her arms.

The other friend marched toward Celia. She attempted to dodge him. He didn't move as lightning-fast as vampires, although, he seemed pretty close to it. He had her pinned to his chest, her arms up in the air in the half-nelson position, in a matter of seconds. She tried to kick at him, but he was too close for contact.

Alec advanced on Grace first, his fingers curled around some kind of black object. His friend had her slammed against the trunk of a minivan. Alec jabbed the thing in Grace's neck and the friend jumped back. An electrified sound filled the space and Grace's entire body convulsed.

Celia screamed. Grace dropped to the ground amid the tattered bags. She didn't move.

The friend's large hand covered Celia's mouth to silence her. A sizzling noise like the bacon from earlier crackled from his palm. He yowled, and then pushed her away. Celia fell hard to her hands and knees.

"What the fuck was that?" he bellowed.

Celia stumbled to her feet. Alec stood in front of her. His eyes were golden too, his face scrunched together in hatred. He jabbed the hard, rectangular thing into Celia's side. A high-pitched charge buzzed in her ears. Electric volts shot through her.

This was worse than Growly's attempt to scare her. So much worse. All her muscles locked, her teeth clamped shut, and her body shook uncontrollably. Her shriek of pain came out in a rattled mumble. The savage gleam in Alec's monstrous eyes, his angry sneer, were the last things she saw before everything went black.

Seven

C**elia came to** an hour later. Her body felt like it was on fire. At the same time, someone drilled a hole into her skull. Her eyes refused to open. She tried her other senses to figure out what was going on.

Her wrists and ankles were bound to the chair, the metal edges of the arms digging into her inner wrists. A very thin pillow barely cushioned her from the hard seat. Someone breathed heavily to her right.

“Where’s the fucking remote?” The voice was so sudden she probably would have jumped if she had any control over her body.

“Right next to you, stupid ass,” Heavy Breather answered.

A television flicked on. A female sportscaster reported on the NFL.

“You got the Packers?” the first one asked.

“Naw, the Niners. I gotta pick up this spread or I’m in the hole with Joe.”

“You still betting with Joe the Mo?”

Heavy Breather chuckled. "I'd love to hear you call him that to his fucking face."

"Shut up," the other guy said. He didn't sound so confident anymore.

Celia pried her eyes open. The drill into her brain turned into a jackhammer. It hurt so much that she had to stifle a groan. She blinked a few times to clear her fuzzy vision. She tried to gather as much information as she could, without alerting them to her consciousness by lifting her head.

Another chair stood beside her; she recognized Serena's gold gladiator sandal. Her leg was tied to the chair as well. A plaid sofa was to her right. Every once in a while, a sneakered-foot would shuffle in and out of her periphery. A floor lamp in a corner gave the room a soft glow.

Because she needed to know more, Celia slowly raised her head. Relief so sweet swept through her at the sight of Serena on her left, her chin to her chest. Her hair covered her face but her chest rose and fell in an even pace. Grace was bound to another chair beside Serena's. Her head rested on her shoulder at an awkward angle, her eyes closed.

The heavy breather—the one who had attacked Celia—sat on the sofa watching the television. He held a bag of frozen peas in his bandaged left hand. The blond one sat on the floor next to the fireplace. He clicked away on a computer in his lap. From the pauses and amused faces, he must've been chatting with someone.

The door to the room stood open, and Celia glimpsed a dark hallway. Alec entered the room suddenly. She hadn't heard him approach. He looked right at Celia; she couldn't pretend she was still passed out. His crooked grin was nowhere to be seen.

"You're awake," he said stiffly. "Good."

"What's going on, Alec?" she croaked. Her throat was itchy.

The sound of her voice roused the others. The two men looked at her, coming on guard. Heavy Breather tightened his grip on the peas. Both Serena and Grace groaned as they came to.

Alec stood in front of Celia and crossed his arms at the chest. "You ought to be ashamed of yourself. You don't even know how disgusting you are."

Celia gaped up at him. "What the hell are you talking about?"

"You! All of you." He swept his arm out to indicate Serena and Grace as well. "You don't even know how *bad* you smell."

"Smell?" She had to blame the stun gun for her density, because she actually tried to sniff herself.

"You don't even seem the type," he went on. "That's what makes me so angry. I've seen those . . . those repulsive people. They're like addicts, strung out, begging for more."

"What's going on?" Serena asked shakily. Her brown eyes, always so happy, were glazed with tears.

Alec sneered at her. "And you," he spat. "You had the nerve to hit on me? I wouldn't touch you with a ten-foot pole!"

Serena balked.

"Oh, that's original," Grace said with a snort. Alec turned his glower on her, an angry growl ripping from his throat. Grace didn't even flinch.

If only they knew how Celia felt. She had spent time with this man. He had always been so cheerful. It had all been a front.

"What is this all about?" she asked. "What do you want with us?"

"We don't want anything to do with *you*," Alec said. "We want your bloodsuckers." His anger caused the Shifter Smell to sting her nose.

"They'll come looking for their sheep."

Serena sniffled now, her tears streaming black mascara down her cheeks.

Celia scowled at him. "I am *not* a sheep."

Alec inhaled deeply, and then pretended to gag. Celia's lips pursed in anger.

He straightened. "Sure, the smell's fading on you. But these two . . ." He jabbed a finger at Serena, who jumped and choked back a fearful sob. "They might as well *be* bloodsuckers the way they stink."

"Yo, what the hell'd you do to my hand?" Heavy Breather stood with his left hand raised. Water dripped between his fingers and hit his boot. Celia didn't answer.

"I said" — he took a step closer — "what'd you do to my hand? *Yo.*"

Celia kept quiet. Alec stuck his hand out when his friend leaned closer. He looked at his watch. "We have another hour or two until sundown. Sit tight."

He left the way he came.

Heavy Breather returned to his seat and faced the TV again. The other eyed Grace, his bottom lip clenched between his teeth as his gaze scanned her breasts.

"Hey," Celia snapped. He blinked, startled. "Stop looking at her."

His surprise rose for a second before vanishing into anger. He placed his computer aside, then stood. They all watched as he approached Grace.

"Or what?" he said to Celia. He ran a finger along Grace's cheek. "Huh? What're you gonna do?"

Grace moved away from his touch. He grabbed a fistful of her hair. His other hand cupped her breast, his eyes still on Celia.

"Stop it," Serena whimpered. Her bottom lip trembled. Celia tried to stand, forgetting her restraints.

"I don't think you understand who's in control here," he said. He squeezed. Grace turned her head and bit into his forearm.

Their captor yelped. He let her go and pushed her shoulder. Grace's chair toppled backward. Grace's head bounced off the floor with a soft thud.

Celia and Serena both gasped. The man looked at his arm. Her teeth had left a red bruise.

"Fuck," he muttered, rubbing it.

His pal laughed as he lifted Grace's chair back onto its legs. "You probably need a hep C shot now. Maybe syphilis too."

After glaring at his friend and giving Celia the finger, the first guy went back to his computer on the floor.

Celia looked at Serena first. Serena's chin quivered as she tried in vain to control her tears. Celia's eyes met Grace's, and for once Celia felt a connection with her. They were each trying to tell the other that everything would be fine. That they would get out of this alive.

Celia hoped her doubts didn't show through too.

The girls sat in the chairs for an hour and a half. The miniscule cushions were not doing their job. Celia shifted a few times, but it was no use.

Serena had stopped crying forty minutes ago. Now she squirmed in her seat. She glanced between the two kidnappers, but they were ignoring the women pretty good.

She finally spoke up. "I, um, have to use the bathroom."

"Tough shit," Computer Guy replied, without looking.

"But I can't hold it anymore."

"You want her to pee herself?" Celia asked. "Then you'll have to clean the floor."

Computer Guy's glare made Celia's blood run cold. He placed his laptop on the floor and stood. Pulling a pocketknife from his back pocket, he cut the cloth they had used to bind her.

"Try something," he growled at her, sticking the sharp knife in her face. "I'm begging you."

Serena cringed away, but he had a tight grip on her bicep. "You're hurting me!"

"Shut up."

He dragged her out of the room. In the hallway, he kicked open a door on the right and shoved her inside. She tried to close the door. He pushed it open.

"I don't think so. Do what you gotta do and hurry the fuck up."

Serena's whimpers carried over the sounds of the television. Celia kept an eye on Computer Guy as he watched Serena do what she had to do with a little too much interest. It must've been extra embarrassing for Serena, since her romper was a one-piece.

The toilet flushed. Computer Guy reached in and yanked her out before she could wash her hands. Serena stumbled as he pulled her over to her seat.

As Computer Guy retied her to the chair, Alec strolled into the room.

"Sun's down."

Breather lowered the volume on the tube. His eager gaze focused in on Celia. Computer Guy stood beside Alec.

"Now, all you all have to do is call for them. And make it good. I'm looking for a fight."

"You still haven't said why you're doing this," Celia said. She wanted to make sure Victor would be okay if he came here. She couldn't differentiate the Shifter Smell to determine if Alec's buddies were shifters as well.

Computer Guy snarled at her. Alec raised a hand to silence him, and then stared at her, his unnaturally golden eyes digging into her. She was scared out of her mind but she fought hard to keep it from showing. She wanted him to see that his little act disgusted her too.

"My friends here," Alec began, "are always complaining about the bloodsuckers taking over."

"We've told those freak shows this is *our* town," Computer Guy interjected with a thump to his chest. "Vegas used to be all wolf. Now it's overrun with those parasites. They won't leave so we gotta show them what's what."

"This is wolf territory," Breather reiterated, his nose in the air.

"What does that have to do with us?" Celia asked. "We don't live here."

Alec shrugged. "That's too bad. But we have to set a precedent, and it looks like you picked the short straw."

Okay, his little clichés were getting annoying.

"Wolf?" Serena's voice cracked. "What do you mean?"

"We're werewolves, idiot," Computer Guy spat. Serena's mouth fell open.

Alec gestured to Computer Guy, who happily whipped out his pocketknife yet again. "Her first."

When Alec indicated Serena, she promptly burst into tears. Computer Guy smirked when he stood in front of her, the knife at hip level. The point of the knife dragged along her jaw to her ear, then down her neck.

"Please," she whimpered, trying to shift away from him. Her restraints held her in place.

"All you gotta do is call your master, or whatever the hell he is," Alec said.

Serena was crying too much to form intelligible words.

"Do it!" Computer Guy demanded. With his outburst, his knife pricked her where her neck met her shoulder. Serena cried harder.

"Leave her alone!" Celia yelled.

"You shut up," Computer Guy retorted. His free hand flicked out faster than she could react, slapping Celia across the cheek. The impact stung so badly, all she could do was gasp.

Alec took a step forward. "Hey, ease up, Carl."

Celia glowered at Alec. "Oh, *now* you want to be humane? *Now* you care about our fucking wellbeing?"

His eyes widened. After a moment, he composed himself, folding his arms at his chest and stepping back.

Carl, seeing he had permission to do what was needed, chuckled. As he laughed, his brown eyes blazed golden. A chill went right through Celia that she couldn't hide. He turned back to Serena, and when he spoke, his voice was much deeper than before.

"Call him."

Serena's mouth opened a few times, but no words would come.

"Rafael."

Everyone looked at Grace. She shot icy daggers at Carl with her eyes, which was probably the most emotion she'd ever displayed.

"We're in trouble. Help us."

A pause followed, where everyone waited with bated breath, as if expecting Rafael to magically appear. But it didn't work quite like that. The call had to reach the vamp, and since Rafael—as far as what was evidenced—couldn't fly or teleport, he'd have to use more practical means of getting there, after ascertaining her location.

Carl looked disappointed that their goal had been accomplished so quickly. Grace hadn't even whined or cried or anything. He glanced to Alec, who nodded to Celia.

As Carl approached with his knife and smirk, Celia wondered how they knew her *master*, for lack of better term, wasn't Rafael as well. Did she smell differently? In better circumstances, she might've asked, but, alas, Alec was an asshole. Maybe she'd ask her coworker Michael . . . if she got out of this in one piece.

Carl gave her the same treatment: his crotch in her face, threatening her with the knife. Celia stared at him deliberately. His golden eyes narrowed.

"Bitch, don't you know you don't stare a werewolf in the fucking eye," he growled. "That's a challenge."

"To what? Your manhood?" She said it like she was going to laugh.

Carl's jaw clenched. He raised his arm and slapped her again, sending her head to the side so that her chin met her shoulder. That time she whimpered. Werewolf impacts hurt just as much as vampire's. She knew the latter from when she had foolishly punched Victor in the shoulder once during an argument. And there'd been that time Ashleigh hit her in the face.

Celia straightened up in the chair and stared at Carl's chest. Her own chest heaved as she tried to stay in control.

"Now, call him so we can be done with this."

She shook her head.

"No? You're serious?"

She didn't respond. Carl grabbed her face in his hand, crushing her jaw. Involuntary tears sprang to her eyes.

"Don't make this so hard on yourself," he barked at her. "I could care less about you. It's that fangy shit who uses you as a feeding bag that I want."

"You've got it all wrong, you know," she said through clenched teeth. "You don't know anything about me." She directed those words to Alec, because it was pointless reasoning with the other two.

"I don't wanna hear your justifications," Alec said.

Carl released her face. Celia shook her head in disbelief.

"Was anything you said true? Are you really from Atlanta? Do you have a sister? Was that architect stuff all bullshit?"

Alec shifted his weight to his other foot as he gritted his teeth. He looked like he wanted to turn his face from her but was compelled not to. It had nothing to do with Celia, though. It was that same wolfy dominance that made it hard for most to look Michael in the eye too long.

"It wasn't bullshit," he said. There was a note of sadness in his voice. "It was all true."

She didn't know if it would've been better if it had all been a bunch of lies. But knowing he'd been telling her the truth didn't ease her resentment. He might've done that just to keep his facts straight.

Celia rolled her eyes away from him, making him growl at her insolence or whatever, but she didn't care. She was done with him. Her current problem lay with Carl; the knife was still in her face.

"Well?" he snapped. "We don't got all day."

She shook her head again. The snarl that came from Carl was so ferocious, so feral that the three women nearly jumped out of their skins. Thank goodness for the restraints keeping her ass in the seat.

His body trembled, the hand with the knife shaking too closely for her liking. The Shifter Smell magnified. The shape of his eyes shifted, becoming yellow spheres in his face. The women watched in muted awe as light brown fur began to sprout from the back of his hands and neck and jaw, and anywhere else with exposed skin.

Celia had been forcing herself not to think about Victor. The fear that rippled through her at Carl transforming knocked away the walls she had built. She didn't exactly say words in her head, but Victor came to mind as she internally sought some form of solace, so as not to do something wimpy, like scream or pass out.

The sound of bones breaking and bending filled the room, unsettling Celia's stomach. Carl grunted and shuddered in pain. When he opened his mouth, all four of his incisors had elongated into razor-sharp fangs. The rest of them extended to points as his jaw popped and expanded.

"Frankie!" Alec shouted.

Breather jumped up from the sofa. His attention had been averted by the television. He pounced on Carl and wrapped his thick arms around his expanding chest.

Carl snapped at him with his partially formed snout, but Frankie dodged his assaults. Carl's shirt ripped as a furry chest burst through the cotton material. The thighs of his jeans tore along the seams as well.

Frankie grunted in his struggle to drag the changing man from the room. Alec finally had to grab hold of his legs. They carried the snarling, bucking man/wolf out of the room. A door slammed shut, and the growling decreased.

Celia checked her heart rate before inspecting Serena and Grace. Grace was as white as a sheet, which was saying something since she was already so pale and always so impassive. Serena wasn't crying, but her body shuddered as if she were cold.

Celia opened her mouth to needlessly ask if they were okay. She stopped before the words left her mouth.

Serena's face had suddenly gone blank. Her entire body relaxing, she focused on something beyond the wall straight ahead. Then she tried to stand. When she couldn't, she looked down at her restraints. Confusion made her frown. She tried to stand again with the same result.

"Serena?" Celia asked. "What're you doing?"

Serena strained to lift her arms, ignoring her.

"Rafael must be calling her," Grace said. Celia was confused. "She's trying to go to him," she clarified matter-of-factly, as if Celia were dense.

"She needs to stop." Celia eyed Serena's wrists, which were already beginning to bruise under the cloth. "She's going to hurt herself. Serena? Serena, can you hear me?"

"She won't listen to you," Grace replied blandly. "And she won't speak to you."

Celia looked at Serena's wrists again. The off-white cloth gradually turned red from chafing her skin. Fuck, she had no choice.

Celia closed her eyes. She wasn't sure if Victor had heard her earlier, but this would be clear.

She visualized her boyfriend. *Victor. Please, we've been kidnapped. Tell Rafael to stop calling Serena. She's going to hurt herself trying to get away*.

She took a deep breath, telling herself he would get the message. That affirmation didn't soothe her, but she opened her eyes anyway. Serena continued to struggle against her binding. She didn't seem to register the probable pain of the cloth rubbing away at her skin.

The memory of Milo calling her came rushing back. No one had been able to stop her, either. Celia had just mindlessly gone to where he had been waiting for her in the Public Gardens. The thought of that night made Celia clench her teeth.

After a few minutes, Serena paused. She had been gazing at her left wrist. Celia raised her eyebrows, waiting to see what she would do.

Serena blinked. Then her face crumpled in pain. A wave of relief washed over Celia. It was the greatest feeling in the world at the moment.

Victor had heard her. He'd found Rafael.

"It's okay," Celia told Serena. "You're okay."

Serena didn't cry this time around.

A loud crash outside the room shook the floor. The growling, which had started to die down, filled the room as if Carl was there in front of them.

A door opened, then slammed, and Alec stood in the threshold, his entire body quivering like a plucked violin string. His eyes darted around from each of them until they settled on Serena's wrists. He groaned as he disappeared into the dark hallway.

He returned a moment later holding a blue bed sheet. He stomped over to Serena while ripping off four strips from the sheet like it was paper, then tied the strips over the red and white bindings until all they could see was the blue.

When he stood, his face was flushed. His beautiful hazel-green eyes were more yellow. Did the smell of her blood make him . . . hungry? Celia cringed at the thought. If her knowledge of vampires was minimal, her knowledge of werewolves was basically non-existent.

Alec's nose flared slightly in frustration. It seemed a struggle to pull himself out the room. He closed the door behind him.

Celia sat back in her chair. Victor would find them. He'd help. She repeated that to herself over and over and over.

Eight

Victor found the house empty and silent when he rose at sunset. He located his cellphone, which sat charging in the kitchen. There were no messages. He called Celia, but she didn't answer. He tried Hastings.

"She was on the Strip," Hastings said. "I haven't received a call yet."

Victor was quiet for a moment. He tried reaching out for her, but found something wrong with their connection. He could only barely feel her, as if she were just beyond his grasp.

"Is something the matter, sir?"

"Probably not," Victor said slowly. "I'm just surprised she hasn't called yet. Are the reservations ready for tonight?"

They were going to have their anniversary dinner at Delmonico, followed by a comedy show. The rest of the night would entail champagne, strawberries, and the hot tub.

"Yes, sir, for seven-thirty."

Victor glanced to the empty living room. "When did you speak to her last?"

"Around noon, sir."

The house phone rang.

"I'll call you back." He picked up the cordless from its base on the counter.

"Hello, Victor."

Victor stifled his sigh. "Rafael."

He chuckled. "Still angry, are we? Life's too short for grudges, friend."

"What can I help you with?" Victor said tightly.

"It seems that my girls were with your girl this afternoon. They haven't returned yet. Are they there?"

Victor frowned. "No. I only just discovered Celia isn't here."

"Hmm, late riser, no? Esperanza has a, what do they call it? A *text* message. It is from Serena."

"She said that they might be late," Esperanza replied in the background. "And that they might bring Celia back to the house with them."

"I'll be there shortly," Victor said. He hung up then appeared on Rafael's porch. A human opened the door when he rang the bell.

"May I help you?" the man asked politely. He was careful to keep his eyes on Victor's nose.

"I'm looking for Rafael."

"One moment."

He didn't close the door, since it was unnecessary. Victor couldn't follow him inside. Grace's careful choice of words had worked; the magic that kept vamps from entering without express permission was invisible but it pulsed in front of him all the same.

A minute later Rafael appeared in the hallway with the man. "Victor, my friend."

"You may enter," the human said.

Victor crossed the threshold and trailed behind Rafael into the living room. It was pristine. No balloons or streamers, confetti or wine glasses. You'd never guess anything untoward had occurred there just the other night. Victor wasn't concerned by any of that, though.

Esperanza stood by the window wall, checking her phone. The light from the porch fell across her pale cheeks. Elena was draped over one of the sofas as if posing for a *Vogue* layout. Her black silk robe wasn't completely cinched, and she wasn't wearing a bra. Victor turned from her.

He hated being in her presence, mostly because of the memories of their time together. Looking back, he hated the person—the monster—he had been with her. How much he had enjoyed the bloodlust, the bloodshed, the uninhibited, boundless existence. Life was simpler without a conscience.

"This is quite bizarre," Rafael said. "The girls are usually here when we wake."

A knot of apprehension tightened in Victor's gut. He cast around again mentally, but it was the strangest thing; he couldn't feel her at all anymore.

"They probably went shopping," Elena replied with a shrug.

"They would've come back before sundown," Esperanza said. "We have that show tonight."

Rafael's expression shifted from concerned to angry.

"They're in trouble," he said, his voice as flat as a board. "Grace is calling to me. And Serena is in distress."

Esperanza's brows furrowed in worry.

"What have they gotten themselves into this time?" Elena asked. She ran a hand through her hair. "Honestly, Father, they're more trouble than help."

"That's not true," Esperanza snapped. "Do not start, *hermana*."

"Please. All they do is spend Father's money. I do not understand why we are still holding on to these two."

"Elena."

The eldest sister's tone was commanding. Elena rolled her eyes, but she kept quiet.

Victor reached out for Celia again. He was met with a sort of . . . wall. He didn't understand it.

"Can you tell where they are?" Esperanza asked Rafael.

He didn't answer. He had gone stock-still, staring off into the middle distance. The others were quiet as they waited, Victor the most on edge. As an old vamp, Rafael didn't have to say his commands out loud. The vampires who spoke their commands, however, usually did so for finesse.

Just then, Victor experienced a tremble from Celia. Her fear washed over him, making his top lip curl over his teeth. He just needed to concentrate to pinpoint her location.

Celia's voice filled his head, telling him to make Rafael desist his call for Serena, which he did. Rafael gave him an odd look, though he did what he said. Victor found it strange too, this ability of hers to communicate back.

Just then, his cell rang. He snatched it out of his pocket. It was Hastings.

"Have you heard something?" Victor asked immediately.

"No, sir, but I know where she is." He gave him directions.

"Come on," Victor said to the others. He was confident in Hastings's directions, but he was also fairly certain of where Celia was, now that whatever barrier had been shielding her was gone. Another odd occurrence, but he would deal with that later.

Elena stopped Victor's trek to the front door.

"Victor, *amor*," she said in that husky voice that used to send a shiver of pleasure through him. "Your precious human has been kidnapped. You cannot think you can go into a fight unfed."

He glowered at her because she was right. Feeding would make him stronger. Her lips spread into a mischievous smile. She waved her hand, indicating the sofa. Victor remained where he stood.

Elena disappeared from the room. When she returned, she was dressed in leather pants and a V-neck t-shirt.

She also had three humans in tow. She grinned at Victor, and then directed the humans to stand in front of him in a line.

"Guests choose first," she told him.

Victor clenched his teeth. He didn't like how they were displayed, like on the auction block. However, there was no time for an argument. He took the first woman's elbow and pulled her aside. Without preamble, since the humans would either already be under a vampy spell or they very much enjoyed being drunk from, he swept her brown hair from her shoulder and bit her neck.

He managed to keep his noises to himself, because he didn't want to give Elena the satisfaction. And she was watching him intently. Her smirk was gone, disappointment and anger raging in her eyes at his clinical feeding.

With a huff of indignation, she grabbed the face of the man who had answered the door. She pulled him down to her height and kissed him passionately. He was just getting into it when she cocked his head to the side and bit into his throat roughly enough to make him grimace. His large hands gripped her tiny shoulders, but he couldn't push her away—one, she was a vampire, and two, he wouldn't want to offend her, especially if there was a chance she or one of her sisters would turn him.

Victor left the room. A minute later, the humans rushed past him in the hallway, then up the stairs. The second woman of the group had her hand cupped to her throat, but the red bruise was visible.

Esperanza and Isabel stood in the foyer. Isabel held the hand of a blonde human. The human gazed, unfocused, at the marble floor. The youngest vampire ran her hand through the woman's hair, fixing a few flyaway strands. The woman's makeup looked like it had been applied with a paintbrush: her cheeks were deep red; her rouge ran outside the creases of her lips; her eyelids were smeared with black shadow.

Isabel hummed as she lifted the woman's hand, bringing her wrist to her mouth. Other bruised puncture marks occupied her neck and arms. Esperanza groaned as she placed a hand on Isabel's shoulder.

"It's time to go."

Isabel shrugged off her hand. Esperanza grabbed her jaw instead, pressing her fingers between her teeth to make her release the woman's wrist. Isabel snarled at her sister, blood dripping from her lips.

"¡Basta ya!" Esperanza nudged the woman with her free hand. "Go upstairs."

"No!" Isabel shouted around her sister's fingers.

The woman stopped short.

"Cállete." She squeezed harder on Isabel's jaw. "Go!" she repeated to the woman. She did as she was told.

Victor had taken a step forward to help, but Esperanza dragged Isabel to the powder room while chastising her in Spanish.

Rafael came down the stairs as Elena exited the living room and the women emerged from the restroom, cleaned and sighing for different reasons. The vampires all had pinkish tints to their skin as they headed into the night.

The windows of the white Lexus GX were way too dark to be legal. The five of them climbed inside. Victor navigated from the passenger's seat.

The drive took forty minutes. None of them knew the area; all they had were Victor's directions.

They pulled onto a long, dirt road. Any signs of habitation had disappeared ten minutes ago. Now, only the dark desert stretched out on either side of the road.

After another ten minutes, the road turned right. Five or six ramshackle houses were spaced evenly on both sides of the road. Many of their roofs had caved in; one of them was missing the front door. A rusted tractor sat beside the last house. Up ahead, three more houses were grouped together. Lights shone in the last one's windows, yellow squares hovering in the darkness.

Rafael steered the SUV onto the shoulder of the road, concealing it behind a mobile home with two flat wheels. The moon sat high in the sky, but was shielded by a line of puffy clouds.

The vamps advanced on their target from behind the other houses. Rafael, Elena, and Isabel hid in the shadows of the house across the street;

Victor and Esperanza crouched down on the side of the occupied house.

A rocking chair on the sagging front porch swayed ominously in the night breeze. A red Mariner and Serena's Cadillac were parked on the vamps' side. Now that they were closer, the hum of a generator broke the silence of the night.

Victor glanced to Rafael, who sneered back, his fangs showing. Victor smelled the blood in the air too. It was faint, but it was there. He also smelled the women. The Mariner stunk of wolves. Victor's gums tingled as his fangs slid out in fury.

The front door burst open. Two giant wolves sprang from the porch, landing in the center of the road. The black one lifted his head to the sky and howled.

The vampires emerged from their cover at a run. The wolves hesitated only a moment. They were probably stunned at the number of vamps.

The black one was in for even more of a surprise once Victor jumped in the air and landed on his back. His talon-sharp nails dug into the scruff of the wolf's neck and ripped at his flesh.

The wolf yelped and bucked him off. Victor landed on his feet in front of him.

Isabel whizzed by and into the house. Good. Now Victor could give these wolves his full attention. He squared his shoulders and flexed his fingers, telling them to bring it on.

* * *

The women had been sitting in relative silence. The television still played in the corner. Celia learned the New England Revolution had lost their recent game. She hadn't even known soccer was in season right now. It wasn't one of the sports normally played in Cage's.

She closed her eyes after a moment. Her mouth was dry. She tried swallowing a few times. Her side ached from the Taser burn and her left ankle was itchy. She rubbed it against the binding, but couldn't quite alleviate the itch. Serena's stomach grumbled in hunger beside her.

A sudden crash on the other side of the door made Celia's eyes spring open. Heavy feet thundered across the floor, only they sounded like dog paws with overgrown claws scraping the wood. Another loud crash followed, and then a scary howl pierced the air.

"You think they're here?" Celia whispered.

"I don't know," Serena whispered back, her first words in some time.

They all stared at the door, as if willing it to open, or at least become transparent so they could glimpse what was happening. Their backs were to the window, but the curtains were pulled closed anyway. Celia looked over her shoulder just in case, then went back to staring at the door.

When it swung open, Celia gasped in surprise. Isabel stood in the doorway, her sharp eyes appraising them. She stooped in front of Grace first and ripped off the restraints. The door was open, but Celia couldn't see down the hall from her angle.

The ravenous barking from outside escaped into the room through the busted front door. One of them was hurt; he was whining.

No, wait. That whining was much closer than the other sounds.

Celia craned her neck until she saw the chocolate brown wolf on its side just outside the door. His breathing made his body shudder. His ribs must've been cracked.

Celia gazed in wonder at the small girl as she knelt in front of her to untie the restraints. Her dark hair was in a ponytail at the nape of her neck. In her red-and-black plaid skirt, fishnet stockings and black baby tee that was supposed to make her appear rocker tough, she instead seemed incredibly young and fragile. Even so, she had taken out the wolf all by herself.

Celia shook herself. Of course she had. The girl was a fucking vampire.

Now free, the women stood, stretching their tight, sore muscles. Celia grabbed the cloths that had bound her and tied them around Serena's raw wrists.

"Thanks," she murmured.

"There is door this way," Isabel said, or at least that's what Celia thought she said. Her accent was so heavy, and she spoke so quickly, that Celia wasn't sure if she had been in fact speaking Spanish.

Serena and Grace seemed to understand because they were right on her heels as she exited the room. Celia stepped over the ball of fur collapsed on the floor and rushed to catch up to them. She kept as close to Serena as humanly possible without actually climbing on her back.

Isabel led them down the hall and to the left, where they entered the kitchen. The wood paneling was separating from the walls, revealing the crusted plaster beneath. The appliances were dingy and a thick layer of rust-colored grease coated the stove and counters.

An ancient machine on one of the gross counters chugged halfheartedly. Coffee dripped into a stained carafe resting on the hot plate. The kitchen was a few degrees warmer than the rest of the house; someone had been using the oven to bake a pizza. The aroma of pepperoni and green peppers, mingled with coffee, filled the room. She also spotted a deck of cards on the table, a game of solitaire in process.

Fucking bastards, Celia cursed in her head. The three of them had been cooped up in the other room, mouths dry and heads aching with dehydration, while they were in here, drinking coffee, getting ready to eat.

Isabel crossed to a door beside the fridge. It was locked, but one jerk of her arm and it popped open to a melody of splintering wood.

The night seemed darker out back, with the only sources of light provided by the house. A wooden fence marked the property. Most of the boards were broken; planks of wood lay in the dirt as if they had jumped free of their constraints.

Isabel strolled purposefully along the fence while the women crept behind her, keeping their heads ducked. They practically ran to keep pace with her.

As they approached the front, the grunts and groans and growls increased. The two wolves were still on their feet, if only barely. The black one favored his right side and you could see why. In addition to the gash to his neck, he bled from his left side where fur and skin had been ripped away, revealing the pink muscle beneath.

A few yards from him a vampire lay prone on the ground. Celia's heart stopped.

It was Victor.

He wasn't moving. Three long, ugly slashes cut across his back. Wet blood glistened on his face and neck in the light spilling from the house.

The wolves had planted themselves between Victor and the others, who were in bad shape too. Rafael and Elena hissed at them, though they were unsteady on their feet. Esperanza was on her ass, cradling her arm. Because she wore a tank top, Celia could see something was wrong with her left shoulder. The bone protruded under the skin where it had dislocated at the collarbone. With clenched teeth, Esperanza pulled down on her left arm and the bone popped back in place.

Celia had to fight the urge to run to Victor. She glanced around at the two standing vamps, willing them to take out the wolves.

"Celia!" someone hissed.

A gap had formed between her and the others when she had slowed down to gape at the fight.

The light brown wolf's ear twitched backward at the sound. He turned, his golden eyes landing on Celia. She froze. If wolves could smile, that was one evil smirk he threw her way.

Celia's logic finally returned to her. She pitched forward in a run. His legs were stronger.

"Celia!" Serena screamed.

Isabel ran toward the wolf, but he was too close. She wasn't going to reach him in time. His massive paws pounded the earth. Celia closed her eyes, braced for impact. His breath scorched her cheek.

The wolf rammed into her, knocking the wind from her chest. They crashed through the soft wood of the fence.

Celia landed on the ground hard. She was certain she had died. There had been no sharp teeth sinking into her. He had snuffed her life too quickly.

She couldn't be dead, not yet. She didn't want to die. There was so much she wanted to do. Travel, have sex in an airplane, buy a house. Say goodbye to her family. Maybe start her own.

All of these wishes and regrets circled her head. All the things she could've done at some point in her life. But here she was, lying in the dirt, surrounded by darkness.

Although . . . if she was thinking . . . how could she be dead? Plus, her right leg was stinging, all up and down her shin. So was her right arm where the bruise had come into contact with the fence. The commotion around her rose to normal levels.

Celia's senses gradually came back to her. The pain from her body registered in her brain and she choked back a cry.

The furry beast had tumbled over her when they hit the ground. A furious growl rose up from somewhere beyond her head. Giant jaws snapped in response.

Celia lifted her head very slowly. Her vision cleared after a moment. She saw Serena a few yards away. Isabel held her back with an arm around her waist. Serena's frantic gaze alternated between Celia on the ground and the action beyond her. Celia looked too—and immediately wished she hadn't.

Victor rode the brown wolf's back, like he was a pony. His hands gripped either side of the wolf's head. The wolf snarled and snapped. Victor jerked his hands and broke the wolf's neck.

A look of permanent surprise etched his face as he flopped to the ground. A small puff of dust circled his snout. Victor waited a moment to make sure he stayed down before he climbed off.

Gradually, the fur began to recede. The wolf's body shuddered in tiny spasms. The bones shifted beneath the pale skin that was now visible. Carl lay naked and motionless, his blond hair over his shoulders.

Victor came to Celia's side. She stared blankly up at him. Blood and dirt stained his skin and clothes, but the grotesque slashes were progressively mending.

He knelt down. Gently, he scooped her up in his arms and carried her back to the yard. His skin was ice cold against her thighs. Celia thought she was going to be sick. Rocking in his arms wasn't helping.

"Are you all right?" Serena asked, when they were close. Celia could only nod.

The black wolf lay on his belly behind Rafael and Elena. Once he saw Victor and Celia emerge from the cloud of dust the fight had kicked up and not his cohort, he tilted his head to the sky. The anguished howl he emitted penetrated Celia down to her bones. Elena rolled her eyes at his grief.

The group went over to Rafael. "Are you hurt?" he asked, examining Serena and Grace like a physician. Tiny scratches littered his face. His shirt and pant leg were ripped, and dried blood caked his chin, neck, and arms.

"We'll be fine," Grace answered.

They left Alec there in his wolf form, bleeding and struggling to breathe. Celia gazed at him over Victor's shoulder. He didn't look good, and she wondered if he would make it through the night. She couldn't decide how she felt about that. Alec and his cronies had kidnapped them to kill their vampire companions. They would have probably disposed of the girls as well. He had manipulated and betrayed her.

Though she considered him complete scum, she couldn't wish him dead.

As she watched, Alec shook his head a few times, and then licked his wounds. The clouds moved across the moon, sending down a spotlight across the yard. He howled again. The cry carried across the night as the moonlight disappeared again.

Elena stretched her arms high above her head. Her shirt was torn in the back and her pants were dirty. "What are we doing tonight? I need to work off some of this adrenaline."

"Let us do dancing!" Isabel chimed.

She took Elena's hands. They both laughed merrily as they spun in circles up ahead. Their supernatural speed caused a small tornado of dust and sand to form in the neglected road.

The rest walked in silence to the GX—all except Serena, who had begun to cry again. Grace took her hand, and Serena buried her face in her shoulder.

At the SUV, Grace reminded them of their car still parked at the cabin. Elena and Isabel raced to retrieve it. Their laughter and cries of joy in Spanish echoed behind them.

They waited in the car. Rafael clicked his teeth impatiently. He glanced to the clock, then looked at the rearview mirror.

Five minutes later, the Cadillac pulled up next to them.

"What took so long?" Rafael demanded.

Elena rolled her eyes to the roof of the car and poked a thumb at Isabel. Isabel's mouth, chin, and chest were wet with fresh, dark blood. She smiled gleefully at her father.

"*Quiero otro lobo. Me gusta* wolfy wolf. Woof! Woof!" She held her hands up, her wrists bent in a begging dog imitation.

Rafael gritted his teeth. His gaze flicked to Celia and Victor through the mirror. He then waved his hand at the other car, dismissing them, and pulled off. Celia saw Elena smirk. She said something to her sister, who then licked her lips like a child trying to get the last of her treat, no matter that her tongue couldn't reach.

Celia stared out the window on the trip back. Her side sang from the impact with the hard ground. She didn't want to think about anything. Instead, she focused on the dark horizon and the drone of the wheels on the road.

Rafael dropped them at the house. Celia jumped down to the

pavement. She noticed Elena watching them from the Cadillac. There was something appraising in the way she looked at Celia.

Victor climbed down after Celia. She didn't wave goodbye to them; she just couldn't manage.

They continued inside, going straight upstairs to the bedroom. All she wanted to do was crawl into bed and sleep for a week. However, the shower called her name even more persistently. She needed to be clean.

Celia sat on the bed with a groan. The alarm clock told her it was only about 11:00.

"We should go home," Victor said grimly. "Pack your things."

She looked at him. He leaned against the wall, his arms crossed at the chest, surveying her. Most of her did want to leave after tonight. She didn't know how she could enjoy the rest of the trip without worrying someone might jump from the shadows to snatch her away.

But that teensy-weensy part of her that didn't want to go just yet nagged a bit louder. This was her first *real* vacation. They were out of danger now the wolves were handled. Plus, they only had one more day.

She voiced all of this to Victor. He didn't look convinced.

"We can always come back," he reasoned.

She shook her head. "I know, but I think we're okay now. I swear I won't go off with any strangers." She tried to smile at her little joke, but it didn't happen. Even her cheek muscles ached.

"Is that what happened today?"

Celia grimaced. "It was Alec—this guy I met in the casino. I saw him a few times. He was just getting close to me because he smelled you on me. He ran into us at the casino, tricked us into going to lunch, and then kidnapped us to force us to call you all." She shook her head in anger as she recalled the events of the night.

"Why did they want you to call us?"

She shrugged. "Something about territory. They're trying to get rid of the vampires. They wanted to use you as an example."

Victor's jaw was clenched, so how he managed to mutter, "I should've killed him myself," was a wonder.

"Don't say that. It's over now."

"He tricked you, Seal."

She shook her head again, her exhaustion making her body heavy. "Yeah, well, shit happens."

Victor eyed her. She used the moment to shuffle over to the dresser, where she searched for a change of clothes before heading to the bathroom. She crossed to the shower stall, dropping her pajamas on the counter on the way.

She paused at the mirror. The woman staring back at her was bruised and battered and dazed. If she had Victor's blood, the cuts and scrapes would disappear by morning, her side no longer sore. Except that was the least appealing idea she'd ever had. Pain seized every inch of her body, but she'd take it. At least the stinging reminded her she was human. That she was still alive. She needed that at the moment; she felt so numb inside.

The water was hot and glorious, sending tingles through her as her cells jolted awake. Five minutes and the tight muscles in her back and neck relaxed. She wasn't even bothered by the stings from the water pelting her cuts. She closed her eyes with a sigh and rested her forehead against the tiled wall.

She might've drifted off; there were no thoughts, no bad dreams. Just comforting blackness engulfing her.

After a while, she woke up slowly. Aware she was no longer alone, her eyes opened.

Victor stood just outside the bathroom. From his profile, Celia saw he had cleaned up and his cuts were gone. There was no trace of a fight anywhere.

He had been staring at the floor. When she turned, he looked at her face.

"We can stay," he announced. Celia's smile was minuscule, but she was relieved. "I know you don't get away often."

"And we don't want to waste your plans."

"I don't care about that."

There was a pause, with only the sound of the water splashing at her feet.

"I couldn't feel you today," Victor said softly.

She tilted her head to the side. "What do you mean?"

"I can always feel you. Our blood exchange created that connection. But tonight, I couldn't sense that you were in trouble . . . I couldn't even find you at first. Hastings had to perform a Locating Spell."

Celia stared at him. His expression was solemn, and she could tell this really concerned him.

"I . . . don't know what to say." She racked her brain, trying to recall if she had done anything differently. She had been terrified and afraid for Victor at the same time. She hadn't wanted to call him if she knew he'd be in danger.

And then Computer Guy had begun to change. She had needed Victor.

"I, um, I tried not to think of you," Celia said.

"Why?"

"Because I was trying to protect you. I didn't want them to hurt you."

Victor paused. She thought she saw a glimmer of a smile. "Well, you blocked me out."

"Oh." She would be the first to say she didn't know much about vampire magic, so she had no explanation for how she had managed to stay off Victor's radar. That hadn't been her intention.

Victor's gaze drifted downward. She looked down too, and realized that her left shoulder was up at her neck and her knee bent against the tiled wall. She was shielding her body from his view.

Victor crossed to the shower. She shrank back into the corner, not out of fear of him, but because she didn't want him to see her like this.

He slid the glass door open and stepped inside fully clothed. The steam lifted his hair from his forehead. His black eyes reached out to her in earnest. He rubbed her cheek, then leaned down and kissed her temple.

"Victor," she whispered, shifting from his touch. He took gentle hold of her jaw so that she wouldn't move away.

"Let me take this from you," he whispered back. "You don't deserve this."

She thought about the potion she'd ingested earlier. Maybe Hastings would do it again.

A hard knot formed in her throat. She didn't like the vulnerability. At the same time, she hated relying on others for her safety. It just occurred to her how often she needed others.

Victor watched her, waiting for permission. Tears had pooled in her eyes. Victor seemed to think it had to do with her pain. He brought his wrist to his mouth and bit.

Celia took his blood and immediately felt better. Well, physically.

When she looked down, the bruise on her arm began to fade to a light purple right before her eyes. The red spot on her side lightened; the many cuts and the long scrape on her shin all sealed themselves.

She offered her own wrist to him. The last of the paleness in his skin disappeared.

Victor smiled, hopeful. She kissed his lips.

After dressing in her pajamas, Celia went out into the room. Victor stood over the bed in different clothes, pulling the covers back for her.

"Are you better?" he asked cautiously.

She gripped his hand. "I am."

Victor tucked her in, and then kissed her forehead.

"Sleep well," he whispered.

"No, wait," she said, before he vanished. "Stay with me."

Victor climbed into bed and wrapped her in his arms. She rested her cheek on his warm skin and closed her eyes. He stroked her hair. She was asleep in a minute.

* * *

Victor had become adept at locating Akeem, it seemed. He found the vampire in the Monte Carlo. Akeem sat at a blackjack table in white linen pants and a white t-shirt. Two other men—one donning a cowboy hat and fringe jacket, the other in all-black with dark sunglasses covering his eyes—were on Akeem's left. A pretty, older woman in a sparkly gold dress sat on his right. Her stack of chips surpassed the others'.

Victor waited while the dealer flipped his cards. The man in the cowboy getup had twenty-one.

"Victor," Akeem said without turning around.

Victor got right to it. “How can I contact Ava and Wesley?”

Akeem placed his bet of two hundred dollars. “Looking to move?”

The dealer was a tall, lanky man with bad skin. His sharp eyes darted to each of the players, as he passed out the cards with a flick of his wrist.

“Do you have a phone number?”

Akeem chuckled and glanced back at Victor. “Are you always this serious? Aren’t you on vacation, man?”

The dealer gave the man in the glasses a third card. The woman tapped a French-tipped nail against the felt table. She was given another card. Akeem stayed. The cowboy considered, and then he stayed too. The dealer looked to the others, but neither indicated another hit.

The dealer flipped his card. He had nineteen.

The others followed suit. Akeem had twenty-one.

He nodded with a grin. The dealer slid his winnings across the table.

Akeem, sensing Victor still behind him, pointed toward a table along the east wall.

Wesley was seated at a blackjack table with two other men. Ava crossed to the table from the cashier’s counter. A tray of chips rested in one hand, a glass of brown liquor in the other. Her sun-kissed locks were up in a ponytail. Her short black shorts accentuated her very long and lean legs. She’d had a tan before becoming a vamp.

She placed the chips at Wesley’s elbow, then sipped her drink, her free hand resting on his shoulder. Victor thanked Akeem and headed over.

By the time Victor made it to the table, the game was over and Wesley had won five hundred dollars.

Ava glanced Victor’s way when he approached. “Hello. You’re the one Curtis has been hanging with.”

At Victor's quizzical stare, Ava smiled.

"I think he's going by 'Akeem' right now." She shook her head. "What's the point in changing your name so much? Who cares really? Anyway, I'm Ava. This is Wesley."

Wesley held a hand up in greeting.

"Victor."

"Visiting?"

"I leave tomorrow."

Ava's thin, pink lips poked out in a pout. "You don't like Vegas?" A grin followed to let him know she was joking.

"Can I speak to you in private?"

"Sure thing."

They walked away from the table and the gamblers, until they found a private corner. Victor told her about what had occurred earlier. Ava's lips twisted to the side in distaste.

"Fucking wolves," she finally said. She took a drink from her glass. "Wesley knows how to find where the pack is centralized. We'll handle them. Thank you, Victor. Is your human okay?"

"Yes."

She eyed him a moment. "Are you sure you wouldn't like to relocate here? We could use some extra manpower."

"Sorry," Victor said, with a polite smile. "I'm good where I am."

"If you change your mind . . ."

"I know where to find you," he said, finishing her lead.

She gave him a pleasant smile and pushed off the wall. He watched as she ambled back to Wesley's side, remembering that a council of vampires used to run this part of the country. From New Mexico up to Washington, the council of five vampires had held reign.

One of the males had been a man named Frederick, a tall, thick vampire, like a giant teddy bear with skin the color of beeswax. He'd had a bald head and a lazy left eye. Victor recalled how he always had a smile on his face. Nothing had seemed to get him down.

Victor had come to know him when he had spent some time on the west coast. That had been roughly ten years ago. He'd just bought the house where he and Celia were staying when he'd run into Frederick playing a high-stakes game of poker. A large crowd had gathered, piquing Victor's own interest. Frederick had won without the use of his vamp control, he had told Victor later.

Victor had lost contact with Frederick five years ago. It hadn't occurred to him to be concerned until just now. Akeem had said Ava and Wesley were the leaders now. And Ava sure acted that way.

Victor headed back to the other tables. Akeem was still there, perched on his high-top chair, tapping his finger on the table. His chip pile was only slightly smaller than when Victor had left.

"When did Ava and Wesley move up?" Victor asked.

Akeem didn't lift his eyes from the table. "Um, I don't know. Fairly recently. Like within the last five years."

"What happened to the council?"

Akeem shrugged. "I told you, when I come to town I keep my head down."

"Surely you heard something."

"Sure, you hear things. They gave up their power. They were forcibly disbanded. Things to that effect."

"Shh." The cowboy threw them a harsh scowl.

Victor didn't like the sound of that. It meant Frederick was probably *dead* dead. The entire council would have to be dispatched for someone else to fully take power. This news saddened him.

"I hear Ava's pretty badass." Akeem leaned to the side, speaking softly to Victor. He kept his eyes on the table. "One of the stories was that she snuck her way before the council and took out all of them. I don't know how she got in or how she got rid of them all. Someone said something about a katana. Someone else said firebomb. Someone said she kept their heads. She brought Wesley in later to help her with rebellions in New Mexico."

Victor hadn't heard about those.

Akeem went through three more rounds. The woman sighed blithely, tipped the dealer, and left the table without a backward glance. A black satchel full of chips dangled from her wrist.

Victor checked the time. He had just begun to stand when Akeem declared he was finished. After passing the dealer a fifty, he smiled at Victor.

"Where to, chum?"

Victor's hesitation was visible.

Akeem tilted his head. "Damn, where did these trust issues come from?"

"Experience."

"No hotel rooms, I promise. How about that?"

Victor only rolled his eyes and turned away. Akeem strolled next to him, chuckling to himself.

Victor.

They had just passed one of the lounges. Victor stopped at once, without thinking about why, and glanced over his shoulder. It was an unassuming façade, just darkly tinted windows and double red doors.

Three women stood at the entrance. A rope sectioned them from the passersby. The women were preoccupied with finding their IDs in their purses; they hadn't called him.

The bouncer, a tall, burly man, glanced at Victor as he waited for the women.

Victor crossed back to the bar. Akeem followed curiously, but Victor had forgotten he was there the instant the female voice hit his ears. It had hooked his brain like a lure. He went past the bouncer and into the dark bar.

"Hey!" the bouncer called. Akeem placed a hand on the man's shoulder and caught his gaze.

Victor continued inside, searching for the owner of the voice. He slithered through the people dancing in clumps in the center of the dark bar. The strobe lights glistened across their dewy skins. They laughed and shimmied and grinded to "Womanizer."

Victor slipped through the crowd, stepped off the dance floor, and followed the booths to the back corner of the bar. This section was cordoned off by another black velvet rope. White crystal beads hung from the ceiling, concealing the section. Another bouncer stood in front of the rope. His stony eyes looked at Victor, assessing him in a quick scan.

"Private party." His gruff voice cut through the loud music and came at Victor like a punch.

Victor didn't move—a sentinel waiting for his commands. The man took a step forward.

The beaded curtain shifted behind him. A lithe hand slid up the man's shoulder, halting him. A woman stepped beside him.

"It's okay, Flip."

Elena's dark red lips curved into a delighted smile when she saw Victor.

Flip unlatched the rope and stepped aside. Victor still didn't move. He stared at Elena in confusion at first. If his heart could, it would pound against his chest as it became clear why he had come here. The confusion cleared from his face as panic steadily began to rise.

"I didn't think you'd hear me," Elena said simply. Her eyes didn't betray anything except excitement.

"What're we waiting for?"

Akeem had come up behind Victor, rubbing his hands together. He peeked around the bouncer at the eight or so humans lounging in VIP.

Elena pulled aside the crystal beads. Akeem went inside. She looked at Victor expectantly.

He entered.

Elena took another shot and slammed the glass on the table. The humans hooted. They were all at the swaying-in-your-seat, giggling-at-everything stage of drunkenness. A Mexican girl, wearing a crop top and tight jeans, grinded against a man shorter than her. Another couple hooked up in the corner as if they were the only ones there. One man poured the last of the Grey Goose into as many shot glasses as he could, while the man beside him slid a hand up his inner thigh.

With the loud music and the heat and the dim lights, they could've been in another world. A world without boundaries or judgment, and their sun was Elena.

The young woman sitting next to Elena had been bouncing her knees for the last two minutes. She finally screwed up her courage and lunged at Elena. Her arms wrapped around the vampire's neck as she pressed her mouth against hers. She'd overshot her lips a bit, her top lip hitting Elena's cheek.

Elena grabbed the woman's chin a little too roughly and sat back. The woman gasped in surprise. Elena studied her a second, then pulled her closer. Her tongue stretched out slowly and traced the salt from the woman's lips. She groaned, her hands reaching out for Elena but stopping before they touched her, as if she didn't dare. Elena pushed her tongue between the woman's lips.

The humans cheered again. Akeem lounged on one of the other sofas with his arm draped on a woman's shoulders. She nuzzled his neck. He smirked at Victor, who sat alone on the opposite sofa.

Elena fixed her smudged lipstick then crossed the room. She sat beside Victor, close enough that when she bent her knee across the seat, it rested on his thigh. Her arm rested across the back of the sofa. Her fingers inched over his shirt up to his neck. She propped her chin on his shoulder, her lips close to his ear.

"I've missed you, Victor."

He stared straight ahead, his gaze flat. "I'm sure you've found other replacements."

She sat back a little so she could see his eyes. "Other replacements? Why do you say it that way?"

"I was just a thing to fill that void inside of you."

"Now, now," she teased. "There's no need to be vulgar."

"You know what I mean."

She giggled. "I knew you were a chef and a teacher, but I didn't know you became a shrink. Shall we analyze your motives behind dating a human? I mean, she smells delicious, I'll give you that. But she acts as if you two are a real thing."

"I love her."

Elena snorted. "Yeah, right."

He didn't respond.

"You don't actually believe I was using you, do you? Like you are some . . . throwaway human? Don't you remember England? The towns we traveled through?"

Victor leaned away from her, because whenever she spoke, her breath tickled his neck. With Celia's blood, his skin was extra sensitive. He wanted to leave this bar, but he remained where he sat.

"Too far back? I hope your memory isn't failing you. Well, how about Versailles? Eh? And Bora Bora?" She sighed contentedly. "God, I miss that warm water against my naked skin."

Victor's jaw clenched.

"How about China?" she went on, running a finger along his chin. "The ferris wheel in Guangzhou?"

"Elena."

"Don't you remember" — she leaned forward with a devilish light in her eyes — "that couple in Sky Bar in Malaysia? *They* approached *us!*" She threw her head back with a laugh. "Humans can be so uninhibited sometimes. At least while on vacation, when there's plenty of alcohol."

She waved her hand out, indicating the humans currently doing things reserved for the privacy only a secret hotel room could provide.

"Elena," Victor said again, turning his face toward her. His glare was icy. Just below his anger, fear circled his abdomen. He really couldn't move. His urge to push her aside and flee was being held at bay, against his will.

He could be stuck again.

Elena's fingers raked through his hair. "You drank so much that night. Remember making love while they watched? Our bodies incredibly warm, covered in their warmth. We fit so nicely together.

"Don't you remember, Victor?"

Her voice snapped taut at the end like a rubber band. They sat there a moment, glowering at each other. Akeem peeked over often. He could probably tell something was wrong. Victor displayed the rigidity of a caged animal—like he wanted to be as far away as possible but couldn't move from his spot. Elena enjoyed his captivity, though she seemed angry as well. With his concern, Akeem wasn't paying attention to the lovely young lady currently nibbling his ear.

"I don't want this," Victor said. "Okay? The past is the past."

Her hand tightened in his hair. She pulled, jerking his head back against the seat.

"It doesn't have to be," she purred. Her lips were only a few inches from his.

Victor had winced when she gripped his hair. He took a deep breath to steel himself. "I will never be that way again. Nothing you do will make me and you know it. Or don't you remember *that?*"

Her eyes narrowed. "I could make you."

"And for how long will that be enough? I'd only be a puppet. It won't be real." He shook his head. "I don't want this." There was malice and resentment and dread in his voice.

Elena's nose trembled, like it used to do when she had the ability to cry. Suddenly, her mouth opened with an angry snarl, her fangs extending. In a flash, she bit down into his neck. Her hair fell into his mouth. Her nails dug into his scalp and side as she drank from him.

He reached out to knock her away, though he was certain he wouldn't be able to harm her. She released him before he could try.

With a low hiss and his blood on her lips, Elena jumped up from the sofa and stormed out of the VIP area. The beads clinked together, the sound heard over "Waking Up in Vegas" as she pushed them out of her way. She knocked the velvet rope right out of the wall, taking a chunk of concrete with it. Flip sidestepped her just in time to avoid being knocked over or hit by the swinging rope.

Victor took a breath, and then another. His blood ran down his neck, beneath his collar. Thanks to Celia, the wound closed almost immediately. His spine relaxed. The constraints holding him to this spot were now gone.

Leaning forward, he grabbed some napkins from the table. He left without speaking to Akeem, even when he shouted after him.

Nine

Celia's eyes opened. Her body seemed to float above the mattress. There was no pain, only the vaguely pleasant sensation of lightness.

Downstairs, she found the house silent. Hastings wasn't in the kitchen, and hadn't left a note.

Disappointment had just started to fill her when the front door opened. Hastings glimpsed her with the beginning of a smile, but it dropped away once he saw the radiance in her skin. She wore a camisole, which showed the bruise was gone from her bicep.

He slowly closed the door. "I suppose we have to perform the potion again."

She told him about last night. Hastings's face was a blank canvas.

"Say . . . something," Celia said, searching for some answer in his expression.

He took in a breath, let it out and said, "Werewolves. I didn't know any were here." He walked to the kitchen.

Celia followed. "They were trying to start a turf war."

"I'm sorry that happened."

"It was my fucking anniversary, Hastings."

"I know."

"I just wish . . ." She trailed off. Her fingers grazed the smooth, cool counter. "I wish I knew how to protect myself better. I didn't use to have these problems, you know. I just went to work, went on the occasional date, hung out with my friends. I didn't have to worry about vampires and werewolves. I certainly wasn't kidnapped and tortured. I just . . . I don't know what to do."

Hastings had been listening silently. His brown eyes considered her. There was warmth again, which helped to calm her. He turned for the fridge and began gathering the ingredients for the potion.

Later, Celia decided she had to go somewhere. She couldn't just sit in the house on her vacation. It was unconscionable. She chose the MGM.

Hastings dropped her off a bit reluctantly. At least he had that one thing in common with Victor: he'd prefer she stay within the confines of the house.

She stopped off at the restrooms first. As she was exiting, she spotted Leilani's long legs. The witch was a few feet in front of Celia, heading to the elevators.

Celia halted. She glanced back to the restroom, thinking she would pop back in until the coast was clear.

"Celia?"

Shit. She faced forward.

Leilani had turned back to the casino, as if she had forgotten something. She closed the distance and squeezed Celia's arm. Celia shied away from her touch.

Leilani frowned. "Are you okay?"

"No, I'm not."

Her hand dropped to her side in a deflated way. "But I thought . . . after last night . . . You were talking to me and . . ."

"I was drunk," Celia said drily. "I would've been cheerful with a fucking coatrack."

Leilani bristled. "I really am sorry. Please, I'm meeting the girls right now. Come with me? I want to show you that we're not terrible people."

Her eyes were wide. In them, sincerity shone brightly. The conversation with Hastings, the feelings of vulnerability, all of that circled Celia's mind. It was time she learned more about these supposed abilities she possessed. Might as well use the resources presented to her.

She fought her qualms as she followed Leilani into the house. Kiele, Makala, and Thomasina were all there. Leilani had called on the ride over, letting them know Celia was coming. Instead of sitting casually on the sofa, chatting about their day, they were all straight-backed and not meeting each other's gazes.

"We're here," Leilani announced, though the tension crackling even more was plenty announcement.

"Hi, Celia," Makala ventured.

"Hello," Celia replied tightly.

"Have a seat," Thomasina said. "Let's talk a little."

Celia sat between Makala and Kiele on the sofa. Leilani plopped down on the floor in front of the TV with her long legs stretched out in front of her.

Thomasina leaned forward. "I want to apologize on behalf of all of us," she began in her soothing voice.

"For fucking *drugging* me?" Celia snapped.

Thomasina's gaze alternated between the other witches'. "None of us knew just how . . . inexperienced you were with our ways of practicing."

"I've only been able to stop vampire magic and sometimes see into their heads. I told you all I had never practiced anything."

Celia paused. The witches stared at her in disbelief.

"You hang with vampires?" Kiele asked. Her mouth hung open and the whites of her eyes were visible.

Celia shrugged. She hadn't thought it was a big deal, since they used vamp blood in their rituals.

"How do you get blood?" she asked.

They looked at Leilani. "I'm the one who knows some," she replied. "They like how my blood tastes." She cleared her throat. "It tastes different to them."

"Oh," Celia said. "Right." She remembered the light that shone from Leilani's body as she made out with the vampire Mason.

Celia's eyes widened. "Mason!" she exclaimed, pointing at Leilani. "He's your friend? The one whose blood I had?"

Leilani shifted, tugging at her skirt. "No. Last night was the first time I'd seen Mason in a month."

Celia's face fell.

"You can see into vampires' heads?" Makala asked. "You can hear their thoughts?"

"Something like that," Celia grumbled. "I can see what they see. I usually experience it, as if I'm there. I don't know, it's weird."

"That's kind of cool," Makala said, with a huge smile.

"I guess. Except it only works if I've had the vampire's blood." They seemed puzzled. "I have a boyfriend," Celia said matter-of-factly.

"Vampires always want sex when they drink," Leilani informed them. Makala nodded as if enlightened. She'd been hanging on every word.

"It sounds like you possess the Inner Eye," Thomasina replied. "We can help you strengthen it—if you like," she added gently. "You're what we call Umami. They have connections with supernatural beings. That's why you can glimpse vampire minds. It was a very useful ability decades ago, when witches were battling vampires. It's kind of obsolete nowadays. I'm really surprised the ability is still around."

"What do you mean, still around?" Celia asked.

Thomasina shrugged. "You know, with evolution and such. You'd think all of the Umami died out."

Celia frowned. "What happened? Why were witches fighting vampires?"

"Back in the early eighteen hundreds, vampires were multiplying at a steady rate, especially in the States. I've heard stories of humans fighting them, but they didn't make a terrible dent in their population. Many witches took up the task once they realized they could."

"Humans knew about vampires?" Celia asked.

"Sure. It was still widely believed to be legend, but many people knew they were real. Vampires had worked their magic to stay in the shadows."

"Go back to the part about the witches," Makala said excitedly.

"The first Umami was discovered in eighteen-twelve, I believe." Thomasina slapped her own thigh lightly. "Oh, I wish I had my grimoire."

"What's that?" Celia asked. "It sounds familiar."

"A witch's spell book. It's been passed down in my family."

"We have them too," Makala said. Kiele and Leilani nodded in agreement.

"My mother has ours," Leilani replied, "or I'd show it to you."

"There were passages about Umami," Thomasina continued. "The first one led a crusade throughout Europe, fighting vampires. Until the vampires wised up and found out what she was. She was killed a year later."

"That's sad," Leilani said.

"It's easier to make vampires than witches. They were able to regroup, so to speak. The last Umami I knew about died in nineteen-twenty. There were two sisters with the ability. Collins was their name, Melissa and Doreen Collins. They lived in Massachusetts."

"That's where *I'm* from," Celia said. "Boston."

Thomasina nodded. "They lived toward the central part of the state. Melissa was twelve when she first had a vision. Her mother was a witch, and had told them since they were babies of the existence of vampires. They were bringing wood inside because of the impending rain when it first happened; Melissa knew a vampire was approaching.

"She grabbed her sister and got inside the house just in time. Their mother thought she was psychic, only her powers didn't work with other humans. It was only after that vampire returned to their town two months later did they figure it out.

"Melissa was able to prevent two deaths before that vampire killed her."

Kiele gasped. "What? How did he get her?"

Thomasina shook her head gravely. "He'd seen her on the scene each time."

"Damn," Kiele mumbled.

"He set up a scenario. He captured a young girl on her way home and did all kinds of terrible things to her, hoping Melissa would come to her aid. When Melissa received the vision, she tried to get help, but her mother wouldn't allow it. She didn't want her daughter harmed. Melissa snuck out."

The other witches sighed.

"Doreen's ability became evident two years later. Only, she didn't tell anyone. She joined her mother's coven, as was expected of her, when she turned sixteen. Once she started practicing regularly, however, she could no longer hide her ability. The coven leader, Edwin McAllister, saw an opportunity.

"See, he had lost a son to a vampire who'd taken him while he was swimming. He asked Doreen's mother to let Doreen live with him and his wife for a week to hone her craft. Doreen's mother was reluctant. Edwin had to resort to blackmail. Doreen's mother's, uh, promiscuity wasn't as secret as she had thought.

"Doreen stayed with the McAllisters for a full week. They made her practice and practice without much rest or nourishment. At the end of the week, when Doreen's mother came knocking, he refused to give her back."

"Bastards," Makala whispered.

"There was a fight and Doreen's mother was badly injured. Doreen had to stay with the McAllisters, or else Edwin would kill her mother. He used

Doreen to locate vampires in the area. She was miserable. She was a prisoner. Edwin, afraid she would run away, didn't even allow her to leave the house. A costly mistake."

Thomasina paused to take a sip of her water. The others were on the edge of their seats.

"One night in August of nineteen-twenty, a vampire came to town. He was fierce and quick when he dispensed death. An Irishman, who'd gone mad, was the story from the few survivors he left behind. They say Doreen knew the moment when he arrived; she knew his path would meet the McAllister house.

"The coven had been performing a ritual when the vampire attacked. He killed them all before they could protect themselves. Except two," Thomasina said, raising two fingers. "Doreen warned a young witch named Claudia not to come to the circle that night. She wasn't a member of the coven, so her absence wasn't unusual. The other's name was Marguerite. She had been sick in bed with pneumonia. The Healer wasn't expected for another day to help her.

"Everyone else, including Doreen, died that night."

The room was completely silent when Thomasina finished speaking. The other witches stared at each other in amazement. Celia was astonished.

A sudden thought had her narrowing her eyes. "I hope you all don't have any plans like that."

The witches laughed in unison.

"Of course not!" Thomasina cried. "You're welcome to leave whenever you want."

"And we don't have a vampire problem here," Leilani added. "I mean, there're plenty around, but they just mingle. Back in Hawaii is a different story. That's why we came here."

Well, as long as that was settled. "So, Umamis are rare?" Celia asked.

"The plural is 'Umami,'" Thomasina corrected gently. "And yes. Although one wouldn't know unless they are around vampires. The ability seems to be coupled with them specifically."

"So it wouldn't work on other people? Like shifters?"

"I believe it will."

Celia scrunched up her nose. "Would I need their blood too?" Why drinking other blood was more disgusting than vamp blood was anyone's guess.

"That's the thing, dear," Thomasina said. "You shouldn't need to ingest blood for your Inner Eye to work."

"I guess that was just your trigger," Kiele offered.

"As far as I know," Thomasina said, "neither Melissa nor Doreen Collins ingested blood to track vampires. Witches and vampires tend not to mix. Their blood has magic in it that must've affected your ability."

"And the Collins sisters had visions from the vampires?"

"Melissa spoke of images and dreams that couldn't possibly be her own," Thomasina replied. "She could smell things and hear things not in the room. She could *feel* that she was someone else. And then she knew in her heart where that person was."

"That sounds like how vampires can feel their humans," Leilani offered. "They always know where they are once they've drunk from them a few times."

That was familiar to Celia. She was quiet for a moment, taking it all in. She thought of Milo and Clarice, who were surely still causing problems. And what about those mysterious couples' murders plaguing the news?

Plus, she needed to learn how to protect herself.

"What do I have to do?" she finally asked.

The witches exchanged glances again.

"There are a few rituals we could try," Thomasina said.

Oh, great, Celia thought. *More fucking experiments.* The last experiment to test her ability had left her overwhelmed by the three vamps. Not to mention, she was none too thrilled at the prospect of graphic dreams about the witches.

Thomasina was watching her. The AC kicked on, the vent located above her head. Her gray hair blew softly around her head for a moment.

"And you're not using vampire blood?"

"No," Thomasina answered.

"And my Inner Eye, or whatever it is, will only work on supernatural things?"

"The Inner Eye can work on anyone, as long as the witch has perfected her ability. But whatever it is that makes an Umami an Umami only works with supernatural beings, yes."

"Why are Umami different?" Makala asked.

"The Inner Eye is used for premonitions and divination. Not all witches have that ability, although nearly all have some form of clairvoyance, since we tend to read each other's energies.

"Umami can go a step farther, since they embody the entire vision—sight, sound, smell, touch. From the accounts I've read, it appears they can reach out to others without the need of a personal object. You see," she said to Celia in particular, "when calling on premonitions, like with almost every kind of spell, the witch needs a piece of the person. Some object that is significant to the person or a part of them, like hair or even nail clippings.

Umami just need to call on the person's energy.

"There are a few theories about why that is. The one most people go with is that a witch with a powerful Inner Eye had an affair with a vampire. This was in the late seventeen hundreds. Her husband was a witch too. When he found out about the affair, he told the coven. They punished her by hanging her above the grave the vampire slept in during the day. They'd put a spell on her to contain her powers. She'd been able to fight the spell, but by the time the vampire woke, she'd stopped struggling against the noose. He cut her down and gave his blood. And then he fled with her.

"No one knew exactly what happened to her. There was a lot of speculation, starting with the boy who allegedly witnessed the vampire rising. He said she was conscious enough to take his blood.

"And then rumors started that a doctor two towns away—about three nights travel by horse—had taken in a comatose woman. Her case was tricky because, you see, she was pregnant.

"The doctor called in a local witch—Lydia was her name, Lydia Porter. He called her for help with the unusual case. She couldn't make heads or tails of the woman's condition. She still had vital signs, even though she wasn't breathing. And her stomach grew with the baby, though the doctor said it wasn't getting enough nourishment. Lydia Porter performed a few Protection Spells; it was all she could do."

"What happened?" Kiele asked.

"Her water broke six months later. The doctor had to open her up to get the baby, who he feared was dead. Only she wasn't. She screamed her little head off. She had the most radiant brown skin, and her hair was already thick and full of curls."

Celia's hand absentmindedly went to her own hair.

"Lydia reported that a vampire would visit often. He named the baby Jane," Thomasina continued. "The next day, since the mother still had no vitals, they buried her. The doctor and Lydia cared for the child. Two days after they buried Jane's mother, it was reported that the grave had been disturbed. Her body was gone."

"She became a vampire then," Kiele said. "Right? That's why she wasn't breathing?"

"How could that happen?" Makala asked, her lips twisted to the side. "I mean, isn't it that once you're bitten you become a vampire, like, right away? How could she have stayed alive for six months without food and water?"

Thomasina nodded wisely. "It is bizarre. To answer your first question, there's more to becoming a vampire than a bite. The vampire has to give the human blood, and the human's body goes through a three-day change.

"For your second question, perhaps there was some residual magic. Maybe Lydia Porter did a ritual. Maybe a combination of that and the vampire's blood. I don't know. There are no concrete documents that I could ever find, only hearsay and brief mentions in grimoires."

"So, she just disappeared?" Makala asked.

"No one ever saw her or her vampire lover again. Although, some say you could see strange shadows outside the doctor's house, even when Jane came of age."

"What happened to Jane?" Celia asked.

"She learned magic under Lydia's tutelage. Lydia was pretty tight-lipped about Jane's birth. The one time she decided to confide in someone, however, they told the entire village. What did that person know? She just thought it was a fantastical story. But word got back to Jane's mother's village. The coven came after her. Lydia and Jane were forced to go into hiding."

Thomasina sighed, and took another gulp of water.

"There were stories that popped up of a witch who talked with animals that I believe was Jane or her offspring, but there's no way of knowing for sure. It was such a long time ago, and Lydia and Jane were good at staying hidden."

"Wow," Kiele said, shaking her head. She looked at Celia. "You're probably one of Jane's descendants."

Celia didn't say anything. She had that dazed feeling you experienced when you stepped out of a movie theater and it was still sunny out.

Thomasina reached over and rubbed her knee. Celia looked up at her. "Shall we go outside?"

They all headed to the backyard. The tiki torches were still set up in the grass. Makala went around lighting them while everyone else sat in a circle. Leilani came out with an arm full of items. Thankfully, she was still clothed.

In the center of the circle, Leilani lit three sticks of incense and stuck them in the ground. She then opened a vial and poured the liquid in a circle around the incense.

"What is that?" Celia asked.

"Frankincense, and the oil is acacia," Leilani answered. She closed the vial. "Acacia helps strengthen psychic abilities. Frankincense just helps to get into a meditative state so you can concentrate better."

"What are we doing?"

"It's another form of cleansing," Thomasina said. "Have you ever meditated before?"

Celia shook her head.

"Just relax. Close your eyes." Celia did as she was told. "Breathe in and breathe out."

Thomasina began to chant. Her words were too soft for Celia to understand. After a few moments, she stopped trying to hear them and focused instead on her breathing. The scent from the sticks of incense filled her nose, her lungs. Her muscles relaxed.

"That's it." Thomasina's voice floated somewhere to her right. "Now, open your eyes, but try to maintain this peaceful state."

Celia opened her eyes slowly. The others were doing the same. The trees surrounding the property swayed together, though there was no breeze. When she looked at the others, she noticed the bluish light radiating from them. It wasn't as pronounced as Leilani's glow had appeared to her last night, but she could see it. Their energy.

When she looked down at her lap, the same light emanated from her arms. It swayed like smoke. The places where the sun touched shimmered like diamonds.

Celia smiled. She was reminded of the calm she felt under Michael's spell. Only, his was more palpable and intoxicating, where she could hardly breathe. At the moment, she wasn't aware she was breathing.

"Now," Thomasina said, her voice soft, dreamy, "we just want you to learn how to be at ease in your own head. That way you can draw forth your magic easily when you need it."

Thomasina and the others each dug into their pockets and produced knives. Celia's calm lapsed at the sight.

"It's okay," Thomasina said quickly, as if she could sense Celia's uneasiness.

It's okay, Celia.

Stunned, Celia looked to Leilani beside her. Leilani's smile was warm, her dark hair waving around her shoulders. She handed Celia another knife. *You're in good hands.*

"But how . . . ?"

"We're sharing each other's energy," Thomasina answered. Celia finally saw how the wisps of their energies were mingling, creating a willowy dome around their circle.

I don't understand.

You will, Thomasina responded without moving her lips. She flipped open her knife. Celia's discomfort rose even more. *We have to give of the earth in order to use her elements.*

And now Celia could hear Makala and Kiele in her mind. They chanted like Thomasina had.

Thomasina made a small cut across the pad of her index finger. She leaned forward and allowed two drops of blood to hit the ground where Leilani had poured the acacia oil. Sparks sputtered from the sticks of incense where before there had only been a bright orange. Celia didn't think that was her imagination.

Thomasina nodded once and gestured to Makala beside her. She did the same, then Kiele, with the same result. Leilani was next. Then they all looked to Celia.

Celia looked down at her knife. The pretty handle was made of ivory. The knife wasn't long but the blade looked sharp.

This didn't seem right. She wished she could call her aunt. Meg would probably think she had gone batshit crazy. Mostly, she would listen and try to advise her as best she could.

"It's okay," Makala coaxed. "It doesn't really hurt."

That nagging feeling persisted. It wasn't the pain of the cut that bothered her. She didn't like the idea of using her blood in this manner. Sharing blood had always been associated with binding. What would she allow to bind with her if she went through with this?

When her hesitation stretched on for a full minute, Leilani nudged Celia with her elbow. "What's wrong?" She looked to Thomasina for guidance.

"Celia?" Thomasina asked.

"I . . . I'm sorry. I'm scared."

"We all were," Makala said. "But once you understand, once you feel your power . . ." She smiled at the group. "It's amazing!"

"Look!" Kiele said.

A few rocks had risen in the air. They twirled in place at eye level. Celia watched, captivated. At first, she knew the others had performed this. But soon she could feel it from herself; wanting to try it out, her mind had reached for the rocks. They spun faster at her command.

Makala and Kiele giggled, but their voices faded. The wind whipped around the rocks as they whirled in the air.

"Um, guys," Kiele said. "Something's . . . different."

A few branches lay on the ground. In her mind, Celia wished for them to rise. They answered her command and joined the rocks.

"I can't feel the circle." Makala's voice sounded far off.

A large, white butterfly fluttered above their heads. Its wings flapped the air to its own internal beat. Celia wondered if it would come to her. The rocks had done what she wanted, would the butterfly too?

It flew away from the yard. She focused on the butterfly, willing it back. Suddenly, it stopped moving. Its wings still flapped but it couldn't fly higher.

That's right. The voice, strong and clear, sounded like hers. Her pulse pounded in her ears, drowning out the other sounds.

The butterfly came toward her now.

"Celia," Leilani cried breathlessly. "You have to stop!"

Celia raised her hand to offer the butterfly a perch. The butterfly, only a few inches from her palm, spun in erratic circles as it struggled against its invisible constraint.

Strong hands grabbed hold of Celia's shoulders and shook her hard. Celia's breath hitched. The rhythmic thrumming in her ears ceased, and the sounds of the yard returned. She blinked at Thomasina. The older witch was in front of her on her knees.

The butterfly paused. Its wings flapped harder than ever as it took off away from them as fast as it could go.

Celia frowned at Thomasina. The witch's energy—the silvery wisps—waved only about two inches from her skin now, when before it had nearly clouded the yard. The same was true of Leilani when Celia looked around at the others. Kiele and Makala had none. The two looked around, down at their laps and palms. All of the witches' faces had paled in horror.

Celia looked down at her own hands. Her energy had grown exponentially. It was no longer silver, but a darker steel gray, radiating from her like shadowy sunbeams.

The *power* cursing through her was like nothing she had ever felt in her life: a pleasurable tingling starting from her belly. The rocks and butterfly were just the beginning. She could have anything. She could *do* anything. She was certain of it.

When she stood, the others shrank away. Celia took in a deep breath, the air filling her down to her toes. Without a backward glance, she walked away from the broken circle.

Celia strode out of Leilani's house and continued down the street. Somehow she knew she was headed in the right direction.

She came across a small dog in one of the front yards. It had found a shaded space at the front of the house, where it sniffed at a gnawed rawhide bone. Its head popped up when Celia stopped at the fence enclosing the house.

She smiled. "Hey there, cutie."

She stooped down in front of the fence. Poking her fingers through the diamond shapes of the chain links, she called it over. The dog stared at her without blinking.

"Come on, it's okay."

The dog stayed put.

"Hey, it's okay." Her frustration rose. Why wasn't it coming closer?

Come here.

The tingling in her gut intensified. Her energy trembled in response. The dog whimpered as it got to its feet. It moved closer to the fence.

The dog tried to plant its feet in the dirt. Dust and pebbles jumped up around its paws. It was being dragged forward by an invisible leash.

Seeing it struggle, Celia straightened. The dog stopped moving. It hesitated, as if trying to be sure it was free, before rushing off around the house.

Celia frowned as she contemplated the dog's fear. She turned away from the yard.

A man exited the house across the street. His steps slowed when he caught sight of Celia. She smiled. He smiled back.

"Would you mind terribly giving me a ride?"

He doesn't mind one bit.

The man drove her to the Strip while they blasted dancehall music from his stereo. When he leaned toward her, his lips pursed for a kiss, Celia laughed, and got out of the car.

She sat in the casino, playing cards.

She had gotten the chips to join in on the game by persuading a man to hand them over. Like with the man who'd given her a ride, it was like she possessed vampire-type compulsion. She had walked up to him and asked nicely for a few chips. He'd handed over five fifty-dollar chips without a single question.

Celia was winning at this table. Not because she was exceptionally good at the game, but because she had the confidence she would win. It emanated from within her. Or, hell, it could've very well been her newfound power. She seemed able to see everything clearly. And the voice whispering to her, the one that sounded like her own, urged her on.

Her phone rang.

"Hey," Victor said when she answered. His concern was evident in just the one word. "Where are you?"

"Out."

"Well, I see that." He forced a laugh. "Our flight is in two hours and you still have to pack. What's going on?"

She sighed. "I'm trying to have a little fun during the vacation I'm on with my boyfriend who I can only spend half of that time with. That's what's going on."

Where had *that* come from? She hadn't thought it; the words came out as if from someone else entirely.

He deserves it.

"What's wrong?" Victor asked immediately.

"Nothing."

"Ma'am, please, no phones at the tables." The dealer nodded toward her phone. He had paused in handing a card to the man on Celia's left, who glowered at her for violating game etiquette.

"Gotta go," she said and hung up.

"Thank you, ma'am," the dealer said curtly.

Ma'am? "Do I look like a 'ma'am'?" she asked, her words icy.

One of the other men chuckled. The dealer's brows rose.

Celia held his gaze as the power tingled in her stomach. He coughed, his cheeks puffing out and his lips shuddering as he tried to hold it back. He raised a fist to his mouth as another cough fought its way up his throat. A third and a fourth came. His eyes had started to water and his cheeks burned bright red.

Everyone stared in astonishment as he doubled over. People gasped, jumping to their feet. The woman at the far end went around the table. Someone else signaled for one of the security guards. Two of them hurried to the table. The dealer's coughs had transformed into a gasping fit. He clutched at his throat as if fighting to breathe.

The guards were maneuvering him away from the table when the dealer's eyes met Celia's again. He'd been looking around without really seeing. But when his eyes connected with Celia's, dawn erupted across his face. She'd never seen such terror. It hit her like a ton of bricks, knocking her free of her trance.

The man's gasping turned into deep breaths as his body accepted the air in grateful gulps. He stumbled between the two guards as they led him away. A female dealer had been waiting fretfully. She watched them go then stepped up to the table.

Celia had been the only one still in her seat. She slowly got to her feet.

"Ma'am!" the dealer called after her. "Your chips!"

Celia didn't stop until she was outside. The arid air couldn't shake away her confusion.

Why had she done that? And why wasn't she as upset about it as she should be?

Because he deserved it.

But he hadn't meant anything; he was only being formal. It was his job.

He deserved *it*.

"Hey, sweet thang."

The raspy voice had come from behind her, interrupting the persistent voice in her head that sounded too much like her own. She ignored the man and began to walk away.

"Let me talk to you a second."

A large hand seized her elbow.

Instead of fear, anger rippled through her. Whipping around pulled her arm free of the man's grasp. He was an inch or two taller than her, an Angels' baseball cap on his head. The bill was bent down on the sides, shielding his face. He wore a dingy tank and black shorts. His smarmy grin revealed a missing tooth right in front.

He reached out toward Celia's face. She slapped his hand away before he could touch her. That angry tingling started up again in her gut.

Who does he think he is?

She could see the man crumpled in a ball on the ground, writhing in agony. The vision was as clear as day.

The man's grin fell away. He looked like he had just eaten something that wasn't agreeing with him. He grasped his stomach as his face fell in on itself. He stared at her with the same terror she'd seen in the dealer. The look had the same effect, releasing her from her anger.

The man's mouth flapped open and closed a few times before he stumbled away. Confusion clouded his wide eyes, because he knew she had caused this inexplicable pain, but how could she have?

A group of gabbing women exiting Dylan's Candy Shop interrupted his retreat. Someone cried out in pain when he treaded on her foot. He pushed his way through and broke out into a run.

The magic inside of Celia made her float down the street. When her phone rang again, she knew it was Victor. Could he feel her, for lack of a better word, tantrums?

She stepped into Fat Tuesday and ordered a margarita. Waiting to the side, she gazed down at her hands. Her energy floated up from her palms.

"Cute shoes."

The young woman standing next to Celia sipped from a straw stuck in a long blue flute. She pointed at the black crochet flats Celia had paired with pink shorts and a short-sleeved pink plaid shirt.

"Thanks."

"I want some now."

The woman introduced herself as Phoebe. They were talking shoes when her friends joined them.

"You like music?" one of the guys asked Celia, draping his arm over Phoebe's shoulders. His lids had that droopy indication that these were not their first drinks of the night.

"Sure," Celia answered.

"You should come with us!" Phoebe said. "Our friend's playing in this battle of the bands tournament. Have you ever been to one?"

Celia shook her head.

"They're so much fun!"

"So you coming?" the boyfriend asked.

Celia had told Victor that she wouldn't go off with strangers. That was before this power. If someone tried to hurt her again, it was their funeral.

So she partied with this bunch of five friends. Their friend's band was eliminated from the tournament just before 10:00, in the second round, but that was no reason to leave.

They danced and drank and laughed in the sweltering club, until Celia looked down at her watch and saw it was nearly 4:00 in the morning.

"Whoa!" Phoebe cried close to her ear. "Where did the time go?"

They laughed, with sweat glistening on their foreheads and collarbones. Phoebe's hair was pasted to her back. She stumbled into Celia a few times, who almost fell over when she found her shoes stuck to the floor where too many drinks had been spilled.

Blair, Phoebe's boyfriend, appeared with another round of shots—Washington Apples this time. They downed the drinks and Phoebe shrieked happily. Blair lifted her in the air and swung her around. She kissed him, wrapping her arms and legs around his body. Celia and their friends cheered.

They tripped out of the bar in one sweaty, exhausted clump at 4:30

when the tournament ended.

"Oh my God, Celia, you rock!"

That was one of Phoebe's friends, but Celia couldn't recall her name. Her head swam pleasantly. They all hugged her before skipping off down the street.

Celia's phone rang. She ignored it but decided it was time to head back to the house.

Victor swung the front door open before the cab had pulled to the curb. The light from the porch spilled across the hollows of his black eyes. His lips were a tight line, and it was probably a trick of the light but worry lines branched out across his forehead. He looked drained.

"What the hell, Celia?" he demanded when she stepped up to him. "We were supposed to have left at nine-thirty. I've been out of my mind."

"I was just out, Victor." She slid by him into the house. The door slammed.

"You didn't call and I couldn't find you again. It's almost dawn. And what was that comment earlier?"

She put her purse on the table then turned to him with a sigh. He was surveying her, his brows pulled together.

"There's something different."

"Yeah, you're right about that. Look," she went on before he could question, "I'm tired and more than a little drunk, so I better get to bed before I say or do something I shouldn't."

"What does that mean?"

Celia headed for the stairs. Victor flashed in front of her, blocking her path. She wanted to keep it to herself. But the alcohol and power pulsing through her veins fueled her words.

"I was trying to enjoy my vacation, okay? I don't get what the big deal is. I had to spend most of this time by myself anyway, so what difference does it make if that's during the day or night?"

Victor recoiled as if struck. "So this isn't about those wolves? You're angry with me."

She could only hold his gaze. He seemed perfectly able to read her resentment. After a moment, he worked it out for himself.

"Because I can't be with you during the day." His voice was as flat as a board.

Celia threw up her hands. Then it poured out of her from somewhere hidden inside. Somewhere not so far from the surface.

"This sucks, Victor, okay? How have we been doing this for a year? Why did I think this would work?"

He shifted his weight uncomfortably. "Going on vacation, just the two of us," he said carefully, "wasn't going to be easy. That's partly why I had suggested Seattle."

"You can't come out during the day!" she protested.

"I would've found a way. But there's no way around the sun."

She considered that as the angry knot in her stomach stirred. "So our options are to go somewhere dreary and/or rainy, or somewhere where I'd be alone for most of the trip?" She shook her head. "Can't you see how fucked that is?"

"What was I *supposed* to do?" He'd finally lost his cool, his voice a tight rope. It took a second for him to rein it in. His eyes dropped for a few seconds, then returned to hers. "I figured you'd enjoy the nightlife with me."

His voice trailed off at the end. His pain tugged at her.

"I know, I know. It's no one's fault. It just *sucks*."

Half-life.

The word popped in her head unbidden. She could still see Naomi's face, stubborn and unwavering, her wrists shiny with her crimson blood. Naomi had endured her tortured, unbalanced relationship for three years.

"What are you saying, Celia?"

She had to step away from him. His scent, his eyes . . . he was reaching out for her, desperately.

"I'm just seeing things clearly now. I've been in such . . . denial. Without distractions like work and my family, I see that *this*" — she indicated the space between them — "is what we have. Me, here, in the sun. You, there, in darkness. We've been trying damn hard, but it's all an act. It's a stage production, hiding the reality of this dysfunctional relationship."

"Dysfunctional?"

"Yes. Because how long can this work? I don't want to be a vampire." She raised her hands again. With the stirring inside of her the gray wisps surrounded her body like a cloud. "Not when I have this."

"This what?"

He looked at her hands. She let them drop to her sides.

Victor moved closer. "Celia." His hand extended toward her.

"Don't touch me," she said.

At the same time, she threw her arm out to ward him off. An invisible cord yanked backward, and Victor was knocked off his feet. He went crashing through a door to her right, landing on the concrete floor of the garage. When he looked up, and his eyes met hers, he was just as shocked as she.

Tears burned her eyes. She was hurting people.

He deserved it.

No, she shouted back, only the word wouldn't leave her mouth. She ran up the stairs, to the room, and slammed the door shut.

* * *

Victor sat there on his ass for a full minute. He'd received confirmation of what he'd suspected for the past month: Celia was a witch. He finally realized what was different about her. It wasn't just her words—which cut like a silver knife—but her presence. Her brown eyes had been lit with something more vehement than her anger. And her scent was more profound, but not vanilla-sweet. No, it had been similar to the pungent warding smell that rolled off Hastings.

He finally, slowly, got to his feet. Celia's footsteps paced the carpeted floor above him. Crossing to the kitchen, Victor retrieved his cellphone.

Hastings answered after the third ring. "Yes, Master Smith?" His voice was thick with sleep.

"I need your help."

* * *

Celia had settled into rocking back and forth inside the walk-in closet. Her back was against the wall, her gaze directed to a tiny rip in the carpet. She had wrapped her arms around her bent knees. The gown Serena bought her brushed against her arm, tickling her skin.

Why had she said those things?

Because they were true.

She didn't want to hurt Victor.

He deserved it.

"Shut up," she muttered to that voice. Squeezing her eyes shut couldn't push away the anger or the magic consuming her. They were hot like fire now, singeing her insides with their potency. The more she tried to ignore the combination of overpowering anger and magic, the more it demanded to be heard, to be felt.

Tears escaped her closed eyes. When she opened them, her energy swarmed the inside of the closet like a cloud of smoke.

From the main room, there was a knock at the door. Celia continued to sway. The lock clicked.

"Seal?" Victor called.

"Stay back!" she cried. "I don't want to hurt you."

Victor's head peeked around the corner of the closet. After assessing her for a moment, he stepped into the doorway. Hastings appeared next to him, dressed in his usual garb: linen pants, loose shirt. A murky green liquid swished around inside a mason jar he held clutched in his right hand.

"Miss Wilcox," Hastings said, "what happened today?"

He looked around the closet. From the way his eyes swept the enclosed space, it appeared he could see the gray energy rising off her like an abstruse haze. He kept his distance.

"I went with those witches, the ones from the spa. They tried to do a spell with me but then something went wrong." She swiped at her wet cheeks. "The girls . . . they lost their power."

"How?"

"I don't know. I was able to make these rocks float, and then I saw a butterfly and was distracted. Then Thomasina was shaking me, and when I looked around I saw they had lost their energies."

Hastings was quiet as he contemplated.

"Did I steal their magic?"

"Yes," he said.

Celia's shock that it was that simple just added fear along with her anger. "But how?"

"There could be a number of reasons. What kind of spell were they performing?"

"She said a cleansing ritual. They were trying to test out my Inner Eye, or something. They said that I needed it since I'm an Umami."

The hangers on the rails above her began to tremble. Her shoes, which were in a line next to the doorway, started moving on their own. They tapped the floor and knocked into one another.

Frightened, since she hadn't told them to do that, Celia scooted closer to the corner at the back of the closet.

Hastings glanced in their direction, but his demeanor remained calm. "What did they do?"

She described the chanting, the circle, and the blood donation.

"They bound the circle," Hastings said.

"But I didn't give blood."

"They gave you access. That's how you were able to take their magic."

"I didn't mean to!"

One pair of flip-flops did a somersault.

"Not consciously."

"But how could I have done it subconsciously?" Celia stared at the flip-flops, as if they were a spring-loaded trap awaiting her slightest movement.

"I'm not completely certain of that." Hastings took a step into the closet. She tore her eyes from the shoes when he knelt beside her. Her gray energy swarmed him but didn't touch him. The stillness in his eyes let her know to relax, that he wasn't blaming her.

He had taken the cap off the jar and held it out to her. "Drink this."

"What is it?" she asked warily. She'd done more magic in the past week than she'd done in her lifetime.

"It's a Binding Potion. You've consumed more magic than you know how to handle. It'll start to manifest itself in ways you might not be able to control."

She glanced away from his eyes, which was plenty proof that that had already happened. Plus, the shoes kicked into high gear.

Her gaze went to the tattoo on his forearm, the one of the two circles. The circles had melded together, forming one large black dot. The ink moved slowly, flowing like a continuous waterfall across his brown skin.

"There's really no other immediate way," Hastings said. "If I could show you how to control it, I would. But that would take time. And judging by your energy" — he broke off as he looked around the room — "we don't have it."

The floor trembled, as if the earth was shifting beneath the house. Celia reached for the jar.

The potion smelled like rubber glue. After taking a deep breath, she drank all of it. The thick liquid, which tasted like tar, went down her throat like sludge. She choked when the revolting potion blocked her esophagus, and nearly spit it out. Hastings put a steadying hand on her shoulder, and she managed to get down the rest.

"Very good," Hastings replied. He took the jar back and replaced the cap.

The effect was immediate. The grip of magic petered out. The dark gray smoke retreated to her body. The shoes and hangers fell silent. The house stopped moving.

She took another breath. She felt like herself again, if not a little lightheaded from all the alcohol she drank tonight.

"Is it still inside of me? The magic?"

Hastings nodded. He helped her up. When she stood on wobbly legs, the room spun. Her stomach clenched in turn.

Pushing past Hastings and Victor, Celia rushed to the toilet. She was able to shut the door behind her just in time to spare them at least the sight.

Her vomit was mostly liquid, as she hadn't eaten since earlier in the day. Surprisingly, the potion didn't come up. She stayed there for a few minutes, hunched over the toilet bowl, until the earth stopped swaying.

Victor had been sitting on the bed, presumably listening to make sure she hadn't fallen in. He stood when she stumbled out of the bathroom. Hastings was gone.

Victor helped her to the bed. She groaned when she lay down. He removed her shoes and then covered her with the blanket.

She tried to reach out for him; however, the last of her energy had left her. Her arm wouldn't lift any higher than a few inches from the mattress. And then the world went black.

Ten

Celia's stomach flipped—a lovely wakeup call if there ever was one. She waited to see if she would vomit. When nothing happened, she sat up in bed. Her pulse pounded in her temples. Her mouth was dry. Other than that, she was okay. The knot of magic no longer claimed her belly. She no longer felt all-powerful.

She felt hung-over.

Last night's events didn't help matters. When she thought of the power that had all but devoured her, her nausea returned. That magic had been fueled by her anger. Anger she'd been harboring obliviously.

A paper was on the nightstand, a note scrawled in Victor's handwriting. He'd been able to change their flight to early morning.

Sliding her feet into the nearest pair of flip-flops, Celia left the room.

She stood in the living room for a moment. The AC churned softly. Otherwise, the house was silent. When she peeked outside, the street was still. A thick quilt of gray clouds covered the sky. The witch working with

Victor had made the sky overcast to shield him from the sun.

The shrouded sky was incredibly depressing. The tourists would lose a day of sun because of them. She turned away from the window.

The massive amount of food in the refrigerator astounded her. Fresh produce, chicken wings marinating in a bowl, milk and juices, different kinds of cheese, wine bottles, sodas, lunch meat. She didn't dare check out the freezer.

She didn't know if she'd be able to get anything down. She made a piece of toast, bacon, and fried eggs anyway and forced herself to eat it all.

She poured a tall glass of water and sank down into the sofa with her cellphone. She tried Trixie. The call went to voicemail. It was 12:30 in Vegas, so 3:30 in Boston. Trixie was probably at work.

Celia groaned in disappointment. She considered her aunt. For some reason she couldn't make herself call. Once she started, she would have to tell her aunt everything that had happened. Everything she had done. She scrolled through her address book and dialed another number.

"It's never a good sign if you're using your phone during a vacation."

The house had been so silent. She knew Victor was in his room, but she was still alone.

The sound of Jay's southern twang brought tears to her eyes. She lifted her face toward the fan to keep them at bay.

"Nah, I just have a little downtime. What's going on?" She was proud her voice sounded normal.

"Ah, the usual. Slaying and laying."

Celia stared at her phone in disbelief. His words were so ridiculous, so immature, that she burst into laughter.

"Why are you so stupid?" she managed to say.

"You obviously haven't been on the receiving end of this charm," Jay said. There was a smile and a challenge in his voice.

She snorted. "I remember. It wasn't that impressive."

"I've been holding back, ma'am," he drawled. "For your panties' sake."

She rolled her eyes. "Your head's always in the gutter, isn't it?"

"Seriously," he said, after another chuckle. "What's up?"

"Nothing. I just wanted to talk to someone."

There was a pause. "Right." With just that one word, he seemed to understand everything. "I went to a movie yesterday, you believe that?"

She smiled as the tears threatened to blind her. "Actually, no. What'd you see?"

"A zombie movie. It was funny. A little inaccurate."

"Do *not* tell me you've come across fucking *zombies* before."

"Nah, I'm just fuckin' with you."

Celia rolled her eyes as she relaxed. "Who'd you go with?"

"This waitress I met last week."

She could only imagine: They'd probably gone back to her place after the movie, seeing as how Jay had taken up residence in some guy's basement the last time he was in town. Either that or he still squatted in his parents' house in Texas, the one with the missing wall. Neither spot was a very conducive place for getting in the mood.

As if the woman would focus on that if she was in Jay's presence . . .

"You like the service industry, huh?" Celia joked, to cover the sting of envy.

"They're just so easy."

"Hey, fuck you!" she cried, laughing.

"Sorry, but it's true. I should know."

"You need to stop talking. You're already in for one slap, don't add on anymore."

"I'm not scared of you."

"You should be. I may be little, but I'll scratch your eyes out."

"You're not so little." His voice was husky all of a sudden. Celia chewed her bottom lip. Where was this conversation going?

"When you coming back?" he asked.

"Are you in Boston?"

"Yes, ma'am."

"I'll be back tomorrow."

"Then I'll see you tomorrow."

She turned on the television, but grew restless at 3:00. Her mind was elsewhere. When she pulled herself up to shower and dress, she noticed her energy was no longer visible, not that she'd been able to see it before the witches' circle anyway.

Hastings hadn't arrived. She leaned against the counter separating the kitchen from the living room. Her eyes glanced to the cordless phone. A blue and purple decorative bowl next to it held a single key, attached to a black key fob with a Jaguar symbol carved into it.

The Jaguar was parked in the garage. The light from the bulb glinted off the hood. Celia slid inside and took a moment to bask in the beauty of the interior. She wasn't used to this kind of luxury. Victor had driven a Maxima when they'd first started dating, which was nice, definitely more state-of-the-art than her Honda since it had power seats. But this was different. The smooth console, the shiny knobs, the wood-paneled steering wheel. The way the seat seemed to hug her hips.

She carefully pulled the car out of the garage. She missed driving, not that she would complain about being chauffeured. She easily recalled the way back to the highway.

Leilani stood behind the reception desk at the spa, another woman beside her. Celia regretted going there the second she saw her. The witch's shoulders slumped forward, giving her back an unappealing curve. Her long hair was in a disheveled, limp ponytail at the base of her neck, and her uniform didn't seem as crisp as usual.

Both women glanced up when Celia pushed the door open. Leilani stared at Celia as the last of the color in her face drained away. Celia tried to hide her uneasiness and guilt, but failed fantastically.

"Hi, Celia," Leilani said, once she was closer to the podium.

"Can we talk?"

Leilani looked to the woman beside her, who nodded that it was okay. She watched them go with an expression of deep concern. It was understandable; Leilani looked to be at death's door.

Celia followed Leilani down the hall to an empty room. Leilani closed the door behind them and Celia faced her. In the dim room, Leilani's skin seemed gray and flat.

"I don't even know where to begin," Celia said. "I guess with I'm sorry. I don't know what happened. But I want to give it back." She held her hands out as an offering. "Do we have to do another ritual?"

Leilani's gaze fell to Celia's open palms. "It's not that simple."

"Is there more than one ritual?"

"There is no ritual that any of us could perform." Celia's heart dropped. "We'd need a powerful witch to lead it and a bigger coven for the kind of energy we'd have to use."

Celia's eyes prickled again. "I'm so sorry."

Leilani's smile was forlorn. "I can still do some things. It's not terrible." She clasped her left elbow with her right hand, which only served to make her more hunched. A tear streaked down her cheek and dripped off her jaw. She turned her head to conceal it.

"No one could've seen this coming," Leilani continued. "Thomasina wonders if maybe you have Delmi in your lineage. That would explain why it happened so easily."

Celia's eyes widened. "Delmi? Isn't that a bad witch?"

"Well, with them, the power consumes them and turns dark." Leilani scanned her. "You seem okay today. Yesterday, you were practically glowing. I could feel your power. I'd be surprised if regular people didn't notice."

"I took a Binding Potion."

"Wow." She shook her head with sadness and awe. "We *really* wouldn't be able to get our powers back then. Not without a powerful witch."

"I'll get Hastings then!" Celia cried. She had stepped forward but hesitated with touching her. "He gave me the potion; he could undo it, maybe."

Leilani considered it. "Does he know other witches?"

Celia wavered. "I . . . don't know."

"I've never heard of a Hastings. And we're the only coven in the area." Her voice, which had started an upswing of hope, was deflated again. "Besides, unbinding your magic might make things worse."

"How can it be any worse than this?"

"It didn't fully consume you before, or else a Binding Potion wouldn't have worked." She paused. "It might consume you next time."

"I'm sure Hastings could help." She took out her phone, but when she called there was no answer. She tried again.

"Celia, it's okay—"

"It's *not* okay."

"Thomasina has been practicing much longer than me, and she doesn't know how to reverse it."

"Don't say that." Celia redialed. "There *has* to be a way. Things can't just be one way and that's it. There're supposed to be balances in life, right? So if I can steal your magic, I can give it back. Or you guys steal it back. Something will work."

Leilani sighed, her breath leaving her like a dull breeze. "Your death."

Celia stiffened. Hastings's voicemail message played in her ear for the fourth time. She slowly hung up.

"What?" she asked, even though she had heard Leilani perfectly well.

The witch smiled again, but it didn't reach her eyes. Celia's own tears escaped. She stepped forward and hugged her. Leilani tensed at first; Celia hoped that was an involuntary reaction. After a moment, she returned the gesture.

"I'm so sorry," Celia repeated thickly. Leilani's heart thumped against her temple.

Her phone rang. She answered it without checking the display.

"Celia?"

She hesitated, not recognizing the female voice.

"It's Serena."

It was a good thing she had said her name, because Celia would not have known. She sounded so morose, so un-Serena-like, that it took a moment for her words to register.

"Oh. Hi." She looked at Leilani, her eyes wet with disappointment. Leilani nodded, and then headed for the door.

"Hang on," Celia said into the phone. She followed Leilani to the front of the spa, where the podium was empty.

"I'll find a way," Celia said with more confidence than she felt.

"Well, you know where to find me."

Celia turned away, because she thought she might really lose it if she kept looking at what she had done to Leilani. Even though the sun was hidden, the heat outside was still oppressive. She wiped at her face, then brought the phone back to her ear.

"I was wondering if you wanted to come over," Serena said. "If you're not busy?"

"Oh, um . . ." Celia trailed off a moment, considering. Two young men rode by on bicycles. Sweat poured off them. A breeze kicked up, blowing hot air across her skin.

She didn't have any other plans, and she knew if she stayed in the house, she'd just end up slumping deeper into this pit of depression that loomed in front of her.

"Sure," she said.

"Good. The car's on its way."

"I have Victor's car." Luckily his Jaguar had GPS.

Celia keyed in Serena's address. The car idled in the parking spot, the engine purring contentedly. She stared at the glowing display in the dashboard. The GPS voice urged her to drive to the main road.

Her argument with Victor had come back to her. She was nervous now. How could she take it back? The words were out there. Surely the blame could be placed on the increased magic. She'd been possessed by a dark force. He could understand that, right?

She wasn't comforted. The GPS again asked her to drive. She took a deep breath. Then she rubbed her face and tightened her ponytail before driving off.

The house was just as beautiful in the daytime. The palm trees swayed in the afternoon breeze, happily welcoming company. Serena opened the door when Celia rang the bell. A blast of cool air rushed past her.

If it were possible, Celia's heart dropped even farther, down past her knees. Serena's red hair hung listlessly around her shoulders. Dark circles tried to form under her eyes—or that could've been yesterday's makeup smeared during sleep.

Serena stuck her head out the door, screwing her face up at the sky.

"It's not supposed to rain today," she commented.

Then she grasped Celia's hand and led her to the massive staircase. Celia glimpsed the white bandage peeking from under Serena's long-sleeved cotton shirt. She also wore buttercream linen pants that skirted her toes.

At the top of the stairs, Serena turned left. They passed through an open space with a large loveseat and reading lamp before entering a bedroom. A queen-sized canopy bed made of shiny oak sat between the two windows. There were two matching dressers, and a wooden desk beside the door held her toiletries and makeup and jewelry.

Serena released her in the middle of the room, then pulled herself up onto the edge of the bed, where the tattered shopping bags from yesterday's trip lay across the rumpled comforter. As she watched Celia look around, she scratched absently at her left wrist.

"You look okay. Are you okay?"

Celia touched her cheek, where Computer Guy had hit her. There was no bruise, but she felt the impact unexpectedly.

"I'm okay."

"Have you been outside today?" Serena asked. Once again, her voice sounded drained of its usual liveliness. "I mean, besides coming here."

"Just a little." She took a seat on the vanity bench. "I went to this spa, but that was about it."

"You should've gone to Oasis."

"That's where I went."

"Did you see Leilani?" Celia nodded. "She's cool."

Celia waited, expecting her to launch into some fantastical tale involving magic and sex. Instead, Serena's shoulders sagged, her gaze drifting to the open window.

"Weren't you supposed to leave last night?" she asked.

"Yeah, but . . . we missed the flight." Celia glanced away. Serena didn't say anything, and silence filled the room.

"Where's Grace?" Celia asked, to break up the silence before it became too uncomfortable.

"I don't know, out somewhere. I went right to bed last night and she wasn't here when I got up. Rafael wanted to give me blood but I was just too tired."

"Look, Serena, I'm so sorry about that. I didn't know what Alec was and I would never intend for you two to—"

"It's okay. You didn't know."

They were the right words, but Serena couldn't inject any warmth to make them sincere. That just made Celia's guilt return tenfold.

Tears stung her eyes. "If you hadn't been with me," she began, her voice shaky, "nothing would've happened to you. You would've had fun shopping and . . ."

Celia crumpled forward, cupping her face in her hands. So crying during your vacation . . . normal?

After a few seconds, Serena's hand rubbed her back in little circles.

"But then they would've gotten you." Serena's voice was very close; she must've knelt in front of her. "And then you would've been all alone. They could've been a lot meaner if it was just one of you and the three of them."

That was true. But Celia wasn't done blaming herself. She cried for five more minutes. She cried for Serena and Grace and the trauma they had suffered because of her. She cried for Leilani and the other witches and the pain she had caused them. When she finally lifted her head, she saw Serena through blurry eyes, sitting on the floor in front of her. Serena smiled and a ghost of her old self appeared for a moment.

She lifted a tissue box. Celia took a few to wipe her face.

"I'm sorry," Celia said. "I've been kind of a wreck this weekend."

"What's going on? Well, besides the obvious," she added, with a playful roll of her eyes.

Celia sighed. Maybe Serena could give her some insight with her struggles.

"It's Victor. Well, it's us. We had this . . . argument last night. And I said some stuff I can't believe I said." She shook her head. "I guess it all started on the plane when he almost attacked me."

Serena's brows rose. "He *what?*"

"He's a nervous flier and he wasn't himself, and I thought I was past it, but it was really disturbing seeing him like that. I *felt* his hunger."

Celia placed a hand on her chest while staring Serena in the eye, trying to make her see how distressing that incident had been. She hadn't fully thought it through, but now she needed someone else to understand, to tell her it hadn't been irrational to feel scared.

"You felt his hunger?"

Celia hesitated. That was a longer conversation she didn't want to discuss with her. "Through our bond," she said at last.

"I don't think I've ever felt emotions."

Celia only shrugged.

Serena smiled again and patted Celia's knee. "Victor's a sweet guy. So, I can see why you'd be upset. But that happens. *A lot.*" She chuckled. "Oh, I'm sorry!" she added at Celia's astounded expression. She rubbed her knee.

"I forget you haven't been around vamps as long as I have. They lose control sometimes. I think they call it 'bloodlust.' All they see is blood. It takes over and they lose that human side for a while. We almost had to call an ambulance for Grace once, this time in Amsterdam. Elena can get rough. She does it on purpose, though."

Serena's expression hardened. "It's why Grace wants out. Elena's always mad about something, and I don't think she likes us, so she takes it out on us whenever she can. She's the bad part of being a vampire.

"Rafael was so pissed that night. He slapped her and kicked her out of the house." She shook the incident away.

A round of sympathy for Serena and Grace hit her. It was true that they were at the mercy of the Pérezes. No wonder Grace wanted to leave them. One of the vampires could snap and kill them without a second thought.

And yet they stayed. There had to be more to their bond than just money and trips. Even before Grace wanted out, she had agreed to be with the Pérezes. Celia recalled how happy Serena had been congratulating Rafael on his successes. She seemed to genuinely care for him. Was that enough to justify the inherent fear of dying?

And then she realized the similarities of their situations. Victor *was* a sweet guy, but he was still a vampire. One whose dark side she'd seen up close. She remembered his confession, about how hard it was to control himself sometimes with her. How he avoided connections with humans, even other vampires, for that reason. She didn't like that she was a constant test of his willpower.

And yet he stayed around. Something had to be different this time.

Serena interrupted her thoughts. "Like I said, Victor's a nice guy. He probably does a good job of hiding that bit of himself from you."

Celia sighed again. "That's just it though, isn't it? A guy shouldn't feel the need to hide any part of himself from his girlfriend. What's the point of being in a relationship if you can't be open with the other person?"

Serena frowned. "But you just said it was scary."

"Exactly!" Celia cried. "He shouldn't have to hide himself and I shouldn't be scared shitless. Don't you think something's wrong with this picture?"

Serena shrugged. "I think you're making a big deal out of something small."

Celia gaped at her. For a few seconds, she was speechless.

"I'm just saying," Serena went on, "it sounds like he lost control for a moment. They do that, even the old ones."

"The last time he lost control," Celia said, finding her voice, "somebody died."

"That happens too."

"And that's it? You don't care?"

Serena gasped. "Of course I care. But it's just something you come to deal with, being around vamps."

"Well, maybe I don't *want* to deal with it." Celia looked away to stare out the window. From the arch of her brows, Serena still didn't think this was worth all the trouble.

"I don't know how I'm going to face him." Celia said it softly, as if speaking to herself.

"You like him, right?"

Celia looked at her. "I love him."

"So you can make it work. Isn't this your anniversary vacation? You've *been* making it work."

Celia frowned, but she nodded. They had been working hard. She'd have to stay in the present, like she always did. If she was happy in the present, why harp on the future? Why dwell on *what ifs*?

"You're right. It's hard work, but I love him and I want to be with him." And she meant it.

Serena's face lit up with its usual vigor.

"Are you hungry?" she asked. "Come on, the chef will make whatever you want." She hopped up before Celia could say anything and skipped from the room.

Celia stood and glanced in the mirror. She didn't like what she saw—red nose and cheeks, puffy eyes. There wasn't much she could do at the moment, so she went downstairs to the kitchen.

Serena was talking to a short man with a crew cut and beard. His nose hooked to the left and his brow bone bulged slightly from his forehead.

"Dennis will make whatever your heart desires," Serena announced proudly.

Dennis looked to her expectantly. Celia's mind went blank under his stare.

"Uh, I don't know," she stammered. "I mean, I'm not too hungry. Maybe just a turkey sandwich?"

Serena laughed. "That's nothing!"

She shrugged. Serena squeezed Dennis's arm. "I guess it'll be two turkey sandwiches. Oh, with those sweet potato chips too."

"Right away." He crossed decisively to the fridge.

Serena placed her hands on Celia's shoulders and gently pushed her out the door. They went back upstairs, where Serena busied herself with changing the polish on her toes while Celia thumbed through some of her magazines. They talked about trivial things, such as movies coming out, celebrity couples, celebrity deaths. It was a treat for Celia to take her mind off real life.

Dennis brought their plates up personally. The girls sat on the rug, engrossed in an article about the pros and cons of threesomes. Celia's cheeks had flushed when she came across the article. The vision or dream after her experiment with the vamps was still fresh. Unlike how dreams from sleep faded after waking, it was like it had happened the night before. She couldn't even recall the actual experiment with as much clarity and detail.

Celia jumped when Dennis cleared his throat. He had come all the way into the room without attracting their attention. Celia slammed the magazine closed, though she was certain Dennis had gotten a good look at what they had been reading. Her cheeks flamed again as she accepted her plate.

"Enjoy, ladies." He took his leave.

"That was embarrassing," Celia whispered, peeking up at the door.

Serena looked at the magazine partially hidden under Celia's thigh.

"What, that?" Serena laughed. "Please, he's walked in on plenty."

The food was delicious. Dennis had toasted the whole wheat bread and added bacon, goat cheese, and a smoky sauce, and the sweet potato chips were crisp and warm.

"That's it," Celia said, after swallowing. "I'm getting a personal chef."

Serena giggled. "Dennis comes with us most of the time. He can make *anything*. And if he can't, he knows, like, all of the best chefs and calls them for advice. He thinks I don't know that," she added in a whisper. She even put her hand to the side of her mouth, as if he had vampire hearing.

Though she hadn't been hungry, Celia ate nearly the entire sandwich and most of the chips. She sat back against the bed, stuffed to the gills. Sighing happily, she closed her eyes.

"You're up early," Serena remarked, prompting a frown from Celia.

"What—?"

She opened her eyes to investigate to whom Serena was talking. Her words caught in a frightened gasp.

Isabel sat beside Celia, her face in the crook of her neck. Celia jumped so high, she nearly clocked the vampire with her shoulder.

Serena had resumed reading the magazine with the threesome article, since it lay in her lap. She glanced back down to it now, like it was no biggie that Isabel was sniffing Celia. The vampire sat back and stared at Celia with those intense, non-blinking eyes of hers.

"You no smell like wolf no more."

"You *don't* smell like wolf," Serena corrected her. "Honestly, Isabel, you've been alive for how many years, and living in America for how long with English-speaking people, and you still won't learn?" She shook her head. "Stubborn."

"I speak like what I want." Isabel paused, contemplating, her eyes glancing sideways for a second. "Bitch."

Serena gawked at her. The baby-faced vampire ignored her. She bent forward again. Her breath stirred the little hairs at the base of Celia's neck. Celia wanted to shrink away, but held still. Isabel *had* saved their lives. A little sniffing session in return was okay.

Isabel leaned away. Her eyes held a quizzical glint. She'd piled on the makeup once again, this time to match her corset and black leather miniskirt. The holes of her red fishnet stockings were large enough for Celia to glimpse three pink marks on her right thigh. They were cuts, so straight that they could've been applied with a razor. The pinkness faded before her eyes until her leg was completely smooth.

Isabel noticed her gaze, but she didn't adjust her skirt. There wasn't anything to cover anymore. Celia glanced up, unsure of how to voice her concern for the girl.

Isabel's chilly finger grazed the vein pressing against Celia's neck. "Why you no smell good?"

"What?" Celia touched her own neck.

"You no smell good, like before."

Isabel didn't have Esperanza's snaggletooth problem. Her teeth were straight lines. When her fangs slid down, Celia's mouth went dry. Was the vamp going to bite her? Surely she was hungry . . .

"Isa, stop trying to scare her."

Celia's head jerked toward the door at the sound of Elena's voice. She wondered how Serena and Grace could possibly live with a bunch that was so quiet on their feet.

Elena was comfy loveliness in a hunter green shirtdress, the sleeves rolled up to her elbows, and black Capri leggings. Her dark hair was piled on her head in a messy bun. She crossed the room, walking on toes painted a deep burgundy color, and sat cross-legged in front of Celia.

She gazed at Celia for a while. Celia wanted to look away but then pleasant warmth consumed her discomfort. It was like she had sat in front of the sun. Elena even had this radiance that sort of pulsed around her. Maybe the sun *was* there in the room. Could she control that? Bring the sun from the sky into this very room? Was it just for Celia? What an amazing woman—

Just as suddenly as it had appeared, the heat was gone. It left so abruptly that Celia got a chill. Glancing around, she saw the others watching her. Serena looked uncomfortable. Isabel's mouth hung open in a grin, her fangs pressing into her bottom lip. Elena didn't smile, but she was satisfied.

A sick thud hit her in the chest. Elena had compelled her. She hadn't even sensed it happening.

"What do you want?" Celia asked, keeping her voice level. Inside, she freaked out. The thought had never crossed her mind that the Binding Potion would remove *all* of her abilities.

"Oh, nothing," the vampire said sweetly. "It's just amazing to see what Victor finds attractive nowadays. My, times have changed."

Why didn't she just kick her in the fucking shin? There was a nice, vacant spot on her right leg at the moment.

As Elena surveyed her, Celia took in the vampire's beauty. The small features, the pouty upper lip, the flawless skin, the tiny mole on her cheek. The thick, flowing, *luxurious* hair. The exotic accent. She was stunning.

Was this the caliber of Victor's exes? Celia thought of her soft stomach and thighs that touched. Her curly hair that wasn't always tamable. The old burn mark next to her pisiform—the little bone in your wrist that stuck out—that had healed a darker shade of brown than her complexion. How could Celia live up to Elena?

Well, great. What was the point in teetering on the edge? She might as well just dive headfirst into the Pit of Depression. Man, she could use a drink.

"You dated Victor?" Serena asked.

"'*Dating'* is such a mundane word," Elena said, as if the word had gone sour against her tongue. "The kind of bond we shared cannot be described. Humans *think* they have meaningful connections. They are wrong."

Serena gulped.

"We were together for quite a while," Elena continued, "when he lived in London. He was young then, in need of much guidance." She stared Celia right in the eye. "I saw him one night, coming home from the theater. He just looked too delicious to pass by." She cocked an eyebrow. "I do love the chase, maybe more than the prize sometimes. Although, not with Victor. It was fun bringing him home with me."

Celia's face fell as she realized what Elena was saying. Victor had been living in England with his family when he was turned . . .

She didn't know what to do with this information. Victor never talked about when he'd come over. She'd received more information in a week than she'd had in a year with him. There must've been a reason for his secrecy. It had always frustrated her that he wouldn't share, but at the same time she recognized that she'd never pushed him to. She'd assumed it was just too painful for him to relive. Part of her wanted to seek him out right that instant and demand he explain. Her curiosity was the only thing keeping her from storming out of the room.

Elena's lips twitched into a grin. "He didn't tell you about me?" She wasn't angry. If anything, she sounded delighted.

Celia only shook her head. Though that wasn't really true. Victor had mentioned his maker a few times . . . indirectly.

Serena leaned forward in awe. "You turned him?"

Elena's eyes were only for Celia. "He came out of the theater," she said. "He was very handsome in his suit with this long jacket and his top hat and gold chain on his vest—" She pointed to her stomach, indicating where the chain had sat. She chuckled to herself. "His shoes were so shiny."

Yeah, Celia thought. *They would be.*

"I think he was by himself. It was so long ago." Elena shook her head as she tried to recall those little details. "Anyway, he left the building alone. He smelled like . . . the ocean, as strange as that sounds. He was in London. Why did he smell like the beach?"

Celia's teeth clenched in anger at the idea of someone else enjoying Victor's scent. Of course others had, but that was *her* smell; she could be irrational if she wanted.

"I followed him," Elena carried on. "He didn't know I was there, not until I dropped my umbrella. It had rained earlier and the ground was still wet. He turned around and saw me struggling to hold up my dress so it wouldn't get wet on the pavement. The dresses were so grand then, though not as big as they used to be. Today, you can go out in your underwear if you so choose."

Serena giggled. "If only!"

Elena shot her a silencing look. Obviously, she preferred the fancy dresses of the Edwardian days.

"Victor was always the gentleman," the vampire continued, turning back to Celia. "He rushed over to pick up the umbrella. I thanked him and we spoke for a bit. Then it started to rain. We ran for cover, laughing like schoolchildren. He held my umbrella over me and when he smiled . . ."

She trailed off into a smile of her own. Celia's fury rose another notch.

"Since he wanted to be chivalrous, as was the times, he started to court me. I went along because he was fun. The first time he kissed me, we were out for ice cream. I wanted him right then.

"I couldn't carry on for much longer, or else he would've become suspicious. We couldn't do anything during the day, which frustrated him. His family had just come into sustaining money. They were finally able to treat themselves with some—not all—but some of the finer things in life. That night at the theater had been his first time. He wanted to lavish me. But I only lived half a life. So that night, I asked him to come inside my home. You should've seen his face!"

Elena laughed so hard at the recollection that she slapped her thigh. Isabel imitated her sister's mirth. Celia's stomach had been clenching this whole time. Half of her didn't want to hear this. That half also felt guilty, because shouldn't Victor be the one telling her this tale?

The other half of her was fully engrossed in Elena's story. Then, on top of all that, she was jealous and angry to hear of Victor's time with another woman. Since she couldn't decide how to react, her mouth stayed clamped shut.

"He was so surprised, but I let him know it was okay. That night, I took him to my bedroom. He obviously had experience. I do not know why he was so shocked. Perhaps because *I* made the first move. Perhaps he wasn't used to that. Women were supposed to be chaste and reserved, though most were not, I tell you," she added with a roguish smirk. "We just knew how to make the men feel macho."

Serena raised her hand for Elena's attention. "What happens when you're turned?" she asked carefully, so as not to upset the vamp.

Celia was surprised she didn't know.

"I've never witnessed it," Serena said, correctly reading her expression.

Elena leaned back, placing her hands behind her on the carpet.

"You die first." Her tone became professional. "The vampire blood has to travel through you. A few times, you're in a coma. Most times you walk around as if nothing has happened, except you have headaches and cramps and are very, very hungry but no food satisfies you."

"Sounds like that time of the month," Serena quipped, throwing Celia a grin.

"It's worse," Elena snapped, making both women start. "You don't know what's happening or why, because most times you don't remember being bitten. Sometimes there are strange dreams, but you can't make sense of them. By the second day, you're in so much pain that you can't even leave the bed. The third night, you think you're fine because the pain is gone.

"When you rise, everything is the same, but different. The sun hurts. The air tingles. There is no reason to breathe. Your pulse is gone. That is when your maker is supposed to come in, to explain what has happened and to show you the way. To teach you to feed.

"You have to feed as a vampire or you will shrivel and become nothing. Not dead. Not undead. You're nothing. That's what happened to my mother." Elena's voice hardened.

At the mention of their mother, Isabel's fingernail cut into her thigh. She wiped up the little blood that had dribbled onto her skin with her fingertip and brought it to her mouth.

"She refused to eat," Elena said, without acknowledging her sister's behavior. Celia and Serena slowly turned back to Elena. "She withered away, her skin becoming tough like leather against her bones, in a matter of days. She couldn't move—she *wouldn't* move. That was my father's punishment. She didn't care that she was punishing her daughters too.

"*I* was the one to release her. *I* was the one to drive the stake through her chest." Her eyes narrowed. "I was there for Victor." Her voice was laced with ferocious confidence. As if she dared Celia to challenge her actions.

Finding her voice finally, Celia asked, "How did he take it?"

Elena tilted her head to the side. "How do you mean?"

"The change. How did he feel about it?"

Elena was quiet for a moment as she considered Celia's words.

"He was not happy. He ran away that first month, which I allowed for a little while. Then I called him back. I showed him the fun he could have."

Celia wanted to ask her to elaborate, because she imagined all kinds of risqué things based on the few vampy activities she herself had witnessed, like the party downstairs the other night. At the last second she decided she didn't want to know the gory details and closed her mouth.

"How come Victor isn't with you anymore?" Serena asked.

Celia frowned at Serena, who shrugged apologetically.

"He asked me to release him," Elena said. "So I did." She tapped a finger against her chin as if she suddenly remembered something. "But there *was* that summer in oh-five we went through Asia. I had called him again, thinking we could relive the past, but he just wasn't having fun with it."

"How so?" Serena asked quite eagerly. Of *course* she'd love to hear of his sexcapades.

"He used to be so free. Every night was a new adventure. Once he accepted the power he had as a vampire, he didn't care about the who or the where, and sometimes the how much."

Serena's smile disappeared. "Oh." She gave a sideways glance toward Celia.

"He understood our superiority."

Celia's voice was low, yet defiant. She wasn't a fool. She knew Elena had been trying to get a rise out of her from the start. She could hold back no longer.

"Superiority? The sun kills you."

Serena's brows shot up. Isabel grinned.

Elena smiled sweetly. "I can snap your neck before you even realize I'm coming. I could make you jump out the window thinking it was your idea." She leaned in. Her voice was warm, comforting, but her eyes were filled with icy indignation.

"I could make you my slave long after you need someone to wipe your face and ass. You think Victor was unhappy? Wait and see what I'm like when I *don't* like someone."

Celia held her gaze even as she took in those threats. "Sure. But it would only be because of your will. Unless someone willingly submits to you, it's not real. So compel away. You'd never have the real person."

Elena sat back, her nose flaring. She stared Celia in the eye, but time continued to pass; Elena wasn't going to compel her to do something dangerous.

Isabel reached out and rubbed Celia's cheek. "*Tu cara,* it is red."

Celia swatted at her hand and rose to her feet.

Isabel jumped up as well, and Serena stood when Celia looked her way, letting her know she had had enough. The three of them headed to the door.

Elena was there in the threshold, blocking their exit. Celia and Serena gasped as they came to a halt.

Elena's gaze skirted Celia's neck. "I could do the same for you," she said gently, as if offering a prize. "Then you can be boring with Victor forever."

Celia's hands balled into fists.

"Don't you love him?" Elena asked. "Isn't that the plan?" The vampire leaned forward, her lips aimed for Celia's throat. "Otherwise," she breathed against Celia's skin, "what's the point?"

Celia ducked away and rushed out the room. Downstairs, she went right out the door.

"Hey, wait," Serena called.

Celia stopped on the porch. Serena stood in front of her, with Isabel on her right. Serena's mouth opened, but no words came out. Celia shuffled the toe of her sneaker on the top step.

Elena's words still rung in her head. She imagined Victor and Elena wreaking havoc wherever they went. Killing with no remorse. Partying like rock stars, only instead of liquor and drugs, with blood and flesh.

The two of them acting out because of a life they hadn't chosen.

It was hard to reconcile those images with the Victor she knew . . . until she remembered the creature who had snarled at her on the airplane.

A sky blue Audi TT swerved down the street. It came dangerously close to sideswiping the water fountain in the middle of the rotary. The top was down, releasing loud rock music from the tiny car. The Audi jumped the curb as it came to a stop in front of the house. Grace's head jerked forward then back at the abrupt halt, her black hair falling into her face.

After a second of gathering her bearings, Grace shoved her door open. The music and engine were still going when she stumbled out of the car. She crossed the grassy yard toward the house, unaware of the eyes on her. Her navy-blue t-shirt was wrinkled and one of the legs of her jeans had ridden up, revealing the red ring around her ankle. Her eyelids drooped, and she kept reaching her hands out, as if she were going to fall over at any moment.

"Gracie, where have you been?" Serena demanded.

Grace jumped at the voice. Very slowly and carefully, she lifted her face to the spectators on the porch. She looked as solemn as ever, only her eyes were puffy and bloodshot. Her tiny hand took hold of the railing as she started up the stairs.

Serena gasped when she made it to the landing. "You smell like gin!"

"That's because I was drinking gin," Grace replied flatly. She belched in Serena's face.

Serena waved the smell away. "And like sex!"

She squeezed between Serena and Celia, paying no heed to Serena's outraged expression.

"*Crazy bitch*," Isabel chimed.

Serena whipped her face to the vamp. "Hey! Don't do that!"

"*Stay out of my head*," Isabel said with a huge smile.

"Stop it, Isa!"

Grace grumbled under her breath and went in the house.

"You do realize you parked on the lawn, right?" Serena called after her. Grace continued to trudge toward the staircase.

"I will move," Isabel volunteered. She jumped down the stairs, landing silently at the base, even in her heavy, military boots. She then ran to the Audi. She was inside and whipped the car onto the road just as Serena began to protest.

"She's not supposed to drive," Serena said, slapping her forehead with her hand.

They watched in horror as the blue convertible bounced off the curb. It zoomed around the fountain three times, the tires squealing and sending out white smoke, before heading up the road toward the gate, which decidedly was *not* the way to the garage. The car became a tiny blue dot as the gate opened. Isabel jerked the car around the corner, rousing a blast from the horn of a passing car, and was gone.

Celia looked at Serena, who rolled her eyes. "I live with a bunch of two-year-olds."

Celia didn't know what more to say about that. She took the car key from her pocket.

Serena poked out her bottom lip. "You leave tonight?"

"Technically, tomorrow."

Serena grabbed her in a tight hug. "I'll miss you. Will you call me?" She pulled back, staring into Celia's eyes with her wide, bright ones.

"Sure," Celia said, because that was the easier answer. Serena kissed her cheek and let her go.

Celia descended the stairs and got in the car waiting on the driveway.

Her head was a jumble. She chewed her bottom lip as she backed away from the house.

At the end of the road for Tower Heights, as she came to a stop for the gate, the Audi blew through the stop sign on the left, rock music still blasting.

It was fully dark by the time Celia made it back to Setter's Cove. Victor would be waiting for her. Her dread rose. She had been quick to defend him to Elena because she wouldn't let anyone talk shit about the people she loved, no matter what.

That, of course, didn't squelch her anxiety. She recalled Serena's *no biggie* attitude toward her worries. Life would be much simpler if Celia could adopt that outlook. She was well aware that she'd had a *don't ask, don't tell* position for a while. But things had changed. She just couldn't see herself acting in that way any longer.

She didn't *want* things to change. She liked having a boyfriend, who loved her, and cared about her.

She paused at the corner before the house. Discarding the idea of driving around the block a few times, Celia pulled the car into the garage.

Victor was sitting on the sofa when she entered. He glanced over his shoulder when the side door opened.

"Hey." He put down her novel.

"Hey."

"Do you want to get dinner?"

She didn't. She was still full from her late lunch, and if she'd been hungry, she would've preferred making something. She actually would have preferred being in her own home, her sanctuary, with her bed and TV and sense of comfort. She regretted making them stay. Her house was sparkly clean, just waiting for her return. Maybe they could catch an earlier flight . . . maybe Victor could teleport them back . . .

For whatever reason, instead of making him take her home, Celia nodded and went to the bathroom to wash up.

Eleven

V**ictor decided on** a nearby place, a Brazilian restaurant with an outdoor lounge. A strange "fusion" style decorated the interior. A large salad buffet occupied one wall. Waiters in white wheeled silver stakes of meat around tables. Large golden Mandarin monks resided in different corners. Big tropical trees reached up to the ceiling, which was painted like the galaxy. An indoor waterfall splashed into a stone-lined pool at the entrance and a volcano was wedged against the back wall, with orange lights imitating lava.

They both raised a dubious eyebrow at each other. Since it was a cool eighty-five degrees with the sun down, they took a table outside.

"How was your day?" Victor asked gently.

She shrugged. "I went to Serena's."

"How are they?"

"As to be expected."

He was used to more elaboration.

The waitress came to their table. Celia ordered a merlot like Victor. She hardly ever drank red wine because it always went right to her head. Victor's lips pursed in discontent.

The waitress hurried off to retrieve their drinks.

"I spoke with Elena," Celia replied, taking Victor by surprise. She didn't look at him; instead, she took a long time draping her napkin across her lap. She seemed so small at the moment. Her shoulders were hunched forward, almost defensively. Her hair had puffed out into a curly halo. She held her hands rigid in her lap, as if by focusing all her energy on keeping her hands there she wouldn't explode.

"She told me about when she met you."

"How she *changed* me," he corrected. Celia glanced up at the change in his tone. "She led me to believe she loved me. Then she killed me, and I was supposed to be *grateful?*" He shook his head. "She never asked. She didn't tell me all of the consequences. She's the most deluded person walking this earth, always has been. She's manipulative and selfish."

Celia's eyes were wide in shock. She hadn't expected that reaction. Hell, neither had he. Why was she bringing up Elena? Was she accusing him of something? When she had told him Rafael was in town, his plan had been to simply ignore Elena, but his maker had just kept inserting herself.

"I only say that as a warning," he added tightly. "You cannot take what she says at face value. She was turned against her will, and she takes it out on everyone around her, except the person who made her. She was using me. She held me captive so that she wouldn't be alone, just like her father did to her. When she finally realized I didn't want to stay with her, she let me go. It wasn't easy and there wasn't anything nice about that night, but she finally released me."

Celia's voice was tiny. "How come you never told me?"

He sighed. "It was too painful. I don't like the person I was with her. When I realized I couldn't be that way anymore, I got as far away as possible."

"I wish you'd trusted me enough to tell me."

That made him growl. "I'm sorry I kept this from you. I just . . ." The words wouldn't come from his lips. He'd felt them for many decades. He stared at her, her round face, her determined eyes.

He forced out the words. "I haven't liked this life, being what I am. I had a good family. I enjoyed my work. The high of becoming stronger and faster than human men wore off quickly when I realized that Elena only wanted to kill and drink and fuck her way through every village and town we encountered. I hated that cycle. It was tedious.

"When I left her, I was able to clear my head. I saw humans as people again. They were more than just nourishment and playthings. And then I was miserable again because I would never be able to experience what they did. I tried, I honestly did. I had relationships. I held jobs, lived in suburbs and apartment buildings. None of it worked."

He sighed a second time. "The instinct to survive has been stronger than my desire to die. And then there's you. You've made me put aside those self-destructive thoughts. You know me without compulsion. I only wish that I were human to experience life with you more fully.

"But if it weren't for you, my existence would be unbearable. So, again, I apologize for not explaining this more thoroughly to you. It wasn't about trust. I didn't want to overwhelm you with such a confession. I didn't want to contaminate what we have with the despicable things what I am can beget. You make me want to live, Celia. It's wonderful and excruciating all at once."

Tears pooled in her brown eyes, which hadn't been his intention. She used her napkin to wipe them away.

"Victor . . ." she whispered.

"This wasn't how I had envisioned this week. You're no longer here with me and I don't know how to get you back. I need you, Celia. You're my anchor to something concrete."

Victor's eyes darkened as a familiar scent reached his nose. When he looked over her shoulder, another growl rumbled in his throat.

Rita and her two goons crowded around their table, completely blocking the aisles. They were in their usual gear: dusty jeans, plain, solid-colored t-shirts, boots. Did they live in the streets?

A few of the other patrons turned to watch them warily, while eating and sipping tropical drinks from fake coconut shells.

"Victor." Rita's smile made her less attractive. "I heard about your run-in with the wolves."

Victor's glare was deadly. "What do you want? Once again, you're interrupting our dinner."

Rita, startled at his indignant tone, quit her smiling at once. Goons 1 and 2 exchanged incredulous glances.

"You watch your mouth," Goon 2 interjected.

Rita composed herself. She placed a hand on her minion's arm—he had propped his hairy knuckles on the table, leaning close to Victor. Her smile returned.

"Calm yourself," she said to Goon 2. She patted his arm to appease him, as if he had been the one insulted. "We *are* interrupting." She surveyed Celia, who had stopped crying, though her eyes were still wet. "We just need to borrow Victor tonight. I'll have him back to you by morning."

Victor shook his head. "This is our last night here," he told Rita. "I'm sorry, but we have plans."

It was sort of true. They had plans to eat dinner.

"The problem with that," Rita replied, "is that I didn't ask. The wolves are rebelling, and we'll need the extra fighters."

Victor was in no mood to placate a group of local vamps trying to assert their dominance. He might have to pay for it later. For now, he had no intentions of joining in on someone else's turf war.

Rita waited, her patience visibly running thin. That smile stretched across her face in more of a leer.

He fixed her with a firm stare. "I'm sorry" — a lie — "but no."

He couldn't tell if she was angrier at his lie or his negative answer. Her hands balled into giant fists, her gaze narrowed, and Victor remembered the man on the street the last time he'd lied to her.

"Don't you want revenge?" Goon 1 chimed. He tilted his head to indicate Celia, who had been sitting in silence as she watched this display. Now that she was mentioned, her expression darkened in anger at being used as a catalyst.

Victor shot up from his seat. They'd been attracting too much attention. Most of the nearby patrons stared outright. The waitress came over as Victor stood, wringing her hands.

"Would you all like a table?" she asked the vamps.

"No," Rita barked at her, making her squeak in fright.

The waitress took a second to search for her voice. "It's just . . . you can't stand in the aisles."

"Back off!"

"Let's step out front," Victor said.

He walked backward a few paces, ensuring the others followed. He made his way through the restaurant and over to the main entrance. A few people stood around outside, waiting for tables.

Victor continued through the parking lot to a more secluded area near the main road. The cars passing by in the direction of the intersection stirred the wind.

Growly sat on the stone boundary. He stood when he heard them approach.

"We going?" he asked Rita.

"He doesn't want to go," Goon 2 said.

"Those fucking wolves are trying to take over," Rita said. She shook her head. Her dark hair didn't move an inch. "I like it here. I'm not leaving."

"Shouldn't you be more worried about Ava and Wesley?" Victor pointed out.

"Fuck that bitch."

Victor took a measuring breath. "I'm not from here," he reminded her. "I don't want any part of this."

"Even after what they did to your little lady?" Growly asked. He looked disgusted that Victor wasn't enthusiastic about helping them.

Victor gritted his teeth.

"How can you let filthy animals run your allies out of their home?" That was Goon 1, taking a step forward.

Allies? Were they serious? Victor decided not to disabuse him of that notion at this time.

"This isn't a request," Rita said. "You're in my territory. You will fight by our side. I've already spoken to the others."

At that moment, Victor realized just how dangerous Rita was, asserting authority on land she had no right to claim.

"I'll meet you wherever you want," Victor said. "Just let me take her home."

After a pause, Rita nodded her consent and told him the address.

Victor went back to the table. The waitress had deposited their drinks. She stood by now, pen and pad in hand. Celia looked up from the menu when Victor approached.

"Can we go?" she asked.

He sat in his seat. "In a minute, okay?" He wanted to make sure the vamps were gone. "We'll just have the drinks for now," he told the waitress.

Celia sipped from her glass and avoided his eyes. This hadn't been the ideal timing for his confession. He was afraid he had actually widened the gulf between them.

After ten minutes, Victor retrieved his wallet and paid for the drinks. With his hand on the small of her back, he guided Celia to the exit. The coast appeared to be clear, but his nose told him the vamps were still nearby.

He pulled her closer. The icy currents rushed through his veins. He'd teleport in the middle of the parking lot if he was forced to do so. He just needed to get her away.

He was too slow. One second Celia was tucked into his side, the next she was gone.

Victor whipped around as the blur that was Goon 2 streaked ahead of him, across the lot and around a corner away from the big intersection. His speed made Clarice—the fastest runner in Ramsey's seethe—look like a mere human.

The few people in the lot glanced around at the sudden breeze. Rita and Goon 1 strolled over to Victor from where they'd been waiting behind a parked SUV.

"You can have her back once we take out the wolves," Rita said.

"I said I would go," Victor growled.

Rita's smile was lecherous. "It wasn't a *lie*, per se. But it wasn't truth, Victor."

Victor's fists tightened at his side. "Why are you doing this? You don't need me."

"Look, the more fighters we have, the quicker we can destroy them. End of story."

Victor took a step forward, ready to rip their heads off, when a wave of Celia's fear washed over his insides, making him halt.

"Shit," he grumbled. It would take time to find her, time he didn't have. Through clenched teeth, he asked, "What assurances will I have that you won't hurt her? That you'll give her back to me when this over?"

Rita smiled, raising her right hand in the air. "I swear." Since his expression clearly read *you're fucking kidding me*, she added, "I don't lie, Victor. You'll have your human back once we've taken out the wolves."

Victor cast around one last time for any way out of this. Coming up irritatingly blank, he squared his shoulders and set off with the vamps.

Twelve

Goon 2 handed a breathless Celia over to Growly. Dizziness engulfed her momentarily, a result of the turbo-speed journey and the red wine. Growly kept a firm grip on her arm, and when she tried to pull away, he shocked her. A burning smell tickled her nose from where his hand covered her shirt.

She was *so* over the torture sessions, that was for goddamn sure. Her body and mind were exhausted.

Celia took a moment to glance around, and felt sick to her stomach. They were back at the house in the abandoned neighborhood. The moon shone in the sky, large and full, casting a warm, white glow on the neglected yard.

Three bodies had been tossed in front of the fence where Carl and Celia had broken through, forming a macabre doggy pile. Celia gulped back her rising nausea. Alec and his buddies were a gift to the wolves of Vegas.

Six people waited in the yard. They didn't seem bothered at all by the dead bodies. She figured they were vamps. Akeem was among them, as well as Mary, who stared at Celia with a mixture of intrigue and annoyance.

One of them, a tall, muscular man with a long braid of black hair down his back and rust-colored skin, eyed Celia like she was a piece of meat—in more ways than one. In fact, each one of the vampires glanced her way several times. She tried to ignore them, but their gazes sent shivers over her skin. Though it was warm out, Celia felt chilled to her core being back here, back in danger. She wrapped her free arm around her torso, seeking warmth in any way she could.

Another ten minutes passed before Rita, her other goon, and Victor came to a halt in the field. Victor spotted Celia right away, his dark eyes boring holes into her. He looked furious and apologetic at the same time.

Growly snickered. He pulled her closer as a warning to Victor. Instinctively, she shifted away from him.

As a reward, Growly sent a jolt up and down her arm. A cry slipped through her lips, tears burning her eyes.

Growly glared down at her. The nostrils of his flat nose flared as he inhaled her fear.

"Just give me a reason," he hissed at her. She glimpsed his fangs. "I've always preferred dark meat."

Celia held still, maintaining an angry, stolid glare even though inside her heart pounded against her chest. Growly smirked. He didn't buy her façade.

"Yeah, just like that," he breathed, making her skin crawl. He licked his lips hungrily. She turned away from him as she blinked back her tears of frustration.

The wolves' generator must've died because only the moon illuminated the area. A distant howl made her head snap toward the dark horizon behind the house. Glancing around, she saw the vamps were already in their defensive stances. They'd heard the wolves approaching long before that little warning.

She looked to Victor. The moon threw a shadow across half his face as he stared out into the darkness. Every muscle in his body seemed tense and ready. He looked so powerful, so dangerous. Had he fed tonight? His anger at that bitch Rita would probably suffice, but Celia was still concerned. She didn't want him hurt.

As if feeling her gaze, Victor met her eyes. She couldn't tell what he was thinking. Certainly, he could read her fear and worry as if she held a giant, blinking sign. His words from earlier swarmed her brain. She'd never realized how powerful his love was for her. It was heartbreaking to hold someone's existence in your hand.

Celia opened her mouth to say . . . something, but the sound of heavy paws beating the earth interrupted her. Their contact was lost as Victor faced the pack.

Celia and Growly stood a good distance away from the group, in the derelict yard of a house with a wide hole in its porch. Even if she'd been closer, she wouldn't have recognized any of the six wolves that appeared from the darkness surrounding the house. The wolves didn't have shapes; they were just balls of fur jumping at the vampires, who met them eagerly.

Celia tried hard not to watch the ensuing battle, but whenever she heard a yowl or a scream, she had to check on Victor. The third time she looked, he held his own against a wolf the color of golden wheat. The wolf snapped at his face but Victor tossed him aside. The wolf sprang back to its feet, shaking off any disorientation. Then it lunged at him again, and they both ended up on the ground in a cloud of dust.

Wistful noises left Growly in a steady interval. His right hand jerked reflexively, as if jabbing at an invisible opponent.

When one of his companions was thrown to the ground and didn't move, Growly took a step toward her. He stopped himself when he realized he still had to attend to Celia. He glowered at her, and then grumbled something under his breath.

"You could let me go," Celia said. "You can help your friends—"

"Shut up!" he barked. His hand tightened around her bicep. She cringed in anticipation, but no jolt came. Growly was too distracted to torment her at the moment, and she was just fine with that.

Celia looked to Victor once again. He knelt beside the gold wolf, who alternated between pants and wheezes. Drying blood matted its beautiful fur. In a flash, Victor's face buried in the great wolf's neck. The animal let out a low, pained cry but couldn't move away. After a minute, the wolf slumped to the ground.

Celia winced at the sight. Victor stood up slowly, wiping his mouth with the crook of his arm. He only managed to smear his chin even further. He searched for more, his rosy face no longer expressionless.

No, he was . . . excited. The wolf blood seemed to energize him.

He spotted a gray wolf gnawing on the arm of that vamp who'd been eyeing Celia earlier. Victor's lips curled back, revealing his fangs. He jumped on the back of the wolf and wrapped his arms around his neck. The wolf growled. He twisted to his left and bit down on Victor's leg. In response, Victor pounded on his head until it released him. The wolf whimpered. Its front legs shook horribly until it fell forward, its legs no longer able to support it.

Victor climbed off to kick it in its side. And kick and kick and kick. Celia couldn't blink, couldn't even breathe as she watched his cold display. She wanted to call out to him, to make him stop, but her voice was nowhere to be found.

Victor wavered. His eyes searched the grounds until they landed on Celia.

Only a shadow of the Victor she knew remained. The moon reflected in the blood coating his cheeks and neck and chest. His hands were rigid fists. A clump of knotted, brown fur poked through his fingers. His fangs were still bared, and she wondered if her beating heart was what distracted him.

This was the creature who'd frightened her on the plane. The one who haunted her dreams.

The one he despised.

Victor took a step toward her, then halted. His brow creased. She watched as he shook his head.

He peered down at the fallen wolf, whose shuddering breaths caused tiny puffs of dirt to rise. He looked back to Celia. His gray eyes focused on her neck.

With a quick jerk, she pulled away from Growly.

"What—?"

She was already running to the road that would take her away from this place.

Growly took off behind her. After a few paces, however, he slowed to a stop, his attention diverted by a black-and-white wolf pouncing on Akeem. The vampire had some bad cuts on his arms and back. His white clothes were now brown and red, his hair frizzy and spiked with pebbles. The wolf's massive paws planted squarely on Akeem's back, sending him to the ground.

His hands splayed out and a small tornado appeared out of nowhere, encircling him and the wolf. Too weak, the windstorm did nothing more than whip the wolf's fur around.

Growly's gaze went to Celia's retreating back once more, and then he ran at the wolf.

Celia didn't know where she was going. She didn't stop, not even when she reached the crossroad five minutes later. Her legs pumped madly. The wind thrashed her puffy hair around her ears.

She finally slowed to a walk after another ten minutes. The road seemed to stretch on without end before her. A faint howl rose up in the distance, lost in the night.

She stopped to catch her breath and give her legs a break. Patting her pockets, she noticed she didn't have her cellphone. Her wallet was missing as well. She only hoped they were in the house and hadn't fallen out during Goon 2's speedy nabbing.

She glanced around. Her only options were forward into the darkness, or back to the ramshackle neighborhood.

Celia stuffed her hands in her empty pockets and let her feet do the navigating, as she tried not to listen to the sudden shuffling or strange sounds in the cocoon engulfing her.

It felt like an hour before she reached the main road. A sidewalk lined the street, which made the trek less daunting.

She had never felt lonelier than she did at that moment, walking along the highway, no cellphone, no money. Every so often, she'd stick her thumb out to the passing cars. She tried to keep her mind clear. It was the only way she'd make it back to civilization without giving up and collapsing on the side of the road first.

So much had happened on this trip. Had it been only a week? It felt like ages ago that she and Victor had been heading to Logan Airport, ready to celebrate their relationship.

Their relationship . . .

She stopped that train of thought immediately. That didn't erase the tears blurring her vision. She used the back of her hand to wipe her eyes. Her face felt stiff; dirt had caked to her skin from sweat.

After a while, the sky began to change from midnight blue to dark gray. It appeared Corinna had made today overcast as well. Celia had rolled her sleeves up to her shoulders a while back with the rise in humidity and temperature. She'd sweated through her shirt by the time someone pulled to the curb.

The black Accord with the flashing hazards seemed like a good sign. The middle-aged woman driving pushed the door open for her. She didn't know where Setter's Cove was, but was able to locate it with her phone. A talk show played from the radio. The man's soothing voice doled out advice to callers.

They arrived at the house twenty minutes later. Celia thanked the woman as a new round of shuddering tears came over her. She covered her face with her hands. The woman pulled her into a tight hug.

"It's okay, sweetie," she whispered into Celia's hair. Her hands made wide circles against Celia's back. She smelled like coconut oil, reminding Celia of her aunt for some reason, even though Meg was partial to floral scents. The sincerity in the woman's embrace made Celia wish with all of her being she were home, where she was safe.

Celia went inside using the hidden key Hastings had shown her on the first day.

She was enjoying a comforting, dreamless sleep when a hand shook her shoulder. Victor leaned over her, looking amazing for someone who'd just been involved in a huge brawl. His hair was shiny and lustrous, his skin flushed, his eyes the palest shade of gray she'd ever seen them.

The vamps must have won . . . and celebrated.

Celia looked away. She pushed the covers aside and climbed out of bed.

"We have to leave in an hour." Victor's voice was toneless.

"Maybe you should meet me in Boston," she said. "Just so there're no issues."

He took a deep breath and blew it out slowly. Fixing her with a long stare, he asked, "Is that what you want?"

"It might be easier that way."

His expression was unreadable, like it would get at times when he debated something unsavory. She always found that irritating and right now was no different. Since he didn't say anything more, she went to the bathroom for a quick shower. The bottom of the shower stall became coated with her dirt and sweat.

Back in the room, Victor was hunched over his suitcase, stalling or giving her space or something, because his bag was immaculate and didn't need as much attention as he gave it.

"I can't find my phone," she told him, as she pulled on her panties. He left to search for it. After dressing, Celia set about packing her bags. It wasn't the best idea, but she folded the gown in its garment bag along the top of her suitcase. It didn't matter anyway. She would likely just donate it once she got home.

Victor informed her he couldn't find her phone. Luckily, her wallet had been on the bed. His blank expression persisted as he hefted their bags downstairs. Celia trailed behind him.

Hastings entered the house when they reached the lower level.

"Can I help you with that, sir?"

"No, I'm fine," Victor said without looking at him. He continued out the front door.

Hastings turned to Celia and held out a hand. She looked at it, and then wrapped her arms around his middle instead. His sage scent tickled her nose.

"I wish I had more time," she said, stepping back. "Maybe I could've been a cool witch." She smiled, without enthusiasm.

Hastings reached into his pocket and produced a vial of white liquid. The vial was only about three inches tall, with a black stopper.

"What's this?"

"It'll help when you're ready for your powers back."

Celia stared at it. "That will reverse the binding spell? I could give Leilani and the others back their magic?"

He shook his head, quelling her burgeoning hope. "You need a group that is at full capacity. That way when the spell is broken, they can control you. This is only the first step."

She took the vial.

"Please, be careful, Celia," Hastings added, and she looked up at him. "Umami are special. Once you master your power, you'll understand."

She sighed. "You called me Celia."

He nodded in concession, his brown eyes twinkling.

They went outside, where the sky was still in that in between stage of gray, the fight between the sun and the moon.

"You're not hurt, are you?" Victor asked once the car was moving.

"I'll be okay," she said.

"I'm sorry you were put in the way like that. I'm sorry you had to witness what you did."

She paused, considering his words. At first instinct, she would let it pass to avoid an argument. Except, she was too troubled.

"What exactly are you apologizing for?" she asked. "What are you sorry I had to witness?"

Victor frowned at her.

"Because I've been kidnapped—*twice*—and tied up and hit and electrocuted and I'm tired, Victor, okay? And then to top it all off, I had the *pleasure* of watching you fight, and you were just so fucking enthusiastic about it."

He was incredulous. "Seal, are you serious?"

She closed her eyes with a regretful sigh. Oh, she wished he hadn't called her that. Just the sound of the nickname sent a warm shiver through her, reminding her that someone loved her. She fought back the tears before they could sting her eyes.

"I *had* to fight. They would've hurt you—"

"I'm *already* hurting!"

She finally looked at him. Victor had been stunned into silence. That's when she became aware of Hastings. He'd been watching the road, but displayed the tense shoulders of someone trying to be invisible.

Clamping her mouth shut, Celia turned away from Victor and faced her window.

Outside of the terminal, Hastings took their bags from the trunk. Celia avoided his eyes when she slipped the vial into her larger suitcase.

"I really think I should meet you in Boston," she said when Victor faced her. She fiddled with her suitcase.

"Seal—"

"Just . . ." she said, cutting him off, "please."

Victor sighed. "Fine."

He picked up her orange suitcase and thrust it on the platform at the curbside check-in counter outside of their terminal. He then handed Celia her boarding pass.

"I'll see you at home," he said quietly. He stayed on the sidewalk, watching her go inside the airport.

It was going to be a long flight.

Thirteen

It had been a very, very long time since Victor had been able to walk around during the day. After shaking hands with Hastings, he teleported right away.

As part of their deal, Corinna had hidden the sun in Boston as well, for insurance. The gritty potion he had taken just before dawn ensured he'd stay awake throughout the entire day.

The November air was crisp. Though everything was gray, it wasn't nighttime.

Victor needed to clear his head after that cab ride. How could Celia be mad at him for fighting? What was he supposed to have done? The smell of blood, the rush of adrenaline. He had allowed the monster inside to take over his actions. It had been the only way to make it through the night, to make sure she had been safe.

Victor traveled all over Boston. He visited the Commons and the Public

Garden, subconsciously avoiding that spot under the bridge. He strolled through Faneuil Hall, watching the people pass him by as if he were any other human. Christmas decorations were already hung across the plaza and in the shop windows.

The city had an altered vibe during the day, as if the cover of night allowed fewer inhibitions. People smiled differently, without ulterior motives of danger and propositions.

Victor trekked over the bridge into Cambridge, to the mall. He paused on the second floor when he caught a familiar scent.

He peered inside the Verizon store. Trixie stood by a display, talking up two teenaged girls about the newest smartphones. She wore her uniform of pressed khaki pants and black polo with *Verizon* stitched in red on the left breast. Her jet-black hair was up in a ponytail. She pointed to something on one of the phones, and the two girls nodded in agreement.

Victor started to move on. He stopped when he realized someone was watching him, a sensation he wasn't used to experiencing. *He* was the predator. Raising his guard, Victor scanned the store.

A tall, Vietnamese man, wearing the same uniform with a nametag that read "Lee," sat behind the desk at the back of the store. The blue light from the computer screen illuminated his face, but he wasn't looking at the monitor. No, his dark eyes were on Victor.

He knew something was off about Victor; the deep frown creasing his brows confirmed it. Victor stared him down a moment longer before departing.

He left the mall after that, wandering back through Fenway, making his way to the Jamaicaway.

Most of the trees were still in full foliage in the Arnold Arboretum—a garden of trees in Jamaica Plain. Victor strolled down the path, hands in his pockets, as he took in the last of the bright oranges and reds and yellows. The leaves rustled on their branches, waving to the people passing beneath.

A young father out for a walk with his two children had been a bit *too* cautious by bundling them in thick coats and hats, as if it were the middle of January. He laughed along with his two sons as they tossed fallen leaves into the air. The dried leaves trickled down on their heads like so much confetti, and the boys laughed harder. It was a glorious sound that sent an ache through Victor's entire body.

That dream of his was so far from his grasp. He knew that the moment he had died. Being with Celia, he hadn't been able to keep himself from envisioning a full life, with children and a big house and a dog named Rusty. It was a vision that was no longer as clear and defined as it had once been. It was slipping away, that foolish dream.

He watched the family undetected. When he could take it no longer, he left the Arboretum.

Celia's flight was scheduled to land in twenty minutes. Victor made his way over to the Forest Hills train station, a ten-minute walk away, and caught a cab to the airport.

* * *

Celia raised her arms in the air for a good stretch. Her body groaned in protest. She'd fallen asleep against the window, and now she had a crick in her neck. She rolled her head a few times to loosen the tight muscles as she waited for the line of people to move down the aisle of the plane.

An attractive man, with a light brown Afro and skin the color of caramelized sugar, smiled at her from his seat two rows ahead. He wore navy blue square glasses and she noticed how enticingly thick his arms were. His head was still in Vegas, since he wore shorts and a t-shirt.

Celia began to return the smile. She stopped herself at the last moment. He was cute and inviting, but the last thing she needed was male attention.

She still had her headphones on even though the battery had died the moment the plane landed. She used that as a cover. Averting her eyes, she hurried down the aisle, past his row and off the plane.

After grabbing her luggage, she caught sight of Victor through the glass door at the exit. He waited by an idling yellow cab, his hands in his pockets, his gaze directed to his feet.

She paused a moment, surveying him. His shoulders curved forward slightly, the only sign of anything troubling him. His shiny hair was brushed back, his chiseled jaw standing out under his skin. He was so handsome. She wanted to keep this image forever, but she knew she couldn't stand in the airport much longer.

Victor, she thought. She half expected him to look up as if she had called his name aloud. But he kept that pose, staring, unfocused, at the ground.

She longed for his touch. She recalled their first night when he'd opened up about his past relationships. She had been intrigued; she couldn't get enough. They had made love like experts of each other's bodies. That symmetry was what they lacked now. A lot of it had to do with her stolen magic, but there was more to it than that; more that had been simmering just below the surface.

The doors slid open. A second later Victor glanced up, having caught her scent. They held each other's gazes for a minute. When their eyes met, she saw the love and ache there. She remembered her resolution at Serena's. She wanted to make this work. The anger and pain was pushed away.

She finally made her feet move. Wheeling her bags behind her, Celia stepped out onto the pavement. A shiver ran through her as a cool breeze sliced through her flimsy t-shirt. It had been just fine in the desert, but was no match for Boston's impending winter.

The clock in the cab told her it was just after 4:00. With the same tight knot of clouds shielding the sun as in Vegas, it seemed like the day had already drifted well into the evening.

Victor gave the cabbie Celia's address. She pulled off, nearly sideswiping a rental car shuttle that had the audacity to be in the next lane. Celia kept her hands clasped in her lap as she gazed straight ahead through the windshield.

"Celia," Victor murmured. He reached over to take her hand, then halted, his hand hovering over hers. She gripped it with hers. His soft skin was warm.

"I love you, Victor," she said.

"I love you, too. But . . ." Her heart skittered. "I think we need a break."

She peered up at him, thunderstruck. "What?"

"Isn't that what you've been thinking? Because that's what you said the other night."

Celia's surprise turned into shock. "When I was—" She broke off and looked at the driver. "You know? That wasn't me."

"It was, Seal. In vino veritas, right?" His smile was grim. His flushed skin seemed to shine from the tunnel lights that beamed through the windows. "You've been wrestling with our relationship for a while."

"Has it only been me?" she interrupted. Her stupid eyes watered again.

"No. I've considered how I've been holding you back. I've been selfish because I didn't want to lose you, even if I was hurting you in the process."

"That's not completely your fault."

"If it weren't for me, you wouldn't know about . . . my kind."

Victor glanced to the driver through the Plexiglas partition. She tapped her thumbs on the steering wheel in tune with the radio.

Celia snorted. "I'm sure they would've made themselves known sooner or later. I smell, remember? Well . . . I did, anyway."

He only nodded. They were quiet a minute. The cab emerged from the tunnel entirely too soon.

"I just want you to be happy, Seal."

"I am happy."

As the words left her mouth, she knew they weren't true. When she looked in his eyes, she saw he knew too.

"Just be truthful to yourself, Seal. Say everything you've been thinking."

She began to speak, and it all came so easily.

"I thought everything was good with us. I thought . . ." She shook her head. She wasn't sure of what to convey. "I was scared of you. Really scared. On the plane, and then again last night when you were fighting. It made me realize that I had been pushing away my doubts about us for some time now. I love you with all my heart, but I *have* wondered how we can be together."

"This is my fault—"

"It's my fault, too." Celia's gaze returned to his. "*I* tried to stay in the present. I didn't know anything about your past because *I* never asked. I made the excuse to myself that I didn't want you to relive any painful memories, only because *I* didn't want to know the details. I didn't want to know that you've hurt people. I didn't want to know about your exes. I was in stupid denial.

"How can you say that you've experienced a full life with me? Equal partners tell each other everything. The good, the bad, and the messy. But whenever you tried, I wouldn't let you."

She chewed her lip when she remembered Jay's words. He'd gotten angry with her because she wouldn't tell him where the vampires rested. He had been right.

"When things get tough," she repeated to Victor, "or they threaten my bubble, I push them away. I was scared last night and I snapped at you. I'm always snapping at you."

"Well, okay," he conceded. Although she pouted hearing that he agreed, she couldn't argue. "But how come you didn't end this when I told you what I am?"

"Well, you had blown my mind." She rubbed her cheek. "And I liked you."

"I liked you." He leaned closer. "You shouldn't be so hard on yourself. It's natural to have discomfort, Celia. I'd be uncomfortable if you didn't. I don't have to use my imagination to know you didn't like what I had to do—*have* to do—in order to survive. That I made mistakes when I couldn't control myself and allowed my humanity to slip away. That my kind of mistakes hurt people. You made that clear, even if you think you didn't."

"But I didn't talk about it."

"Besides every time we argued?"

Her jaw dropped. Victor smiled, a forlorn expression tugging the corners of his lips upward.

"I want to give you the space you need," he finished. "I have nothing but time."

Celia's chin trembled and her throat constricted. Her nose began to run as the tears spilled from her eyes.

"I wish I could change what I am," Victor said.

She gave him a watery smile. "I don't," she managed to croak. "Then we would never have met."

The driver double-parked in front of Celia's building. A gust of cold air hit Celia's wet face when Victor opened the door. She used the bottom of her shirt to dry her cheeks before she slid out of the seat.

Victor stood at the base of the stairs. Celia looked up at the building. A lovely sense of homecoming washed over her, contrasting with her heartache. She was just so happy to be home. Her apartment was immaculate, awaiting her arrival. She figured she'd go upstairs, make hot chocolate, wrap herself in a fleece blanket, and watch a movie. Something mindless and funny to offset her forthcoming bawling.

Her eyes went to Victor. He'd been watching her. He looked so sad that she actually wished for one of his blank expressions. She couldn't believe she was able to hurt him. He was always so powerful, so formidable. How could little ole Celia rouse such a wounded look?

And then she remembered what he'd said; how he despised being a vampire, but wasn't fatalistic enough to kill himself.

She stepped up to him. Gingerly, she stood on her toes and brushed his lips with hers; a simple, goodbye-for-now kiss. As she drew back, his arms wrapped around her middle. He lifted her off her feet.

Victor's mouth covered hers greedily. Of course she melted into it. He knew the nooks and crannies of her body, of her mouth. He was insistent. She caressed his tongue with hers, even when his fangs extended.

They stayed like this until Celia had to pull away to catch her breath. She panted in his face, staring into his despondent, gray eyes.

In that instant, she wanted to forget about the last couple of days. To go back to before. But this trip had been a wake-up call they couldn't ignore. His nature was too present, too in her face, presenting itself as a constant obstacle.

With his lips parted, she glimpsed his fangs.

Victor's fingers grazed her collarbone. He lifted the tiny heart that hung there on the gold chain.

"My heart . . ." was all he said.

He lowered her until her sneakers touched the sidewalk. Celia's shirt was wrinkled now but at least she was no longer cold.

She picked up her heavy suitcases and hefted them up the stairs. When she opened the front door, she glanced back over her shoulder. Victor's hands were in his pockets, his entire body rigid as if steeling himself to his spot. If he had come inside, he wouldn't have been able to leave.

Celia let the door close behind her.

She grunted as she lugged her bags to the second-floor landing. The hallway was quiet. Kenny would be the only one home from school. Her other neighbor must've found a job, since his *Rock Band* wasn't going.

Celia stopped in front of her door with a sigh. *Moderation*, she told herself. She would learn to pack lightly from now on. She found the key to her door and held it to the lock. It wavered there in the air.

She leaned closer, peering at the deadbolt. The metal around the opening was scratched and stripped. The same was true of the lock on the doorknob.

"What the hell?" she whispered.

She placed her hand on the knob and turned. The door swung open. Celia's heart sped up as she took a careful step over the threshold. She wished she had a weapon of some sort. Maybe she could toss the suitcase, but that would require the ability to lift the damn thing.

She reached to her left and flipped the switch. Light flooded the front entrance.

First, the smell of her Island Paradise air freshener hit her. Then, the state of her apartment assaulted her eyes.

Everywhere she looked, there was damage. The overturned sofa, the coffee table on its side. Her DVD player was missing—even the cables were gone, the bastards.

Slashes cut across her curtains. Her books and DVDs had been pulled from the shelves and littered the floor. The AC unit she'd been meaning to take in for a month, lay on the floor, smashed. The space in the window it had occupied felt more like a gaping hole into her sanctuary, leaving her exposed.

Celia rushed over and banged it shut. As she looked around at the mess, her eyes landed on the cordless phone peeking from under a ripped sofa cushion. She snatched it up and called the police.

After disconnecting, she stood, frozen, by the window. Who could do this? And why?

Her brain couldn't comprehend.

Ten minutes passed before the buzzer sounded. The short burst echoed in the quiet space. She jumped at the sound, and then hurried over to the intercom.

"Boston PD," a gruff voice sounded through the speaker.

She pressed the Release button. Her door was still open, her bags still sitting in the hallway. The two uniformed officers took stock of that as they entered the apartment.

The brown-skinned woman scanned the place. Her nameplate read "Jackson." Her partner, the owner of the gruff voice, and whose nameplate said "Santiago," pulled out a pad and pencil. His dark blue eyes focused on Celia.

"What happened, ma'am?"

"Don't call me 'ma'am,'" Celia said with a sigh. "Please."

They went through a rundown of basic information: her name, phone number, where she'd been.

"So, you came home to this," the female officer said. Her voice carried a hint of sympathy. "About twenty or thirty minutes ago?"

"Yes," Celia answered.

"You have any idea who'd do this?" Santiago asked.

She shook her head no. It wasn't the complete truth. She had a few ideas.

She could discard Milo and Clarice, though. They'd never had permission to enter her home. That left the nefarious Night Hawks. Her cousin Winston claimed membership to the group of hunters who sought to take out vampires in the most painful way possible. Celia wondered if Winston was currently in Brooklyn, where he lived.

She pushed that aside as well. Her cousin, as reprehensible as he could be, wouldn't do this to her. What would be his reason? What would the

Night Hawks gain? Did they know about her connection to their missing members?

Last month, Tilly and her two Night Hawk companions had captured a few vamps, including Annie, the long-haired tomboy who belonged to Ramsey's nest. Celia had pumped Tilly for information that Victor and Ramsey used to locate the victimized vamps. Then they'd had their revenge on the hunters.

Perhaps someone had remembered seeing Celia in the South Boston pub talking to Tilly. Maybe they'd reported her to the Night Hawks and this was their idea of intimidation? Ugh, she was getting a headache.

"Is there anything missing?" Jackson asked.

Celia rubbed her forehead. "I only noticed the DVD player. I haven't looked everywhere. I couldn't . . ."

She trailed off as a new lump formed in her throat. Jackson placed a consoling hand on her shoulder. She was taller than Celia; she seemed more like a big sister comforting the younger one as she led her to the kitchen to take inventory.

The vandals had had a field day in there. Dishes and glasses lay in pieces on the counter. The refrigerator door hung open, its contents thrown to the floor. The glass shards of a bottle of pasta sauce lay on the floor, the red sauce creating a jagged design on the linoleum like a cartoon explosion.

They'd used mustard and ketchup to decorate the inside of the fridge and her stove and her cabinets and her walls. One ambitious shit had made mustard stars on the ceiling, imitating the glow-in-the-dark arrangement on the ceiling of her bedroom. A yellow glob landed on Jackson's shoulder, but she didn't notice. Celia's coffeemaker and her toaster, of all things, were gone.

They moved on to her bedroom, which had met the same devastation. Celia stepped over the mattress that hung off the box spring at an awkward angle and went to her dresser.

Her jewelry box was missing. So was her laptop computer. Someone had used her one red lipstick to draw an ejaculating penis on her mirror. They'd done the same in the bathroom.

Anger and frustration bubbled inside Celia, trying to explode from her in the form of tears. She hadn't thought there were any more tears to cry.

They went back into the living room. Santiago had been trailing behind them, snapping pictures with a small digital camera when they left the room. He was still in the bedroom when Celia plopped down in her brown and pink director's chair, still standing in its place by the window.

"Do you have renter's insurance, Ms. Wilcox?" Jackson asked.

She shook her head, wondering why none of her neighbors had reported a disturbance. There had to have been *some* noise. And Carrie, Kenny's mom, knew she was out of town.

"Is there anywhere you can stay for the night?"

Celia nodded

"And you should check in with your landlord. That lock will need to be repaired."

"He lives downstairs. I'll let him know."

"Do you need a ride?"

"No."

Santiago stepped out of the bathroom. He nodded to Jackson, indicating he was finished.

"We'll start the report," Santiago told Celia. "We'll give you a call, probably tomorrow morning."

"Oh!" Celia said, slapping her forehead. "I lost my cellphone in Vegas."

Santiago stared at her a moment, then made a note in his pad. He shook his head as if annoyed. Celia forgot her gloom for a minute and glowered at him.

"That's okay," Jackson replied. "Is there another number to reach you?"

She gave her aunt's number. Jackson handed her a business card for the Dorchester precinct. "If you can think of anyone who would do this, let us know."

Celia nodded, and then walked them to the door. As she tugged her suitcases into the apartment, she glimpsed the officers knocking on Carrie's door.

"He won't let you in," Celia informed them. They looked back at her. "Kenny, her son, he doesn't answer the door when she's not home."

She walked down the hall.

"Kenny," she called through the door. "It's Celia."

After a few seconds, the deadbolt turned and the door opened a crack. Kenny's blue eye blinked up at her.

"Hi." Celia forced a smile. "These officers wanted a word with your mom. Do you know when she'll be in tonight?"

Kenny's eyes widened in fear. He shook his head, sending his blond curls into a whirlwind. "Mommy said not to open the door. I'm gonna get in trouble."

"No, no, it's fine."

She reached out to touch his shoulder, but he stepped back.

"What's wrong, Kenny?" Why was he so terrified?

"Here, let me." Santiago placed his hand on Celia's arm and moved her aside. Kenny backed away from the door even more.

"Hey, buddy," Santiago replied. He made his voice soft as he bent forward to look the boy in the eye. "We just need to ask your mom about something that happened recently. You didn't hear any noises coming from the apartment next door, did you?"

Kenny took a sharp breath, and shook his head again. "I'm gonna get in trouble!" The door slammed shut. Santiago jerked back just in time to avoid a complete collision with the wood.

Celia looked to each of the officers, as if they held the answer to his strange behavior. "I've never seen him like that," she said.

Jackson nodded. "We're going to ask a few more of your neighbors. We'll talk to his mother later. You should go pack and get to your aunt's house."

Celia returned to her apartment. But when she stood there, gazing at the wreckage, she knew she didn't want to be there a second longer.

Picking up her purse from where she'd dropped it at the door, she lugged her two suitcases back out the door. The hallway was clear; the officers must've found someone home.

Celia stopped off at her landlord's apartment. When she found he wasn't home, she scribbled a note and slid it under his door.

Her black Honda waited for her across the street. She struggled with stuffing the large suitcase in the backseat. When she finally slid behind the wheel, she let out a long sigh.

All she wanted was to hide away somewhere without fights or broken relationships or fucked-up houses.

With a dejected groan, Celia started the engine and drove off.

Her magic is bound but she isn't out of danger. Celia will need to learn her family heritage now more than ever . . .

Read on for an excerpt from

Spicy

Book Four

of the *Bitten* Series

Spicy

A car alarm screeched, bringing her back to consciousness. The alarm beeped off as abruptly as it had started. Celia blinked at the television in confusion. A woman's voice crooned smoothly over the airwaves for a seventies' compilation album.

Celia sat up and stretched. Her leg had fallen asleep. Leaning forward, she picked up the remote and turned off the TV. The room went dark. She shuffled toward the stairs, wincing as the blood brought her leg back to life.

A sliver of light shone from the bottom of basement door. Celia headed over. She reached out to flip the switch only to find it was already in the off position. Her heart fluttered a little. She turned the knob.

The door opened with a soft squeak. One step at a time, she descended into the chilly basement. At the bottom, she realized the source of the light came from a window straight ahead. The neighbor's garage light was on—a cat must have run under the sensor.

Celia looked around, shivering. The neighbor's light illuminated the boxes and storage crates. A desk held an old-school computer with a tube monitor in one corner. A silver file cabinet stood beside it. Dust coated the monitor and keyboard. Meg had arranged the area over ten years ago, when she had been working on a series of children's books featuring a blue jay. Life had taken over and her writing had retired in a dusty cabinet. Celia went closer, remembering how Meg's stories had always been entertaining.

The first drawer of the file cabinet contained fragments of stories separated into multi-colored file folders. She pulled out sheets of paper, some scrawled with words, others covered with sketches.

She moved down the cabinet and found the third drawer was stuck, only opening a few inches. Celia tugged harder, trying to jimmy it. Finally, she closed it and then pulled hard. The cabinet yielded. As it slid wide, the neighbor's light shut off.

"Shit," she muttered at the sudden darkness. Clicking on the tiny lamp next to the computer monitor, she faced the open drawer.

Inside, she found a few boxes and two leather-bound journals, among other miscellaneous items. The first box she pulled out was black with gold stars. Their luminosity had faded with time. She put the box on the desk and lifted the lid. About twenty-five photos were stacked neatly inside. She took out the first one: her mother, Daphne, as a pre-teen, splashing in the ocean.

The next one had been ripped in half. Celia held the two pieces next to each other. Daphne and Meg were on either side of a wooden picnic table. Daphne's hair was loose and curly, while Meg's was in her signature straight, blonde 'do. Neither of them smiled, as if the photographer had forced them to be there. The girls sat far enough away that it could've actually been two separate photos.

Celia examined each of the pictures. They were the missing ones from the photo album in the living room. She halted at a picture of her mother a few months before she became ill. Her skin had been clear, glowing, her hair shiny in the sunlight—a stunning contrast to how gaunt and pallid her mother had become due to the cancer.

She wasn't staring at her mother though. Instead, her eyes went to the hand Daphne held to her chest as she laughed in the frozen moment. A red stone sat on the right ring finger; the ruby ring Celia had found in Meg's room. Her heart thudded and her ears grew warm.

The ring was in her jewelry box.

The one stolen from her apartment.

Tears pooled in her eyes. Her mother's ring. She'd been surprised that Meg hadn't given it to her but she had dismissed her hurt feelings. Meg missed her sister. Why not keep the ring? Of course, Celia hadn't given it back to her either. And now look what happened to it.

She wanted to throw something. It took all of her not to knock the dusty computer to the floor, to kick over the file cabinet, and turn over the desk. She shoved the box with the photos back into the cabinet and slammed it shut without investigating more. Upstairs, she covered her head with her blanket and cried into her pillow. She wished Victor was there to comfort her. He didn't mind when her face became red and puffy. He would rub her back and shoulders until her tear ducts were dry.

About the author

The *Bitten* series offers Uzuri a chance to explore the paranormal. It first came to fruition in 2009, and continues to grow in her mind. Uzuri currently resides in Boston, Mass.

Find out more at: www.uzurimwilkerson.com
Follow her at: www.twitter.com/uzuri_iruzu
Friend her on: www.facebook.com/uzuriwilkerson

Made in the USA
Middletown, DE
13 May 2020